MW01717002

Manon Mouland

SUSAN HOFFMAN

PUBLISHER

AMZ Publishing LLC
Bellevue, WA

Printed by **AMZ Publishing LLC**

1400 112th Ave SE,

Bellevue, WA, 98004

Printed in the **United States of America**

To my mother, Anna Hoffman

Table of Contents

ACKNOWLEDGMENTS

I wish to thank my husband Andre Oppenheim and my daughter Emily Oppenheim for always cheering me on. Thanks also to Anita Aviad for her encouragement and excellent editing advice. Finally, thanks to my writers' group; Alex Raphael, Nadya Seminova and Sonnia Kim for their unending support.

SUSAN HOFFMAN

MANON MOULAND

CHAPTER ONE

My father's plot in Elmwood Cemetery gapes like a fresh wound. Beside it, the scraggy old scab of my mother's grave confronts me with its neglect – a sunken rectangle covered by tangles of Creeping Jenny, with its small headstone, tilted slightly toward the freshly dug hole beside it. April rain has turned to May drizzle, making the sod squishy underfoot. My feet sink into the ground as they lower the coffin to be covered forever.

Since the burial, I've been shuffling around the house, trying to find my place, but nowhere seems like home. I can't come to grips with Dad's unexpected death. Just last week, we were sitting together here in the kitchen, the cheerful sound of nesting birds and fresh spring air wafting through the open window.

"I'm going to a library conference in Montreal," Dad said. "I'll be back on Wednesday." He was in a good mood, and I was glad to have the house to myself for a few days.

But he didn't come back.

He liked to drive the meandering side roads along the Magog River and lost control of the car around a sharp curve on the slippery road.

He's never coming back.

Now, I must steel myself to attend his memorial service. I stare in disbelief at the announcement on the kitchen table:

In loving memory of

Gregory Mouland

June 20, 1946 – May 11, 2005

Lennoxville United Church,

6 Rue Church, Sherbrooke,

Friday, May 13, 11:00 a.m.

Most of the population of Lennoxville is here, tracking their muddy feet through the funeral home. Many are left standing on the periphery of the chapel, and even more spill over into the entrance hall. They've all come to pay respects to their town librarian. I resent them for being here; this was *my* father. *I'm* the one who will miss him forever.

When I enter the chapel, I avert my eyes from the congregation, looking down at the hideous floral pattern of the carpet. One insistent stare draws me, and I look up to see Mary Allidon squeezed between her husband and Stacey Bell, who replaced me as her best friend. Mary must have flown in from Arizona just to pay respects to my Dad. She's wearing a pastel blue summer dress, which I'm sure Stacey admires. To me, she just looks cold.

I feel uncomfortable in this room in this cheap polyester dress from Le Château. My gangly arms and legs feel wooden, as if they have been tacked on to my torso like an artist's jointed mannequin. My careful attempt at smoothing my hair has already failed. Dark chestnut tendrils have escaped the restraints of the scrunchy, so I remove it, and my whole head of hair springs back to its natural frizzy mass. The mascara I applied, for no good reason, is already smudged.

There is no way I can bring myself to speak in front of this crowd, so Sage Hume, Dad's long-time colleague at the library, delivers the eulogy.

"Gregory Mouland was a giant of a man, his enormous heart consistent with his six-foot frame. He devoted himself to his daughter Manon and to this community that he served ..."

She waxes eloquent about Dad's many accomplishments, but often, overcome with emotion, she falters and wipes her eyes. As she speaks, she looks out over the congregation with her pale oval face, pointy nose, and chin. She talks about what a devoted father he was, of his love for me. I sense the furtive, even hostile glances directed at me by those who knew of our difficult relationship. Many of them had witnessed our vehement arguments at the library.

They saw how Dad tried to constrain his rage whenever I misbehaved – almost always. When I was younger, I drew pictures with markers in library books, and when I was older, I carved flowers into the library table. They loved my dad, so when they saw his red face and heard his whispered shout, *"To my office!"* they felt sorry for him for having such an unruly child. They saw how defiant I was. What they couldn't see was that all I wanted was for him to hug me.

Really, Sage? Did he really love me?

Mary is seated in the fourth row behind me. She had been my only friend growing up. The other kids thought I was too weird to hang out with, and they were right. I had no qualms about speaking my mind, even if it meant alienating those I actually wished to be liked by. They treated me with caution and avoided me where possible. I scorned their idea of fashion: cartoon-stenciled hoodies, T-shirts printed with bands' logos, tight trousers, and Converse runners. I preferred quirky mismatched garments from the Salvation Army store. When they swooned over sentimental 'screamers' like Whitney Houston and Celine Dion, I mocked them with screeching parodies. I preferred the soulful vocals of Amy Winehouse and Etta James. In school, I strove to be ignored by my peers. I rejected the efforts of teachers, who thought I was smart and just needed direction, to 'befriend' me. I didn't need anyone's approval, only Mary's. She understood my passions and thought I was special.

After she ghosted me, I never had another close girlfriend. I had boy 'pals', but I didn't really belong among them, and that sense of apartness led to bouts of self-loathing. Once, I cut myself accidentally with an exacto knife and watched in fascination as the blood oozed out of me. This was so satisfying that I began using a razor blade to make hair-thin incisions on my inner thighs just to see that first drop of red trickle out. The pain was soothing, and nobody was the wiser, not even Mary. That was around the time I started experimenting with cubist portraits in shades of blue, painting limbs with slits leaking rivulets of blue blood.

Now, I secretly touch the scars through my dress and am somehow comforted. Mary and I only exchange a brief glance before I look away without saying hello. I fear that if I greet her, I might lose my reserve and devolve into a public display of tears. We have never forgiven each other for that infamous weekend that ended in her feeling abandoned and my feeling betrayed.

As the pastor drones on with his meaningless parables, my mind wanders. We were just seventeen when I convinced her that we should hitch a ride to Montreal for the day. We sat people-watching on the steps of the Edward VII monument in Phillips Square.

"Manon, look at that girl!"

"What about her?"

"She's wearing those new cargo pants with all the pockets."

"Yah, they're okay."

"I want to get my hair cut in that layered, messy style."

I had noticed her, too, but I was more interested in the crop top revealing her midriff, where a metallic glint caught my eye.

"Look Mary, she's got a belly button piercing. How cool is that?"

A boy sat down beside me, ignoring me at first, but then he silently offered me a cigarette, which I took but didn't light up. He was about our age, tall, disheveled, and totally cool.

"Wanna come to my place and smoke a joint?"

I wanted to go badly, my hedonistic tendencies overruling my common sense. Mary didn't, so I suggested we meet by the statue in an hour and I go off with him. His name is Tom. Tom from Baie D'Urfé. That's all I know because we didn't speak more than ten words to each other. He took me by the hand, and we walked for about five minutes to his room in a basement somewhere near Chinatown. It was a bare, dingy place with an unmade bed that exuded body odor. With my first toke of the joint, I had a coughing fit, and when I calmed down, he kissed me. I blissed out, oblivious to everything but Tom's hands. They were rough, and his fingernails were filthy, but when he touched me, my body responded with delicious tremors in my belly.

I lost my virginity, but with my first cigarette, I gained a new vice. I couldn't wait to tell Mary what happened, but when I got back to Phillips Square, I couldn't find her anywhere. I waited and waited, watching the after-work crowd bustle by me. Were they looking at me differently? I felt like I was glowing.

I wandered along Ste. Catherine Street as far as St. Denis, eventually accepting that Mary must have left. Finally, I got the 8:45 bus to Lennoxville, agonizing the whole way about what Dad would say and still feeling the thrill of my first sexual experience. When I got back at 11:00, Dad was fuming mad. He had that red-faced anger that made him look fearsome. His fingers fisted by his side, he shouted, "We had the Sherbrooke police out looking for you, Manon! Mary's parents even organized a search party to scour the river banks. When she got home, she told us everything about hitchhiking to Montreal and how you left her and went off with some boy."

"Dad..."

"Don't say a word. Do you know how much anxiety you caused? Not just for me but for all the neighbors who nervously waited to see if they would dredge your bodies from the river. You're an inconsiderate, selfish girl. Consider yourself grounded. From now on, you are to come straight to the library after school and then straight home with me. And no more allowance."

Really? Was he kidding? I've been saving my allowance since I was twelve, when he took me to the bank to open my own savings account. A couple of weeks without it won't hurt me at all.

He stomped off to bed without even giving me a chance to offer excuses. As usual, when I upset him, I'm the one that feels miserable. Dad was the last person I wanted to hurt, yet I couldn't stop aggravating him. I stayed up that whole night drawing, designing piercings I would never get, replaying my experience with Tom, and vowing never to forgive Mary.

Dad smoothed things over with the police, but our neighbors were not as easily appeased. They saw me as an ungrateful troublemaker and were sad for him.

At the memorial, several people step up to recount stories of Dad's generosity and his decency. A widowed woman tells how he helped her find government agencies that provided social services she didn't even know she was entitled to.

"He improved the quality of my life," she said, "he always made time for me, and he was so patient."

Really? He was patient? Not with me, he wasn't.

Others speak about his knowledge of books and how his tenacity in championing municipal causes led to improvements in the neighborhood. A young woman came in from Montreal to say a few words. Her familiar voice, smooth as caramel, resonates in the small chamber. Dad had helped her find books on writing the perfect resumé and urged her to pursue her desired career.

"With his encouragement and his letter of recommendation, I landed my dream job at CHOM-FM."

Formerly a fan, I am now bristling with resentment for this woman who benefited from Dad's encouragement. I didn't merit his support. He never acknowledged that I had any talent for art. When it was time to choose a college, I begged him to let me go to the École des Beaux-Arts in Montreal, but he wouldn't budge.

"Art school will squelch whatever flair you may have," he said.

"If I have real talent, it can never be squelched." I asserted with less conviction than I felt. Do I really have any talent?

"A liberal arts education will be the key to finding your true muse. Better yet, explore your love of plants and nature. You could go for a science degree, in biology maybe. Even studying Humanities would be better than becoming a flâneur and squandering your academic potential."

Maybe he really believed I had no talent and wanted to save me from my own disappointment. Maybe he regretted sacrificing his own musical talent to establish a more secure existence. Is that what he wanted me to do?

"Besides," he went on, "artists tend to be anarchists. You need to settle down. You're lucky, you have the brains to study and contribute something worthwhile to society. I don't want you to embitter your life by continually creating chaos around you."

"But Dad, what if I can make masterpieces that will live on after we're gone, wouldn't that be contributing?"

"After we're gone, it won't matter, it's this life we need to live as best we can. Great artists' lives often end tragically. Look at Caravaggio, what did his talent accomplish but a wretched life and an early death? I could cite any number of talented artists who lived unhappy lives and died before reaching their full potential."

At his insistence, I ended up at Champlain College, a ten-minute bike ride from home, in the science program – a far cry from the Ecole des Beaux-Arts, let alone from my secret, unattainable dream of attending the Pratt Institute in Manhattan. As much as I wanted to break away, to leave Lennoxville, I could not imagine abandoning him. Dad was my only family, and he only had me.

I reluctantly attended classes with a bunch of science nerds I couldn't compete with, and while botany interested me greatly, the rest was just tedious. I lacked the inherent exactitude and discipline required for scientific study. Learning formulas by rote, memorizing Latin names, and conducting lab experiments were anathema to me, so I dropped out after the second semester. When I told Dad, he replied in his just-about-to-explode voice.

"Quitting is not an option. You're far too smart for that."

"I'm smart enough to know that I don't want to do this for another day." I was fiercely defiant. I wasn't going back.

"What are you going to do? You can't just waste your life dabbling in paint."

"I got a job. I'm starting on Monday as a Junior Associate at Michael's, the art supply store on Wellington St. I'll be working with art in the framing department."

I thought I was so clever, managing to get a job even before I told him I was quitting. And I was thrilled because I would get discounts on art supplies.

"This junior retail position has nothing to do with *art,* Manon. It's just another minimum wage, dead-end job for losers."

Despite his lack of support, I devoted myself to painting. I painted endlessly, never satisfied with the results. My work seemed inconsequential compared with the visions I imagined. Now, listening to these testimonials about how supportive Dad could be, I feel a pang of jealousy for every favor, every hour of attention he had devoted to these people. Why couldn't he have given me this kind of unconditional support for my passion? Why had he insisted on pushing me away from what I love?

My sense of loss grows with each anecdote, and I hunch over, wincing with that familiar sinking feeling in my stomach that I'm no good, the word 'loser' reverberating in my brain.

The room is stifling with the crush of bodies sweating in their raincoats, yet I feel shivery sitting in the front row, aware of all the eyes on the back of my head. I'm bristling and have a strong urge to tell them all where to go and then make a dramatic exit myself.

CHAPTER TWO

After the service, out in the lobby, condolences and platitudes are heaped on me like wet woolen blankets. I'm desperate for a smoke, so I make my way to the edge of the crowd and slip out the side door like a truant. Lighting a cigarette, I see Mary emerge, and I start jogging to avoid her and her sorrow – she loved Dad, too. At a safe distance, I slow down for the twenty-minute walk home to our house on Rue Massawippi, where I have lived with Dad for my entire twenty-five years. I ignore the chirping phone in my pocket.

Once in my room, I strip off the ill-fitting dress that was a fashion mistake from years ago and slip into paint-stained jeans and a faded T-shirt. My footsteps echo in the eerie silence, and I realize what's missing is the musical soundtrack to our lives, the jazz that Dad constantly played. I pick one of the vinyl disks from his collection and place it on the turntable. As Nina Simone's plaintive voice starts to cry 'My Man's Gone', I feel the pain she evokes viscerally. In the kitchen, I put the kettle on as if it were any other day, only it's not. It's just an imitation of an ordinary day because Dad dying is the only thing that's happened in the world.

I set up my easel in the living room in defiance of Dad's rule against painting in there. It has the best light at this time of day, and since there's no one to admonish me, I also light up a Rothman's. Turning up the volume, I listen to Nina tell me, "Old man sorrow's come to keep me company." Indeed, sorrow permeates the place, and despite its usual state of disarray – books upon books, magazines, sketchbooks, art materials covering all the surfaces that Dad or I didn't occupy, the place feels foreign to me. The couch looks shabbier, and I notice that Dad's armchair, with the impression of his large frame still embedded in the cushions, needs re-upholstering. The lone philodendron in the corner needs watering, and the entire place could use dusting.

The still life with Calla Lily I started painting before Dad's accident no longer suits my mood. It's too cheerful. I paint a layer of black over it and stare into the blackness. I mix some greens and browns to begin painting the now dying philodendron, but I get nowhere. Instead, I curl up at my end of the couch with my sketchbook. Then, the tears that had been burning my eyes all morning began to spill. They land on the page where I'd painstakingly copied the Pileated Woodpecker from the large, well-thumbed edition of Audubon's Birds of America, the one that, to Dad's chagrin, I had never returned to the library.

My phone has been chirping insistently in the pocket of my raincoat since I left the Funeral Home. Sage, no doubt, calling with concern. Finally, I decided to text her and find several missed calls from a 212 area code. It rings again in my hand, and I answer in the flat, confrontational tone I use for telemarketers.

"Who is this?"

"Hello, this is Alexander Montgomery." The smooth baritone is unflustered by my challenging tone. "I am sorry I missed you at the memorial service. I wanted to introduce myself in person, but you disappeared before I had a chance."

"What do you want?" I snarl.

"I am Gabrielle Mouland's son," he says as if this explains anything and waits for my response. I am rendered speechless, so after a short pause, he adds. "My mother and your father were cousins."

This information has the effect of a rug having been pulled from under me. I've never heard of another Mouland. I'm flummoxed and free-falling. The tiny scars on my thighs begin to tingle with the desire to inflict new incisions, and my legs start shaking impatiently.

"You must be mistaken; my father doesn't have any cousins."

"Clearly, we need to talk," he says as he inserts himself into my life.

I agree to have him come over right away because he's only in town for the day. Then I quickly text Sage to tell her I'm okay, just need some space.

My attempt to tidy up is thwarted by his prompt arrival. Nothing is more than ten minutes away in Lennoxville. I answer the knock at the front door and am met by a cashmere-clad chest and tailored jacket that defines the broad shoulders of a man in his thirties. His brown hair is fashionably tousled, his square chin protrudes, giving him a conquering air. Standing tall, arms loosely at his side, he is a picture of composure, someone comfortable in his skin. We are opposites. Unlike him, I stand in an atmosphere of wariness and tension.

"Hello, Manon." He pronounces my name perfectly as if he were a Francophone. He takes one of my hands in both of his and, looking directly into my eyes, says, "I'm so sorry for your loss." His condolences, expressed physically in this way, somehow affect me more than all the others I've been receiving this morning. I feel a stab in my heart with each reminder that Dad is really gone.

I breathe in through my nose and out through my mouth, trying to gain my composure and invite him in. When he steps into the small vestibule, I have to move aside to let him by into the living room.

"Please, sit." I indicate Dad's chair, and then, as if I were hostess of the year, I say, "I've made some tea. Will you have a cup?" My heart is flip-flopping in my chest, and questions are bouncing around my brain. I fumble in the kitchen for what seems an excessive amount of time, finding a tray, selecting an unstained mug, wondering if he takes sugar? lemon? Burning with curiosity all the while.

"Manon, I see I have blindsided you. In a way, it doesn't surprise me that you are unaware of our family connection; it has been so in my life as well. It seems our family trait is to be secretive."

He appears to be bathed in a warm Norman Rockwell pallet. His clothes are effortlessly blended in grey and fawn, his fair complexion is toasted by the sun, and his sandy brown hair and blue-grey eyes remind me of Dad.

"Is your mother really my father's cousin?"

"Was. My mother died shortly after my dad a few years ago."

"Oh, I'm so sorry ..." and strangely, added to my loss of Dad is a sense of the loss of what never was. "Why weren't they ever in touch?"

"All I know is that there seemed to be a ghost named Gregory, always with us but never outwardly spoken about."

"You mean my father?"

"Yes, as it turns out."

My father, living as a ghost in Alexander's home while living with me and never mentioning them, puts me in a state of shock. My mouth goes dry, and I reach for my tea, sipping it slowly while I try to understand this news.

"How was he a ghost?"

"I'd pick up bits of hushed arguments behind closed doors and hear his name mentioned often, like a recurring theme."

"Did you ever ask about him?"

Alexander leans back in Dad's chair, looking into his teacup as if searching for some truth there.

"Oh, believe me, I tried. But whenever I asked, I was shut down immediately. Eventually, I stopped asking."

I lean back, too, and tuck my leg under me, settling into this fascinating conversation, aware of how his features combine to make him Adonis-like.

"It was the same with me and my dad. Every time I asked about my mom or other family, Dad diverted to another topic. It was so frustrating that eventually, I also stopped asking." My mind flashes to the many cryptic explanations Dad had offered whenever I asked about his family, ever evasive and maddening: "I didn't know my parents. . . I left home early. . ." Even the stories about my mother's family were short and sketchy.

"What do you know about her?"

"All I know is that she had run away from a Residential School north of Montreal. When Dad met her, she spoke only French because the nuns would punish them if they spoke their native language. She hated French and was keen to learn English, so Dad offered to tutor her. Eventually, they got married, had me, and then after a few years, she died."

"Did she have any family?"

"I don't think so. Dad never mentioned anyone except one friend, Manon, who mysteriously showed up at the funeral and then disappeared."

"So you are named after her?"

"Dad told me that my mother was adamant that I be named Manon."

"Well, it's a lovely name, something beautiful she gave you."

"How about you? Do you have any other family?"

"As far as I know, my only living relative is my father's aunt, who has been in a nursing home near Albany for years. I maintain contact with the facility to make sure she is well cared for, but she wouldn't know me or anything of my mother's history even if Alzheimer's hadn't robbed her of her memory."

"It's frustrating to have no one to turn to for some sense of history, isn't it?

"Yes, frustration was a running theme while I was growing up. I wanted answers and wasn't getting any, so I channeled it to other ways of solving problems."

"How?"

"I became a scientist." He laughs a little, and then his eyes go soft as he continues. "My parents are an enigma to me. I was determined to unravel the mystery of their language of gestures, their meaningful glances, that current running between them, by piecing together vignettes I witnessed through slits of partially closed doors."

"Have you come to any conclusions?"

"When I try to derive meaning from them, I keep coming up against that wall they had built around themselves. Finding you has put a crack in it." He smiles a glorious smile that lights me up with an emotion I can't quite place.

"How did you find me?"

"Since my mother died, I've been doing internet searches for the name Mouland, and on Tuesday, your Dad's came up in the Sherbrooke Record announcing his funeral. I was quite shocked to see his name in black and white, no longer a ghost and yet still a ghost. I was sorry he was gone. I had to come. You are the reward for my perseverance. Now, perhaps we can begin to piece together some of our shared history."

"I have nothing to share. All I know about Dad's family is that his parents died when he was young, and he grew up poor in his grandparents' home in Saint-Henri. He left as soon as he was able to fend for himself. That's it. There was never any mention of uncles, aunts, or cousins. Even my Mom's history is a second-hand account of a patchwork of anecdotes she had related to him." I feel like I've been punched in the stomach. I clutch it now as I sit on the edge of the couch. "I thought it was just the two of us. I didn't know anything about your mother or you." This news, Dad's betrayal in having kept this secret from me, is astounding.

Alexander discreetly glances at his elegant wristwatch and shifts as if ready to leave.

"Unfortunately, I must drive to Montreal now to catch a flight back to New York tonight, but I will be in touch. For now, here is my contact information. We are family now, so if you need anything, you must call. I want us to get to know each other."

I feel the cotton stock of his business card between my fingers and glance at the embedded logo, a gold embossed mortar, and pestle, the company name Worldwide Pharmaceuticals, and then his name followed by CEO and a series of other post-nominal letters. I am dumbstruck.

He leans in close, grips my upper arms, and looks deep into my eyes,

"I'm very glad I came to see you, Manon. I'm really happy to have some family. It's something I've wanted all my life. We will talk soon, little cousin."

The endearment washes over me, and I feel a warmth between us that is a novelty. I want to cling to him even as I watch him fold himself into a sporty BMW and drive off.

It's been a long, eventful day, and exhaustion prompts me to bed early. There is an artificial stillness in the house, a silence that is not the silence of peaceful sleep but one in which my thoughts whirl without end.

CHAPTER THREE

I should be preoccupied with speculation about what having relationships with these mysterious kin might have been like. You'd think I'd be intent on the revelation about having relatives of my own, how this new 'belonging' changes me. Does discovering roots transform me from a free radical, floating aimlessly in the universe, into a grounded person?

But no, I am obsessed only with Alexander.

"We will talk soon, little cousin."

I've picked up his business card umpteen times, intending to call but afraid of destroying this new fantasy by learning it's a terrible mistake. Is it even true? Are we really connected? I'm stuck in a kind of stunned immobility, as if I now need instruction to move on. I am virtually paralyzed to act except for sketching, which is an automatic motor function like breathing.

I begin drawing his features: his high forehead and hairline that peaks charmingly off-center; the bilateral symmetry of his ears, which end in plump morsels of flesh; his straight nose and narrow nostrils perfectly proportioned to his face; his lean, muscular neck. I picture the details of his hands. He has long fingers with tufts of sandy hair between the knuckles and large square nails. Unlike other men I have known, he appears to be without a flaw. I am drawn to him as if by some genetic sexual attraction.

What is wrong with me? My susceptibility to men, regardless of their defects, has ruled me ever since I discovered that I could lose myself in physical pleasure. My serial liaisons had the added bonus of showing Dad, in a twisted way, that I was loved. Mostly, I am disappointed and ashamed of my behavior.

I've known that I'm bad ever since my mother died. Dad confirmed it all through my growing-up years, right up until he died. Wanting Alexander is another level of wickedness. The illicitness of my fantasies makes me feel ill for want of him.

All my life, I've lived with a phantom mother. Now, it seems that I have other phantom relatives. I have never heard the name Gabrielle and wonder what could have caused the estrangement of these cousins. Why had Dad never mentioned her?

I go in search of clues, reluctant to cross the threshold of Dad's room; he was so private that the thought of looking through his personal things makes me shudder. I walk gingerly, looking over my shoulder, expecting to be caught like a thief.

His desk is neatly organized: pen and writing pad, a stack of books, his daily journal, and the yellowing Arts section of a weeks-old Montreal Gazette featuring yet another analysis of Van Gogh's madness. I open the top-drawer containing odds and ends and a folder labeled 'current.' Nothing here interests me. The bottom drawer has dossiers randomly filed, labeled insurance, ownerships, and deeds. One, simply labeled 'documents', contains my birth certificate, his will, and my mother's death certificate, which gives me a painful paper cut as I pull it up - Charlotte Marie Hill Mouland, Deceased November 12, 1984.

Now more comfortable with snooping, I decided to expand my search to his bureaux. In the second drawer of the tallboy dresser, under a jumble of socks and underwear I find a manila envelope containing a few photos. One is of a young Gregory, a lanky teenager standing awkwardly in front of a clapboard row house unit. The siding is painted a gaudy red, and all the trim is painted white, so the square windows on either side of the door look like goggles staring outward. Beside him, a pretty girl in jeans and a frilly blouse is holding his hand. Scrawled on the back in a shaky script: Saint-Henri, 1965. Another picture, taken the same day, shows them with two old, grave-looking people standing behind them. There is an uncaptioned photo of the same girl, older now and beautiful. She is looking straight into the camera, smiling flirtatiously. Behind her, I recognize the iconic Habitat building in Montreal. There is also a faded, hastily written note on the back of one of those ubiquitous pink telephone message slips.

> *"Greg, by the time you read this, I will be on my way to New York with Sebastian and you need not see me again. I have to do what is right for my baby. Please forgive me. I will love you always – Gaby*

I sit on the floor, staring at these scraps of history. Gaby, could this be Gabrielle, as in Alexander's mom? I try to digest the revelations that began with Alexander's unexpected arrival in my life. The mystery of where I belong deepens with this evidence – Dad had a family.

Now that he's gone, our difficult relationship becomes more complicated than ever with this discovery. I miss him, and I hate him for not having confided in me. At the same time, my heart aches for him, for having severed from his family so indelibly that they no longer existed for him. Were there other relations? Does he have brothers or sisters? For that matter, are his parents really dead? Might I have a whole estranged family out there somewhere? Nothing is certain anymore.

The eerie discomfort of being in Dad's inner sanctum prompts me to get up and go outside. Early spring entices me to the back porch, where I've spent many solitary hours thinking, dreaming, and drawing. I sit in the big wicker chair, which surrounds me like re-assuring arms, and light a cigarette, safe in the knowledge that the smoke drifting by Dad's window will go unnoticed.

Our shabby little house, the last one at the dead end of Massawippi Street, is wedged between the old railway tracks, now a bicycle path on the east, and the Massawippi River on the west. It's surrounded by trees, making it perpetually dim and gloomy inside, but outside, it is a garden of delights. The back porch extends out on stilts above the slope that leads down to the river, which narrows like a cinched belt directly behind our house, and almost reaches the other side when the river recedes in the fall.

When I was little, Dad had let me go unsupervised to explore our unfenced backyard, which is just the continuation of the river bank. It was only when I was preteen that he wanted to fence me in. While he didn't nurture my interest in the visual arts, he did encourage my interest in the flora and fauna surrounding us. He would sit here in the wicker chair, reading and watching over me. I carried a little book with me to record changes in the flora by season. Especially exciting was the emergence of fiddleheads in the spring, their stems ending in a curl like a scroll on a violin. Even as a child, I appreciated the shape and structure of leaves and petals, often squinting to simplify textures and focus on shape to see them the way Georgia O'Keeffe did.

A film of moisture glazes my eyes as happy memories emerge of summers spent splashing about on the sandbar with silty sand oozing between my toes. I loved to collect things, and sometimes I would run up the stairs to the porch,

"Daddy, look what I found! What is it?" and Dad had an explanation for whatever it was. Bugs, stones, fossils, and plants all had a story. But what is the story of my family? What could be so terrible that he could not tell me?

My head cleared from breathing the pine-scented air, I summon up the courage to call Alexander. He'll want to know about the note I found from his mother and photos of her from before he was born.

CHAPTER FOUR

As if connected by telepathy, my cell phone rings just as I am about to call Alexander. The vibration moves through my whole body when I see his number on the display.

"Hello? Manon?" My heart skips a little beat upon hearing his voice. "How are you holding up? Do you need anything?"

I wonder if he thinks I'm destitute or falling to pieces being on my own. Whatever he thinks, his concern for me touches me deeply. It stokes a fervent desire in me to put my head on his shoulder, unload my sorrow, and confess all my guilt. What's happening to me?

I suddenly remember my discovery.

"Was your father Sebastian?" I ask.

"Yes, how did you find out?"

I tell him about the pictures and the note.

"So that note must have been written around 1968 or 1969, just before I was born. That's the point in time when the history of my family begins for me."

He is expressing my own sense of a blank past. The empathy we share about undisclosed relations is powerful.

"I feel the same," I say. "Searching for family history is like diving into a void. I float endlessly, reaching for something to hold on to." Suddenly, I'm embarrassed at having exposed such personal sentiments to a stranger. In talking about this, the reality that Dad is gone hits me anew, causing painful lumps in my throat. I try to bring the conversation back to the concrete.

"Do you know of any other relatives?"

An unfamiliar sense of kinship swells in me, and the sound of his voice stirs a longing to be close to him.

"Listen, Manon, I want you to come and spend some time in New York. I think we should talk and get to know each other. Maybe we can piece together some common history." His voice and my visual memory of him melt something inside me. An illicit love, which I am loathe to squelch, is kindling in me. "What do you say? Will you come?"

My infatuation with Alexander Montgomery draws me to him, yet I am reticent to respond. Even a couple of weeks ago, I would have jumped at the opportunity to go to New York City. I've dreamt about exploring its art scene. Now, without Dad putting restrictions on me, I'm a little terrified of my freedom.

"Maybe in a little while."

Days go by without my accomplishing much. I wander around the house, trying to find what holds me here. My room is a child's room. A chaos of things collected, constructed, discarded. My collection of Beanie Babies is still on the shelf. I remember how I had given them life with my imagination. They'd be worth something now if I hadn't insisted on removing the hang tags. My single bed, where I discovered that if I created friction between my legs, where I throbbed, I would explode somehow, in a euphoric burst of sensation, like when you strike a match to create the spark that ignites it to flame. That discovery has served me well since I was eight.

The kitchen was the only place that Dad and I ever really talked. Mornings, reading the paper at the table over tea, we shared opinions about what was going on in the world and in Lennoxville, and of course, we would argue. I would deliberately make specious arguments just to annoy him, like when I told him that I agreed with banning Ulysses in libraries, knowing full well what a sore point book banning of any kind was for him.

"Art can never be obscene," he would explain. "It needs to be understood, which is a good exercise no matter what the subject."

"Ulysses is obscenely boring; no one should be exposed to that," was my smart-mouthed reply.

Eventually, he would clam up, helpless, and I felt some satisfaction in showing him that . . . well, I'm not sure what, just the fact that I succeeded in annoying him was enough.

Like a visitor in a museum, I wander down the hall and stop in front of the drab painting that has been hanging there for as long as I can remember. I don't know how many times I have passed by it, but I clearly remember the first time I looked at it with real comprehension. I was no more than five or six. The painting is dark with a myriad of subtle shades of green, and when I peered into the depth of its forest, the chill of its sunless passages gave me goosebumps. What unknown creatures lurked in its stillness, ready to pounce? What would happen if I wandered in and could never find my way out again? It actually made my heart beat a little faster. I touched the canvas and felt the nubby texture of thick layers of paint. I sniffed the pungent odor of old varnish. I wondered how a brush could make the tree bark rough while the leaves looked waxy smooth and seemed to rustle in a breeze. That's when I knew I wanted to be an artist. Now, as I look at it, I want to get lost in its dark greenness.

Art remains a refuge, but even painting doesn't distract me like it usually does. My work in progress is of a trillium I spied peeking out from under a fern. I render subtle shades of green pastels over a skeleton of veins and draw colorless petals in ink. The painstaking accuracy of it frustrates me. I can never let go enough to draw from my imagination, from my heart. That familiar frustration of never getting it right or good enough makes me feel helpless.

I need to get out, so I gather up the overdue books and head to the library. Sage is in Dad's office. I plop down in my usual spot on the small sofa opposite her. She has known Dad longer than I have.

"Sage, did my Dad ever talk about his family or what his early years were like?"

Sage turns away from the computer and directs her gaze at me. She's been there for me all my life. Even though I never appreciated her, she took every opportunity to draw me out. Now that I want to talk, she jumps right into a little monologue, which makes me realize why I always avoided these 'heart-to-heart' chats where she would drone on about anything apropos of the subject at hand.

"No. As gregarious as he was, talking to people about their lives, Gregory was less than open about his own. I met him the year he came to Lennoxville with his young bride. Your parents were well-matched. Like him, she was a good listener but very private about her own life. She rarely came to the library. All I know is that he came from Montreal to take the job as librarian right after he finished his Master's at McGill. As he had just graduated, his resumé was sparse. Dawson College and McGill, nothing much prior to that."

I tell her about Alexander and the stunning discovery of our family connection.

"Was he that tall stranger who was at the service?"

"Yes. He came to see me, hoping to find out more about his mother, but of course, I am oblivious. We've been in touch, and he's invited me to go to New York."

Sage has that look on her face that she gets when she is concerned about me, usually after Dad and I had some particularly egregious argument.

"Are you going?" She knows I've wanted to go for a long time and that Dad wanted nothing to do with New York City; it was a taboo subject. Now I'm beginning to understand why that city was off-limits – Gabrielle was there. He managed to keep me from going, even on my own, especially after 9/11.

"I'm thinking about it."

"I do recall an incident at your mother's funeral. A family from New York attended. The woman was beautiful and smartly dressed. The man seemed uncomfortable being there. When they approached Gregory, the man gripped his wife's elbow, restraining her from possibly hugging your Dad. Taking exception to the way their eyes met, the guy became belligerent, "Let's go," he growled and began to push his wife towards the door. The young boy with them seemed to be in another world until he laid eyes on you. He noticed you on their way to the exit and stopped. Then he just went over and gently picked you up. Even though you weren't a very friendly child, you laid your head on his shoulder as if it was exactly what you wanted."

"I don't remember that at all. Did you ever find out who they were?"

"Not a chance. I instinctively knew not to ask."

֍֍֍֍

After weeks of mourning and brooding around the house, I need to ground myself in the world of art. The Musée de Sherbrooke has an exhibit of Rita Letendre that I've been excited about since it was announced, so I make my pilgrimage. The guard at the entrance nods at me and says, "Where have you been? We haven't seen you for a while."

"Just busy, I guess."

"Glad you got here to see the Letendres. It's closing next week."

The big room on the main floor is awash in brilliant color. I can almost feel the heat of flames from her large canvases of fire. Moving through the room, I arrive at the back where her arrow series are hung, and I can feel the speed and vibration emanating from them. Airbrushed chevrons that forcefully cut across the canvasses diagonally or horizontally from one corner of the painting to the other, showing me the way forward. I decide to accept Alexander's invitation.

In the weeks since our first brief encounter, he has been an ever-present element of my life. The revelation he brought me has left me constantly on the brink between fantasy and denial. I imagine the family I might have had: Dad finally reconciled with Gabrielle; a happy reunion of cousins, my cousins; visits to New York for the holidays, a family Dad denied me. Then I revert to thinking this can't be real, it is just too strange. This mysterious history is almost worse than no history. And then, if it is real, what about my strong attraction to Alexander? I am miserable for want of him.

I begin to feel excited about the prospect of finally seeing New York and meeting him again. Plans ricochet in my head, with so many things I want to see. There are the museums and the vibrant experimental art scene in Soho and Chelsea, lives and events that I have only read about in the weekend New York Times.

However, the New York of the past few years is not so much the city of the avant-garde as the city of 9/11. The apprehension of experiencing the tragedy of that event in *situ* is mixed with my excitement for all the possibilities ahead. I still get choked up remembering that horrible day. Dad and I were having breakfast with the radio tuned to CBC as usual when the news broke. We immediately turned the TV on to witness the second crash in real time on CNN. Standing side by side in front of the screen, we were stunned by the ghastly images that kept looping nightmarishly as if there were an infinite number of crashes and it was the end of the world. Dad put his arm around me and pulled me close as if to protect me from the impact. This demonstrative act of caring was a rare occurrence. I felt so close to him in that moment that my heart broke for everything all at once, the tragedy taking place before our eyes and the tragedy of all the lost opportunities for me and Dad to show our deep love for each other. Now, I think perhaps pulling me close to him served his own need. In that moment, he was probably thinking about Gabrielle. Four years later, 9/11 caused me to hurt again.

CHAPTER FIVE

Flying over Manhattan is magnificent. The glass towers of the iconic skyline sparkle in the sun on a neat grid of parallel and perpendicular streets. Conspicuously absent are the twin towers that are etched in memory. A large green rectangle undulates in the middle, and the blue eye at its center seems to wink in the sunshine. However, landing at LaGuardia is wretched. Once landed at the shabby terminal, the stream of people rushing to get out captures me in its current. The smell of diesel fills the lower level of the terminal because the doors are constantly opening and closing. The polluted air, the belligerent shouting, and the incessant blasting of horns are daunting for anyone from a provincial place like the Eastern Townships. Even Montreal's Mirabel seems tame in comparison.

I notice a tall man searching the faces of passengers and waving a sign with my name on it. His dark, messy hair, jeans, riding boots and retro tee shirt distinguish him from the Limo drivers in suits and captains' hats, similarly waving signs. When I approach him, he grins.

"Welcome to New York, Manon. I'm Hedley Pritchard. Alexander sends his regrets for not being able to meet you. He had an unexpected, time-sensitive issue he had to deal with and asked me to pick you up."

My anticipation and apprehension of seeing Alexander again is met with harsh disappointment but also with a kind of relief, a reprieve from perhaps realizing that he was just an illusion.

In the two months since Dad died, I've been trying to dodge Alexander's invitations to come here, unable to commit. I still have a lot to work out. It's hard enough grieving for the dad I knew, a complicated man, a peremptory parent, but also the sun-warmed boulder that I leaned on when I felt lost. Having learned that he has lied to me all my life, grieving for him has added a new, deeper dimension to my sorrow. He has left me alone, but truly, I have been alone all my life.

Hedley ushers me through the bustle of the airport into a Land Rover parked by the door. It has a parking tag on the windshield, which he snatches up, folds neatly in half, and adds to a collection I glimpse in his glove compartment. I keep my eyes wide open as he navigates through Queens and then through the congestion of Manhattan. I'm eager to see the sites of the city, which to this point is nothing but industrial ugliness, overpasses, underpasses, and unending construction. He tells me that he and Alexander are long-time friends and that he now works at Alexander's Connecticut estate, managing the stables and taking care of the horses.

Horses! Just the idea of being in the vicinity of these animals that I love gives me a thrill.

Once we cross a bridge, we're in Harlem, and I see clusters of brown high-rise tenements that I recognize from years of watching *Law & Order* with Dad. These gradually give way to low-rise brick apartment buildings clad with iron fire escapes looking like exoskeletons, so different from the elegant exterior stairways of Montreal that curl their way up to second stories.

In less than half an hour, we turn onto Riverside Drive, along the Hudson, where joggers and cyclists command a portion of the road. Unlike the mighty St. Lawrence, the river smells more like an ocean with its fishy undertones that hang in the humid air. Here, the buildings have stone facades with embellishments that people refer to as 'pre-war'. Finally, we arrive at a white building with an arcade of elegant arches in front of a circular driveway. A brass plaque by the entrance states that The Colosseum is deemed a historical building by the Landmarks Preservation Commission.

"Hey, Manon, I hope you don't mind my leaving you with George, the concierge," Hedley says. "I'm not that fond of the city, and the horses need feeding. George will get you settled in the apartment, and Alexander will text you to let you know when he'll be home. I know he's eager to see you. I'll see you again at Elderberry Lane on Saturday."

I process this information and all that it entails. Alexander occupies the rarified world of the wealthy in which I have no place.

❁❁❁❁

"July is not the best time to visit New York," says George. "It's too hot to walk around." I guess making small talk is a valuable trait in his line of work; he's an absolute natural at it. Dad would have loved him. He wants to take me up to the apartment, but I can't wait to explore the city. "Suit yourself, but it'll be hot."

He hands me a card with his number and says, "If you need anything or are ready to come back, I can send a car for you." He ushers me out to the corner and points me in the direction of Broadway. "Just a couple of blocks up, you'll see the gates to the Columbia University campus. Walk through it to Amsterdam Avenue. It's more interesting there."

Just as I turn on to Amsterdam, I see the 'Hungarian Pastry Shop' and make a pit stop in their tiny washroom. I can't resist the pastry display. Trying to pick from the delicious array, I finally order a Gerbaud slice, a gorgeous-looking layered cake with walnut and apricot jam filling covered with chocolate ganache, to have with my café au lait. Since there is nowhere to sit, I take my delicious bounty across the street and sit on the wide steps of the Cathedral of St. John the Divine to eat it as the life of the city swirls around me. The scale, the pace, the superlative of everything, the sense that something extraordinary could happen at any moment, is exhilarating.

I walk alternating between the broad avenues and the tree-lined streets of the Upper West side and feel a strange shift whenever I turn a corner. On the Avenues, hundreds of energetic figures walk in time to some silent metronome, while on the streets, there is nary a person, and I feel like I have stepped into a surreal still life, a Magritte-type of Manhattan where pedestrians can take big bites out of bowler-hatted apples falling from the sky.

I make it down to Central Park, which provides a bucolic respite from the busy Avenue. A huge flat boulder, the size of our garage, invites me to climb to the top. I lie flat on my back and feel the heat of it. Above me, a flawless blue sky is uninterrupted except for five white clouds trailing one after the other like fluffy baby ducks following their mother. I close my eyes and watch an x-ray version of the duck family through my lids. There is more sky here than there is between the skyscrapers on the streets and avenues; it's liberating.

Later, heading south from midtown, I witness organized chaos: huge garbage trucks miraculously navigating around cars double and triple parked, pedestrians jostling around neatly bundled heaps of reeking garbage. It's garbage collection day, New York style.

I come upon the famous red Love sculpture on 6th Avenue and crawl in between the 'V' and 'E' for a smoke. I am literally in love with New York, feeling sophisticated, blowing smoke with flair, and not caring who sees me. Just then, a woman overdressed in a shimmery silver gown leans between my letters.

"Do you have a light?" She sits, gingerly floating onto the base of our statue as if descending from a great height, and shakily lights her cigarette. I look into her eyes and find a strange vacancy there.

"Are you alright?"

"I've been lost in the subway all night," she says, not as a reply to me but as if making a general statement. Then, as abruptly as she appeared, she gets up and disappears among a group of pedestrians crossing against the light in a brief gap in the traffic. Even though horns are blasting at them, they don't alter their pace. Extraordinary things happen all the time in New York City.

At 53rd Street, there's a sign for MoMa. I barely get past the gift shop when I see the sunlit courtyard with bench seating that calls me to the serene, art-filled setting. Once seated, I realize I've lost track of time. When I pull George's card from my pocket to ask him what's the quickest way back, I see I've missed a couple of messages from Alexander: I'll be home by five. And: I'm home. Where are you? Are you okay?

I'm chagrined that I've caused him to worry. It was the same with Dad. I'd defy him by disregarding curfews and then regret making him worry about me. Now, I return his call apprehensively, prepared to be admonished.

"Hey, Manon, where are you?"

"I'm in the courtyard at MoMa admiring a Calder sculpture. They let me in for free because they're closing soon. I've been walking all day."

"I'll come and get you. Be outside in about twenty minutes."

CHAPTER SIX

The courtyard is still bright, with the sun filtering through the branches of the young Chinese Elms. By contrast, out in the street, only a sliver of sky is visible through the tall buildings, trapping the day's oppressive heat between its walls.

A little black sports car pulls up, and Alexander emerges looking fresh and casually elegant in raw silk and linen. I feel shabby and grimy. I'm arrested once again by his good looks. My sketches of him from memory don't do him justice. He is so strikingly handsome that even New Yorkers take sidelong glances to see if he might be a celebrity. It's impossible to imagine we are even remotely related – he being tall, fair and well-dressed, while I'm just average height, with dark hair and dressed like a struggling student. He approaches and quite naturally envelops me in a hug, holding tight like the long-lost relatives we are, but I don't feel like a relative. I only feel his taut body crushed against mine.

"Manon, you had me worried. You should have called."

"I'm sorry," I say, but provide no excuses.

"Are you more tired or hungry? Do you want to go home and take a rest or have something to eat first?"

Other than the Gerbaud this afternoon, the last time I remember eating was the lousy breakfast of soggy egg salad on a squashed croissant at the airport in Montreal, but fatigue trumps hunger.

"I'm pretty tired. Can we just go home?" It feels odd calling his place home as if we are a family that lives together.

Back at The Colosseum, we are greeted by the friendly concierge.

"George, this is my cousin, Manon Mouland. She'll be staying with me for a while. She's new to The City, so be sure to give her any help she needs. Manon, this is George Waters."

"Don't worry, Mr. M, Manon and I are old friends. She's got my number and knows that she can call me for anything."

This time, I get a good look at the palatial lobby with its onyx-inlaid marble floors gleaming under crystal chandeliers. We ride up to the fourth floor in an old elevator paneled in rich mahogany with twelve ceramic buttons and shiny brass fittings. My stomach ascends faster than the elevator. Is it fatigue, hunger, or the nearness of him that's causing this giddiness?

The foyer of his apartment is the size of my bedroom in Lennoxville. The floor is mosaic tiled. There's an antique coat rack with an oval mirror and a wooden bench beside a brass umbrella stand. I feel out of my element and despair that Alexander and I could have anything in common. I fear that at any moment, this relationship will turn out to be a big lie and will end in disaster.

"Come on, I'll show you the apartment. I want you to make yourself at home." He grabs my small suitcase and knapsack from where George had left them in the hall.

We begin our tour through an arched entry into a corridor that must be fifty feet long, passing a dining room and living room on the left and a large kitchen, a powder room, and a small bed/sitting room on the right. We turn left at the end of the corridor and step through a doorway to another smaller hallway. There are three bedrooms in this back wing of the apartment.

The master bedroom, complete with ensuite, has a balcony and five windows facing south and west with an oblique view of the Hudson. Next to it is a 'dressing room'.

"This was my mother's refuge. She loved fine clothes and indulged her passion with frequent shopping sprees. Feel free to explore her closet; you are of similar stature and might find something that fits."

The room is painted claret, and with the late afternoon light pouring in through the west-facing window, it has a warm womb-like ambience. A fainting couch, worthy of an Ingres painting, upholstered in burgundy mohair, sits right in the middle of the room as if staged and ready for the nude model to take her place. There are elegant-legged occasional tables, a mirrored make-up table and a freestanding full-length, gilt-framed mirror just leaning against the wall.

I catch a glimpse of myself in it with Alexander standing near me and see I'm about six inches shorter than him. He towers over me. With the window behind us, my mass of dark hair looks like a storm cloud with no distinct edges. While Alexander takes a call, I venture a closer look at my image, trying to see what he sees.

In this mirror, in this room, I look petite. My large brown eyes have flecks of gold. Dad used to say they'd lighten or darken with my mood, just like my mother's. It's a tiny clue of what my mother might have been like. They are downturned, giving me a mournful look, but my upturned nose gives me an air of defiance. Guys always liked my lips, which are full with a well-defined cupid's bow accentuated by a deep philtrum. Alexander doesn't seem to see them as luscious. He doesn't notice my unchaste vibes directed at him or just doesn't acknowledge them, which is worse.

The dominant piece of furniture is an armoire with double doors and intricate carvings that, I know from watching escapist hours of The Antiques Road Show, must be 18th century French oak. I love this room. I could be happy just lounging on that gorgeous couch, doing nothing.

There is another bedroom, which will be my room, with an adjacent bathroom. As he drops my knapsack on a chair, it flips open, and the oversized, dog-eared Audubon falls to the floor. I can't fathom why on earth I picked this large picture book to bring with me. Perhaps as an anchor to my real world or as an old friend, as if I was a child clinging to a teddy bear.

"I have a first edition of 'Audubon's Birds of America', you know. It's in the library at my house in Connecticut."

"Are you kidding me?" I know how rare those editions are, only 120 of them exist in the whole world, and they're worth millions of dollars.

"I do not kid you. I acquired it a few years ago when it came up for sale at Sotheby's."

The *New York Times* did a feature on Audubon when one of the books sold for over eight million dollars. I remember wondering what kind of person could and would buy such a rarity.

I have already begun to understand how wealthy Alexander is, and now I'm starting to see him in a new light; if he treasures this book, then it would seem we have more in common than I thought.

George's voice interrupts us through the intercom, announcing a delivery.

"I've ordered up some food. You must be hungry." I just now realize how famished I am as my stomach replies with a growl, and we both laugh.

Big paper shopping bags from Zabar's Deli emit mouth-watering aromas. There are packages of smoked fish, a platter of crudités and an assortment of cheeses in one bag, and another contains a tall canister of Foie Gras with Truffles and a long French baguette. And there is cheesecake. Enough food for a party.

My gluttony abated, but I am still hungry for answers. I want to ask all my questions at once. I want to know what his mother's explanations were about my father. I want to know everything he knows, not just the sparse facts about the relationship between our parents. Even before I get to all my outstanding questions, I want to know more about Alexander.

"This place is huge. Do you live here by yourself?"

"Yes, it was my parents' home. After they died, I gave up my little apartment in the East Village and moved back here. Your room was my room growing up." Why am I relieved that he lives alone? "Living here again brings back memories of my mother. She had quite a personality, vivacious one minute and broodingly poetic the next. Arriving home from shopping sprees with bags from Bergdorf and Saks and Neiman Marcus, she would call excitedly, *'Xander, come see what I got!'* (She was the only one who called me Xander) and I became excited too as she pulled her 'finds' from their wrappings, flinging tissue paper all over the room." His eyes soften with the memory, and his face takes on a wistful expression. "She was exciting to be around. I wish you could have known her."

"What about your dad? What was he like?"

"Dad was an optometrist with a personality to match, which is to say he was *not* as exciting as my mom. He owned a chain of retail optical stores called Selby Parkes. You may have heard of them. Their mission was to provide quality eyewear of their own design at reasonable prices. Dad instilled in me the ethic that a business can be profitable and do good in the world without charging a premium."

"How did your parents meet?"

"Dad was at a convention in Montreal when he saw my mom sitting by herself in Phillips Square. He was immediately smitten with her and asked her to have a coffee with him. Then he kept returning to the city until he managed to convince her to come to New York with him."

"Was she reluctant to go with him?"

"She was young and probably a little scared. But Dad always managed to get his way."

He searches for something to show me and pulls a photo album from the living room's built-in shelves. Flipping through it, he finds what he's looking for: a formal family portrait. I recognize Gabrielle from the snapshots I found in Dad's room. She is beautiful in a classic Anglo-Saxon way: fair-complexioned, blue-eyed, with an aquiline nose that looks like Alexander's. His father stands tall and is handsome in a darker, more rugged way. Alexander poses languidly in a blazer with a crest and an open-collared shirt. As a family, they look like they could be on the cover of Life.

"My parents were very close. They didn't need anyone but each other. As a boy, I had to excel at everything just to get their attention. My Mom encouraged me to reach for the moon."

"It seems like you succeeded. How did you manage it?"

"I graduated high school early, and because they thought I was a musical prodigy, they sent me to the Berklee College of Music in Boston. But although I love music, I wanted to be a scientist, like my dad, so I switched to Cornell.

After they died, I began digging around to find some connection to a family that didn't seem to exist until I saw your dad's obituary. It triggered a vague memory of a trip to Quebec about twenty years ago, where I met him. It was never talked about and so brief that I wasn't sure if the memory was real."

Sitting opposite me in an overstuffed armchair, he becomes pensive, studying the pattern in his Persian rug. I study it, too, and feel the same hollow feeling that I sense from him.

"My dad's colleague at the library remembered that visit at my mother's funeral. Apparently, there was some altercation and a sudden departure."

"So, it wasn't an aberration. It actually happened. How long that road trip home felt, with the palpable acrimony between my parents filling the car. You know what? Now I'm remembering that I even met you as a small child. You were a cute little girl with sad brown eyes as big as saucers. Do you remember me at all?"

"No, I don't remember much about that time. I never wanted to think about it, I guess. I thought my mom left because of me."

"Why would you ever think that?"

"Because I was a bad girl."

Alexander leans forward in his chair, resting his elbows on his knees, fingers intertwined and looks intently at me.

"How bad could you have been?"

I'm bent forward, too, my arms hugging my chest, and I become self-conscious, being so close to him that I could just reach out and stroke his beautiful face. I lean back and try to explain the guilt that has established itself as a personality trait. Even today, I blame myself first for whatever goes wrong, whether it was my fault or not. I tell him my secret.

"I always thought it was my fault she went away because I had broken a treasured Meissen figurine, a little goatherd with rosy cheeks and an orange band around his grey hat. She would let me play with it sometimes if I promised to be a good girl. I loved how his hand and his tiny, perfect fingers rested perpetually on the neck of his little white goat. I can still remember being crushed by sorrow when I understood it was gone forever. After that, she rarely took me in her lap, and eventually, she stopped hugging me too. I decided that it was because I had not kept my promise and was *not* a good girl. Soon after that, she was gone from life."

"Do you remember her at all?"

"I was only four when she died, and Dad never really talked about her. I can't conjure her from memory. I have to rely on the only photo album we have, which has mostly pictures of me when I was little. The rare ones of her are out of focus. The only clue that she was my mother is the cloud of dark hair around her head, as unruly as mine." My hand automatically reaches up to smooth it back.

Alexander reaches out and touches a strand of my hair. His gesture causes a large lump to develop in my throat, and I'm fighting to hold back tears. He urges me to continue, so I try to swallow the lump.

"Those few photos of the three of us make up whatever sense of family I have. There is one from Canada Day, 1983. It shows the three of us on the lawn of Parliament Hill in Ottawa. I'm sitting on Dad's shoulders, my mother is looking up at me, and Dad is smiling at her. I'm holding a little paper flag and have red maple leaves painted on my chubby cheeks. We looked like a happy family. I painted that scene during my Norman Rockwell phase when I was about twelve. There is another one of me in my mom's lap, which makes me sad. Her long dark hair had lost its luster by then, her face looked gaunt, and her eyes no longer sparkled with gold flecks."

It's strange that I am uttering these thoughts to a man I have just met. How is it that I feel safe unburdening myself to him?

"How unfortunate that you had to process that grief through guilt."

I never thought about it that way. My heart feels large inside my chest and beats exaggeratedly. It wearies me.

The evening seems infinite, intimate, and I never want it to end, but my fatigue rules, and I seem to be drifting in and out of this precious moment. I struggle to stay awake, especially now that I have shared this familiar ache, which is as comforting as pressure on a bruise.

The following day, I sleep until noon and awake, angry with myself for having missed the opportunity to have breakfast with Alexander. He's gone, but New York City awaits.

I do my best to wrestle my unruly mane into a bun and find something other than jeans to wear. I haven't brought much with me, so I try to dress it up with an old silk blouse from a second-hand store in Montreal. I step out on the balcony for a quick smoke and see a greenish slip of the Hudson in a gap between the Elm trees dividing Riverside Drive. There's a lot of activity below me: a steady stream of cars turning on to 115th Street, joggers and cyclists in their designated lanes, and many pedestrians walking their dogs. The dogs all have a New Yorker attitude. They trot along in designer chic or amble beside their people, pooping at will on the concrete, oblivious of honking horns and skateboards whizzing by.

Today, I really want to make it downtown, so I ask George how to get there by subway.

"It's easy as pie, you just stay on the '1 Line' till you get to the Canal St. station, that'll put you right at the bottom of Soho. It'll take about 40 minutes."

This time, I send Alexander a text to let him know I've gone out, heading to Soho. He replies instantly, saying we'll meet up around five and head out to Connecticut.

I descend into the murky labyrinth of the New York City subway for the long ride downtown. It's dank and smells of awful things I can't identify. I find the southbound platform and board the train along with a small group of students, all intently engaged in some esoteric argument about postmodern architecture. I eavesdrop until they leave the train, and I feel envious of their privilege, camaraderie, and the University experience I wanted, so different from my brief stint at Champlain College in Lennoxville.

As we get further south, the car becomes more and more crowded. I worry I'll get trapped by the crowd and miss my stop. Finally, I arrive at Canal St. and emerge from the subterranean dimness into blinding sunshine.

The area is alive with people. What's their hurry? Where are they all going? They all seem to have a mission. I am accosted by street vendors offering all kinds of wares: beautiful jewelry, colorful scarves, gadgets for things I can't even fathom, and art. An eclectic display of everything from portrait caricatures to abstract expressionist paintings imitating the style of the 'New York School' group of artists. I envision myself settling on a stool under a canopy displaying my work. Would anyone stop to look at it, let alone buy any of it?

I happen upon a vintage clothing store with an interesting array of garments hanging on a rod on the sidewalk. I go inside to browse through the racks of unique clothing. The store smells of old perfume and dry-cleaning chemicals. The fabrics feel luxurious, all made of natural fibers: cotton, linen, cashmere, silk, and fine merino wools. Each item has a history, which the chatty owner is eager to share. I pick up a tunic-style dress with exquisite hand embroidery.

"That's an Elsa Schiaparelli from the 1920s. It has all the original nacré buttons. I think it might fit you." I look at the price tag and know it's unattainable. Then I spot a pair of baggy fawn-colored trousers that I love. "Those were Katherine Hepburn's. They are made of the finest summer-weight wool and lined in satin. It's a rare find." The price tag on it is in the four digits. I make a vow to pay more attention to what I wear.

The time has gone so quickly, and it's already almost 5:00 p. m. when I get another text from Alexander: *Grab a cab and come back to the apartment, we'll have dinner at Elderberry.*

CHAPTER SEVEN

It's about a forty-five-minute drive to Greenwich, Connecticut. Alexander drives with easy, lazy confidence; his hands relaxed on the steering wheel of one of those low-to-the-ground British two-seaters seen in James Bond movies, which can rapidly fill with sexual tension. The tension is already there, on my part at least. He hasn't noticed my wanton attraction to him or given any sign of reciprocal desire. That he is unattainable makes me want him all the more.

Speeding along I-95, the vibration of the road transfers to me. I sneak sidelong glances at Alexander's profile, thrilled to be sitting so close to him, sharing this small space, enveloped by his intoxicating masculine scent.

"Do you like horses, Manon?" he asks.

"I did go through a 'horse' phase when I was little. Dad used to take me to the country fairs in the fall, and I always went straight for the pony rides. It's all I wanted to do. I would lean forward in the saddle, dangerously close to slipping off, so I could lay my cheek on the pony's neck and hug him the whole ride long. I'd whisper, "You're the best pony in the whole world," and when he wiggled his ear, I thought we understood each other. I went round and round so many times that Dad had to cajole me into giving other kids a chance."

"That's so sweet! What about later? Did you do any riding?"

"I wanted to but never really got the chance."

"Well then, you'll be happy to know that I have a stable with four beauties that Hedley looks after. He can give you a few lessons, and you can ride all you want."

"Really?" I ask stupidly, as excitement tingles in my veins. "I would love that."

Then Alexander abruptly changes the subject.

"Do you smoke a lot?"

The bucket seat I'm strapped into suddenly feels like a trap.

"Not much," I reply brusquely, wanting to shut this topic down. How does he even know I smoke? I've never lit up in front of him. I must reek of nicotine. Embarrassed and annoyed at what feels like an accusation, I make an awkward segue; "How did you find out that your mom and my dad were cousins?"

"All in due time, Manon, now listen to me. You need to quit smoking, for all the reasons you already know, but also because I won't have my newly discovered relative compromising her health." And just like that, Dad is in the car lecturing me about my bad behavior.

"I won't smoke in your house, I promise."

"The promise I want is that you'll quit. I can help you with that. Will you at least promise to try?"

"Okay," I say, wondering if I would trade my guilty pleasure for Alexander's approval. "Yes, I will try." Then suddenly changing the subject, I ask, "Do you have a girlfriend?"

"Nobody special. How about you? You must have at least one special relationship."

To my regret, I've initiated a problematic topic. What can I tell him about my love life? Nothing. How can I explain that I prefer to be alone, and that the casual relationships I've had are based solely on my sexual cravings. I'm sure he would disapprove of my self-indulgence.

My longest relationship was with Richard, a guy I hooked up with during one of my forays to Montreal. He was a bit older than me and could turn my legs to jelly with a mere glance. Richard was a trainer at Blue Bonnets Raceway, highly respected in his world as a horse whisperer. Horses were a part of him. He drew me like a magnet and played out my most depraved fantasies with me. When we made the rounds, inspecting the horses before their training runs, I clung to him, still role-playing.

On the backstretch, people are insulated from the real world and united by their love of the animals. They adhere to their own moral code where smoking, drinking, gambling, and all kinds of sex are accepted norms. It is a mysterious world where I felt like an outsider, a role I am used to. Despite that, I felt a heady zest being in that environment: early mornings and late nights, the smell of straw and dung, the proximity of the horses and Richard.

Ultimately, Richard became a bit too rough, even for me, so we parted after a few months. I never mentioned Richard to Dad, but he knew. I knew he knew because he was impossible to live with during that time. I'm not about to reveal this sordid bit of my past to Alexander and risk him shunning me.

"No, not really" is all I can come up with.

We have talked practically the whole way, so I'm surprised when we finally pull into a driveway between two stone pillars that flank the long, low brick walls of his property.

"Are we at your place already?"

"Welcome to Elderberry Lane."

The gravel driveway is edged by shrubs laden with clusters of plump purple orbs glistening in the sun. About fifty yards from the entrance is a lovely Colonial-style building with whitewashed siding, a pillared porch, and a wood-shingled roof complete with dormers.

"This looks like a Martha Stewart dream house!" I blurt out like a star-struck fan.

"I'm glad you approve." He turns his wide smile to me and looks genuinely pleased.

As he pulls up to one of the three garage doors, the front door opens, and we are greeted by a stout middle-aged woman, neatly attired in a dark green chemise dress with a smock-style apron over it and sensible shoes. She has penetrating hazel eyes and a wiry hedge of auburn hair tinged with grey strands that spring from her temples. Her expression is flat.

"Mrs. O, this is Manon Mouland. Manon, Mrs. Ogilvy is my secret treasure. She takes care of this place and me with impeccable efficiency." Mrs. Ogilvy looks intimidating, and I'm not sure whether to shake her hand or curtsey.

The smell of roasting potatoes and fresh-cut hydrangeas reaches my nostrils as we enter a large foyer. There is a cozy den on the left and a formal dining room on the right. Light streams in at all angles from the many windows. The floors are gleaming hardwood, and all the walls are white with dark mahogany trim, the neutral background to a collection of stunning horse paintings. Seeing them, I recall my own sketches from Blue Bonnets; one day, I'll do a painting like these. I'm impressed by the décor and the soaring ceilings. Alexander places his hand on the small of my back, urging me forward, and my spine tingles as we enter an enormous open space.

"This house was built in the '30s," he says. "Through the years, it has been restored as close to its as-built condition as possible, but when I bought it, I had the kitchen gutted and tried to recreate a French Country style."

I note every detail of the large kitchen on the right, taking my time running my hand along the speckled stone countertops as if I were a prospective buyer. It has gleaming blue and white tiles and is complete with quaint crockery pieces and copper molds of roosters. I follow behind him to the breakfast area and look out the French doors to a large patio overlooking an expansive, verdant landscape. The view is like a Camille Corot painting.

"This is breathtaking," I say, rooted to the spot.

"Come," he says, taking my elbow and leading me into the Great Room. The ambiance is warm and inviting. A long sofa, a cozy love seat, a big comfy armchair, and an ottoman are all plushly upholstered in leather, suede, and velvet fabrics. "This fireplace is open on the other side in the library, which I'll show you later. It's where I keep the Audubon." Deep navy blues and various shades of brown create warmth, with the printed textiles of cushions, bolsters, and blankets adding texture. A wall of shelving to the left of the fireplace houses a turntable and a multitude of vinyl albums. To the right, there is a closed door.

"What's in there?"

"I use that as an office when I work at home," he says. "I keep it locked for security reasons, but please explore the rest of the house freely. Make yourself at home."

The atrium ceiling makes the space feel huge, and looking up, I can see the second-floor landing beyond a mahogany railing. The atmosphere smells woodsy from the smoky fireplace, freshly hewn birch logs, drying pine cones on the hearth, and the suede and leather upholstery. Mixed in with these scents is the sweet fragrance from bouquets of pale pink and blue hydrangeas placed around the room. This mixture of scents is what Alexander smells like.

I trail behind him around a corner where there is a washroom, a butler's pantry, and a mud room by the side door, and we circle around to the kitchen once more.

"I'm starved," he says. "I'll start up the barbeque and grill some steaks."

I follow him outside, where Mrs. O is setting the table. Alexander gets busy at the barbeque, and I sit in awkward silence, watching Mrs. O laying plates and cutlery for three. I wonder if she will join us and am about to inquire when she asks,

"Where exactly is Lennoxville?"

"It's in an area of Quebec called the Eastern Townships, a borough of the town of Sherbrooke, like the boroughs of New York but on a miniscule scale." I try a little levity and fail. Mrs. O has fallen silent again as she tosses the salad.

"Almost ready," calls Alexander, "Mrs. O, shall I get the roasted potatoes?"

"Yes, and turn off the oven." Who is this woman actually that she can boss her boss around?

"How did you come to know Alexander?" I ask her, and she is surprisingly forthcoming,

"Mrs. Montgomery hired me as a private nurse to Alexander's father when he was diagnosed with ALS." Alexander never mentioned that his dad was so sick, and my heart sinks.

"That must have been a while ago. How is it that you decided to stay with him?"

"Alexander and I need each other. I look after him, and he takes care of me." This answer generates more questions, but dinner is served, and after a brief toast with red wine, we fall upon the toothsome meal in silence.

֍֍֍֍

After dinner, Mrs. O retreats, and Alexander gets busy in the kitchen. He assembles apothecary jars and begins to measure ingredients in a blender.

I perch on one of the stools by the counter, where I have a good view of him and I can't take my eyes off him. I observe the expertise with which he performs his task, his lithe movements – his buttocks. Finally, he hands me a glass.

"Drink this, it'll help ease your withdrawal symptoms now that you won't be smoking anymore."

I take a tentative sip and am surprised at how creamy, smooth, and delicious it is.

"Mmm, it's good. What's in it?"

"It has elderberry juice and an herbal mixture of Ashwagandha, a natural substance known to help calm the mind; CBD, which activates serotonin receptors in the brain blocking reward mechanisms; Passionflower, which is reported to ease the mental symptoms of withdrawal; and Damiana made from the dried leaf of an American tropical shrub that has been shown to be beneficial in relieving tension. Side effects are minimal. You may notice a heightened libido from the Damiana, which is sometimes used as an aphrodisiac." The last thing I need, being around him! "Okay now, let's make this official: give me whatever cigarettes you have left." When I hand him a half-full pack, I feel surprisingly hopeful. If I can give this bad habit up, can I also let go of my other vices and become a better person?

We spend the rest of the evening on the patio. It's on a knoll overlooking a kidney-shaped pool at the foot of it. The water twinkles in the last rays of the sun and reflects a peach and mauve sunset that Corot himself might have painted.

"Mrs. O told me she was a nurse and that your dad had ALS."

"Yes, Mom found her through a contact at one of her charities. She liked how Mrs. O was protective of Dad. Unfortunately, after only a month of looking after him, Dad choked to death on a piece of bread he'd snuck behind her back. There was nothing she could do to save him. She still can't forgive herself."

"Oh, how awful!"

"Yes, it was a very difficult time. It will be five years this September. After that, I insisted she stay on to look after my mother, who had plunged into a deep depression. Mom ultimately overdosed a month later, and Mrs. O was devastated. She was ready to quit nursing. I liked her and was grateful to her for her devotion to my parents. I asked her to stay, and then she came to Elderberry and has been looking after the place ever since."

Alexander pulls a short length of rope from his pocket, and his fingers begin to work, forming a complicated knot.

"I'm so sorry..." My hollow words hang in the air.

These revelations, especially Gabrielle's suicide, hit me so hard that my heart feels too big in my chest. How Alexander must have suffered. And then I think of Dad and wonder if he knew. My family history is unfolding, fraught with criminality, incest, and suicide.

CHAPTER EIGHT

We move to the lounge chairs by the fire pit, and Alexander builds a pyramid of twigs and small birch logs. His manner is efficient, and his movements are elegant. Finally he puts a long match to the structure and blows gently until a small flame erupts. He sits beside me and retrieves the bit of rope from his pocket, undoes the previous knots, and begins anew.

"What are you doing?" I ask, indicating the rope.

"It's a hobby of sorts. I started it a few years ago to distract myself when dark thoughts began to intrude. The intricacies of the various stopper knots, hitches, and loops serve both as a mental and physical diversion. There is always a new knot for me to master."

I'm unaccustomed to how easily Alexander expresses his feelings. Dad and other guys I have known were all very closed, forcing me to guess what they felt. When he talks about his parents, his eyes soften, and he looks almost vulnerable. He's been so earnest about his desire to learn about his family; it connects us somehow, and this connectedness complicates my feelings toward him. Mostly, he lights me up with a deep, slow-burning desire. He places one long leg across his thigh, creating a clear view of his crotch. I watch his lips and imagine his kiss, but I give my head a virtual shake. Now, I want to wrap my arms around him to comfort him, knowing the pain he must be carrying. He's lost his parents, and so have I. We are connected.

"In the years since my parents died," he says, "I have been trying to think of some way to delve into their past. I wanted to find someone who may have known them in their younger days, but it was no easy task because neither of them had any close friends. All they ever needed was each other."

I detect a note of bitterness, and my own resentment of Dad's secrecy surfaces.

"My dad also shut me out. I don't have anyone to turn to either. Even Sage, who knew him before I was born, has no knowledge of his history."

"When I returned from your dad's funeral, I thought of going through the guest book from my own dad's funeral. It was mostly filled with business associates. My mom didn't have a guest book, only cards of condolences, mainly from people involved in the charities she supported. However, there was one card that sounded personal, and the diction was kind of familiar. Wait, I'll show you." He pockets his bit of rope and goes inside.

When he returns, he hands me an oversized card with an ostentatious bouquet of pink roses and purple irises on the front. Inside in a practiced and perfected script, the message reads;

> *"Alexander, my grief for the loss of the lovely lady that was your mother is profound. I send my sincerest condolences – Rosalia Menendes."*

"It reminded me that every once in a while, my mother would go to high tea with her at the Plaza. It was one of the few things she did without my father. I hoped that maybe Mom would have confided in her and that she might be able to shed some light on who my parents really were."

"Did you find her?"

"Yes."

"Did she remember anything?"

"We'll see. We're having lunch with her on Monday."

On Saturday, I finally meet the horses, and Alexander tours me around his three-hundred-acre property. In the barn, there are stalls for ten horses, but only four are currently in residence. Behind the barn is a charming little whitewashed bungalow, not visible from the house, its window boxes foaming with trailing red geraniums. This is Hedley's house. To the left is a tennis court.

As we enter the barn, a flock of sparrows flutter in the rafters. Hedley is mucking the stalls,

"Mornin'," he calls, thrusting a pitchforkful of hay.

"Good morning," Alexander and I say in unison.

The chill inside the barn makes me shiver, but seeing the horses warms my heart. As we advance to greet the first one, they all become animated, sticking their heads out over the webbing, nodding, and snorting. I think they're curious, or maybe they're just happy to see Alexander. Three of them are retired Thoroughbreds, equine royalty. The fourth is a Quarterhorse. Alexander greets each one in turn and introduces them by name.

"This is my horse Artemis, better known as Arty. He's a gelding." Arty has a striking white blaze on his face, contrasting his chestnut coat. Alexander pats him vigorously, and he responds with persistent nudging until Alexander produces a carrot.

"This is Banjo, also a gelding. He's as gentle as they come. He will be your horse, Manon." I hear his words, but the concept of 'my horse' is too fantastic for me to comprehend. I'm blown away.

Banjo is more sedate than the others. He has large, gentle eyes, a perfectly shaped white star and stripe on his forehead. The edges of the star reach almost to the corners of his eyes. His mane, tail, and the tips of his ears are black in sharp contrast to his lustrous red-brown coat. He looks elegant, as if dressed for a special occasion. He nuzzles me, and I'm immediately charmed by him. As we approach the third stall, Hedley interjects,

"This is my horse, Cassandra. We call her Cassie. She's a filly. Isn't she beautiful?" Hedley reminds me of Richard, loose-limbed and rhythmic in his movements. Like Richard, he shares an intimacy with the horses that somehow makes him incredibly sexy.

Cassie has what they call a dish face with a pretty curl of an irregular star on her forehead. She obviously favors Hedley, resting her chin familiarly on his shoulder. The fourth horse is a palomino gelding named Fred.

The horses eye me curiously, snort, and nod their heads. Alexander coos to them in a seductive voice, compliments them, and tells them how beautiful they are, and they nuzzle him affectionately. I watch his large hands patting their necks, stroking their noses, and shamefully, I envy them.

"Manon, would you like to take a ride? I'll show you the trails."

"I – I don't know how," I admit.

"Today, you can ride with me. Later, Hedley will teach you the basics. Hey Hedley, would you mind saddling Arty while I show Manon around?"

We walk around the paddock over toward the tennis court and are greeted by a couple of black and white Border Collies who interrupt their play and bound toward us when they see Alexander. They can barely contain their excitement as they leap and jump up on him. He rubs their backs and pats their heads.

"Good dog, Bobby!" Bobby licks his hand while the other jumps on him, vying for his attention. "Down, Macy, good girl." Once they've calmed down, he turns his attention to me again.

"Do you play tennis?"

"I tried to once or twice. I was never any good at it. Do you?"

"After riding, it's my favorite form of exercise," he says, and his glorious smile lights his face. "I play with Hedley whenever I get the chance." I imagine him on the court with his bursts of power, his well-defined calves, glutes, forearms, and shoulder blades. I see how this form of exercise has very pleasing benefits to his physique. "If you like, I can teach you to improve your game so you can enjoy it too."

When Hedley brings Arty around, I get a better look at him. Standing out in the open, he is towering above me. Along with the white blaze on his face, he has white stockings on his hind legs and a tail so long it almost touches the ground. He flicks it back and forth, eager to get going.

Alexander mounts gracefully. I let out an involuntary squeal as Hedley gives me a leg up onto the saddle behind him. I'm up so high, pressed so close to Alexander, that I feel positively giddy.

"Manon, don't be nervous. Arty is a very experienced trail horse; just wrap your arms around me, and we'll go at a nice slow pace. Relax, you'll always be safe with me."

Hugging him from behind, I press myself against his muscular torso. The heat through his t-shirt transfers to me, spreading like wildfire, making my cheeks burn.

We enter the forest, and immediately, as if entering an air-conditioned room, the summer heat dissipates, and a cool stillness envelops us. I go from hot to cold to hot in the dappling of light and shade. My senses are swathed in the green odor of oak leaves, damp moss, and the redolent scent of detritus dug up by Arty's hooves. I am heady with this olfactory mixture, with the strobe-like effect of light through the leaves, with the regular rhythm of clopping hooves and the contact of Alexander's back against my front.

It seems that Dad, in dying so suddenly, has crashed and opened a portal to another world for me. I've entered it naïvely thinking that I have landed in a kind of utopia where all my dreams are actualized, and everything is possible. This new world is nothing like the world I inhabit. In my small-town life with Dad, I lived on the edge of truth, suspended above a void, uncertain of what came before me. Now, I am plunged into a new reality without Dad having my back. Now, the void has ghostlike figures swimming in it. My world has morphed into the vivid reality of Alexander's world.

CHAPTER NINE

We arrive at Sarabeth's on West 59th Street at the height of the lunch hour rush. Rosalia is already installed in a private alcove. Alexander recognizes her and whispers to the hostess, who ushers us through the noisy, bustling restaurant that sounds like buzzing bees in a hive: diners, servers, bus staff, and groups of hungry patrons waiting for tables. We are ushered through to an alcove that, by some trick of architecture, is suddenly a lot quieter.

"She's in Joan Rivers' nook," she informs us proudly, adding that "Joan Rivers was a regular here," and to further impress us with her 'insider' information, she adds, "She lived down the block on Columbus Circle."

As we approach, Rosalia greets us dramatically, throwing her arms up, sending her cashmere Pashmina flying, releasing a whiff of sickeningly sweet perfume.

"Alexander, look at you; so handsome and accomplished. The last time I saw you, you were a mere boy vying for your mother's attention." She looks him up and down approvingly and then at me judgmentally. "And who is this, your girlfriend?" Her gaze takes in my ordinariness, and I squirm. She reminds me of Cruella deVil, with her hair dyed jet black except for one conspicuous white streak.

"This is Manon Mouland, my second cousin. She's visiting from Quebec."

"Don't tell me this is Gregory's daughter!" I am shocked and irrationally angry with her for her casual use of my father's name.

"What do you know of my father?"

She winks and says suggestively, "Oh, I know a thing or two about him and Gabrielle."

I bristle at her tone, but Alexander is rapt and leans in to absorb every word she utters. After navigating through the menu options and listening to updates on Alexander's career, Rosalia holds forth on everything from her political views to her contempt for the tourists that flood the city, with their gawking wonder and boisterous children in tow.

Alexander puts the menu down, ready with his selection, and he launches into his line of questioning.

"How did you and my mother meet?"

"At Bergdorf's. I helped her pick out an outfit for the opera, which, as it turns out, we were both going to attend. After that, we went to high tea at the Plaza and had such a good time that we vowed to meet there regularly. Gabrielle always bounced in, full of excitement and dressed to kill. She was lovely and endearing, and she fluttered like a bird released from her cage, unsure of where to settle."

"Did you also know my dad?"

"I met Sebastian at the opera that one time, but he wasn't very friendly; he didn't like Gabrielle's attention diverted by anyone. He had her on a short leash. If she lingered over her tea in defiance of the schedule he imposed on her, there would be consequences.

What's the worst that could happen? I asked her, and she just raised an eyebrow and smiled mischievously, leaving it to my imagination. I think she liked challenging him."

Alexander stiffens and refrains from asking any more questions. I wince at the image of something lascivious. I can no longer concentrate on the food I carefully selected from the bountiful menu.

'Cruella' carries on glibly, unconcerned with Alexander's reaction to this aspect of his parents' relationship. I glance at him. He seems to be in perfect control, but I see his jaw tightening. For a moment, he looks positively menacing, and I wonder if this might be what his father might have been like. With a slight shift in posture, he looks ready to leap out of his seat.

Then it's my turn to have my equilibrium upended as she turns her attention to me and says in a slow, gossipy manner, relishing the effect she is having on us,

"Gabrielle was so besotted with Gregory that Sebastian forbade her to ever mention his name." Then she releases a bomb as casually as a dropped hanky; "Gabrielle never was a hundred percent sure of who Alexander's father was."

Alexander and I exchange a brief glance, in which we silently agree that we've heard enough. He calls for the bill and makes ready to leave. He is visibly upset now; his warm grey eyes have turned to cold anthracite, and his lips are as taut as his posture. He's a coil ready to spring. My heart is torn with empathy for him and with the painful revelation of my father's illicit love affair.

Instead of staying in the city, we head back to Elderberry because Alexander wants to go riding to clear his head. On the drive back, the tension in the car is no longer sexual, and the silence is immense. It's not simply the physical silence that fills the small space of his Aston Martin DB5. It's something deep and ominous, like a storm cloud about to unleash a deluge.

He goes straight out to the barn, leaving me standing alone in the middle of the Great Room, looking out at the landscape beginning to brown in the July heat. Moments later, Alexander emerges atop Arty. He leans in, melding with the animal, and gallops away. Arty's hooves pound on the turf, and my heart mimics the rhythm. The implications of Rosalia's blunt statement thumps in my brain ... my dad might also be Alexander's dad ... he was not the dad I knew.

My whole body is clenched like a fist as the permutations unroll; my moral stalwart father is lost; the family I gained is also lost, and if Alexander is my half-brother, then my feelings for him are incestuous.

Thinking does me no good. My thoughts crash into each other, one displacing another. I venture into the library to quiet my brain. Libraries are a sanctuary to me. I had spent so much time there while Dad worked that it was home. My spot was on the old grey sofa opposite him. Dad always handed me books he thought were appropriate, but I had my pick of books from the whole library, and I'd choose ones with drawings I could copy, like Audubon's Birds of America, Maria Merrian's Metamorphosis Insectorum Surinamensium or Dr. Alice Roberts' The Complete Human Body. As I sketched, I'd interrupt him with questions like, "Daddy, where are my grandparents? Where are my cousins? Who is there to love me?"

"I love you, Manon." But he didn't hug me when he said so. Now, Dad is dead, and I'm left with all these unanswered questions.

Alexander's library runs the full length of the building. It is furnished with the traditional tufted leather couch and armchair. In addition to these predictable furnishings, there is also an unexpected pommel horse with a saddle on it, lending its raw scent of leather to the room. In the middle of the long wall is the fireplace, which is open to the Great Room on the other side.

There are big glossy art books and books on photography open on the rectangular mahogany table in the middle of the room. Surprising to find in a private library are illustrated books on biology, botany, and anatomy with diagrams that I love to study and copy. Sage always said I should be a medical illustrator. Drawing diagrams in accurate detail requires discipline, steady fingers, and an aesthetic eye. Anyone who saw my work was always impressed, but not Dad. He would look at my arabesque florals and say, "Good copying," suggesting they were unoriginal. I knew that even though they were exquisitely executed, they were flat and unimaginative. My studies of Audubon's birds are beautifully rendered but as lifeless as the birds themselves. Dad didn't see the value of them.

I see the Audubon on a custom-built stand at the far end of the room but tease myself, taking my time getting to it. I pull a heavy volume of The Illustrated Atlas of the Human Body with Leonardo's Vitruvian Man on the Cover. This drawing of a man, with his arms and legs apart, in two superimposed positions inscribed in a circle inside a square, taught me about human proportion. I stop at the pommel horse and rub my hand on the saddle. I wonder if Alexander ever sits on the smooth seat, which feels warm to my touch.

Finally, I approach the Audubon. Printed double elephant folio size, it is about three feet by two feet, but opened as it is on its stand, it spans four feet across, so much larger in life than it appeared to be in pictures. The birds are all drawn life-size, giving large fowl like the Great Blue Heron a real presence in the room. On the opposite page, lighting up the room is the brilliant Prothonotary Warbler. The splendor of their yellow feathers inspires me to paint; they make me happy.

An *Esquire Magazine* on an end table catches my eye. Alexander is on the cover with the headline: *Alexander Montgomery Vows to Change the Pharmaceuticals Industry*. I go on to read the interview by Nora Weber.

> *It is safe to say that profit is the main driver of Big Pharma. However, Alexander Montgomery, the founder and CEO of Worldwide Pharmaceuticals, is determined to create a new standard of ethics for the pharmaceuticals industry, prioritizing philanthropy and altruism in equal measure to profit making. He has drawn criticism from rival businesses who wonder how he manages to fund his research.*
>
> *I spoke to him recently at his home in Greenwich to find out what the buzz about Mr. Montgomery is.*
>
> *NW: Mr. Montgomery, the industry seems to be fascinated, perhaps even intimidated, by your astounding accomplishments and your big ideas. I'm very interested in exploring that, but first, would you tell us a little about yourself, your early life, and why, with so many talents, you turned to pharmacology and not music, for instance?*
>
> *AM: Well, I was born in Montreal, where my mother was from, but within a few days of my birth, we came to live in New York, so you can safely call me a native New Yorker.*
>
> *NW: What made your parents move to the City?*
>
> *AM: Oh, my Dad was American. He met my mother while at a convention in Montreal and was so smitten that he kept returning for months until he managed to convince her to come away with him.*
>
> *NW: It sounds like your Dad had great powers of persuasion. Do you take after him?*

AM: I suppose we were a lot alike in that I also manage to get my way when I set my mind to something.

NW: Is that what accounts for your astonishing career, from musical prodigy to successful entrepreneur and executive of a Fortune 500 pharmaceutical company in matter of a few years?

AM: You might be on to something there. I suppose tenacity does contribute to success.

NW: What kind of childhood did you have?

AM: I grew up in a privileged middle-class home as an only child. I was fortunate that my parents afforded me the opportunity to explore whatever my interest of the day was, whether it was sports, music, or more intellectual pursuits. I was very curious and excelled at everything I tried. I would say I had a very good childhood.

NW: Your resume reads as if you are the consummate Renaissance man. A BSc from Cornell, your MS in Biology from MIT, and a PharmD from UCLA in San Francisco. But you started out at the Berklee College of Music in Boston, where I understand you were touted to be the next 'big thing' in the music world. You were the whole package: talent, looks, a beautiful baritone singing voice, and a passion for your instrument. What made you switch?

AM: I guess my intellectual curiosity was not satisfied. However, the guitar is still my constant companion. I continue to practice with the same diligence I apply to everything else.

NW: Why the guitar?

AM: Since I was a toddler, I was fascinated by the guitar and wanted to emulate the sounds I heard from my parents' eclectic record collection. I particularly loved the music of Manitas de Plata, the famous Roma guitarist. You may know him as the 'Picasso of Flamenco'.

NW: No, I've never heard of him. Do tell me more.

AM: His intricate fingering is difficult to master, that's what made it exciting for me.

NW: So, by the time you were 30, you had become a successful pharmaceutical entrepreneur with your own manufacturing company. How did you manage it?

AM: After graduating, I quickly realized that I could do more by making medicine than just dispensing it. I had learned a lot about business from my Dad, who successfully built a chain of optical stores. It was practically a no-brainer. Once I made up my mind, I just did it.

NW: You are one of the most eligible bachelors in New York. Is there a particular reason you are not married?

AM: Perhaps one day I will make that leap. For now, I'm happy to enjoy the company of the many interesting women I meet.

NW: Is one of them, Susan Richards, an employee of your rival Biotech Pharmaceuticals?

AM: The female company I keep is a private matter. It has nothing to do with my business.

NW: I only ask because you had been seen about town with Miss Richards until rumors of corporate espionage were spreading through the pharmaceutical industry. Can you comment on the validity of those rumors and why you suddenly severed your relationship with her?

AM: No, I won't contribute to a rumor mill.

NW: What about the rumors about Miss Richards' claims that you caused her bodily and emotional harm?

AM: Like I said, I don't waste time on gossip or give credence to rumors.

NW: I understand charges were brought and then dropped. Can you tell me why you stopped seeing her so abruptly?

AM: "No."

NW: "Are you with anyone now?"

AM: "No."

Alexander Montgomery has already opened an experimental free dispensary in the Bronx and has plans to have this business model become the norm not just in the U.S. but around the globe, hence the name Worldwide Pharmaceuticals. He is currently in discussions with the government of Central African Republic to build a distribution center there that would ultimately expand to other regions, a bold and ambitious plan.

❁❁❁❁

Alexander returns and joins me on the patio, looking invigorated, his calm restored. He seems to have pulled back from whatever brink he was on, as though his thoughts, actions, and emotions have realigned and once again revolve around a solid core with a kind of gravitational force. However, my thoughts and emotions are still in disarray with Rosalia's disclosures and the Esquire interview. My new-found family doesn't seem to be magazine-cover-worthy after all.

Alexander studies his boots for a long spell as if choosing the right words to say.

"Manon, I'm sorry I left you here by yourself to deal with these revelations. I was thrown off balance by Rosalia, and riding is what gets me righted."

As shocked as I am by what I've learned, my feeling for him is not revulsion but an overwhelming empathy - a wounded Alexander hurts me.

"I know how you felt. Learning your mother's secret must be as overwhelming for you as it is for me. Our pain stems from the same source – a betrayal by our parents."

With the insight into Alexander that I've just gained from the magazine and given his treatment of me this afternoon, my admiration for him is tempered by doubt. It's confusing. I've had a glimpse of his fury and imagine how he can hurt people with it. I tell myself not to be such a baby. He is not the flawless person I thought him to be, so what? None of us are perfect.

"I shouldn't have left you alone. I promise I will be there for you from now on. You are a precious gift, and I will take care of you, always."

An early evening gust of cool air makes me shiver. Alexander wraps his arms around me and holds me tight. It doesn't take me long to accept his apology as a healing balm for my hurt feelings. If anything, I have gained deeper sensitivity to him, and not even Rosalia or Nora Weber's accusations can change how powerfully I am drawn to him. I have a physical reaction to his touch, and now the attendant guilt for how my body reacts makes me miserable. How will I ever get 'righted'?

"In a way, I'm glad that Rosalia was able to shed a little light on the close and unique bond between my parents," he says. "The passion and the underlying tension between them was always an enigma to me."

"The note your mom left my dad makes sense now. If they loved each other, if they were lovers . . ." We have not spoken the ineffable yet, but Alexander says it aloud;

". . . then I might be Gregory's son."

A heavy silence descends between us. We are reluctant to look into each other's eyes to see what we might find there.

"We have to get DNA tests, clear up how exactly we are related. I know some labs that do this kind of testing for law enforcement. I could ask a friend of mine at one of them to perform an SNP for us."

"A what?"

"A Single Nucleotide Polymorphism array." The words slip easily from his lips, and I'm reminded of his scientific side. "They're not commonly used for relationship testing, but still, it might give us some insights. What do you say?"

"Yes, if you can arrange that, let's do it."

CHAPTER TEN

After Dad died, I took leave from my job and spent countless idle hours puttering around our empty house, trying to figure out where my place in the world was; without Dad, this wasn't it. Nothing rooted me to Lennoxville except the Massawippi bungalow and the Elmwood Cemetery graves. Being with Alexander, here at his home, feels like I have something to hold on to. It frees my artist's soul to soar.

There is a three-week wait for the results of our DNA tests, so I extend my stay, spending time both in Manhattan and at Elderberry. Anticipation has me alternately prickling with anxiety and contented in oblivion. I yield to the pleasures of Alexander's world, floating in the waters of Lethe, possibly aided by the potions he's mixed for me, in a hypnotic forgetfulness, my mind empty of worry and sorrow.

Life at Elderberry is at a different pace from the city or the rhythm of daily life at home in Lennoxville. It's busy but not fast. Here, I wake up early with the sunrise. My room has an east-facing bay window and is decorated in yellow and white with green accents. I lie languorously in the queen-sized bed among the folds of fine linen under a multicolored quilt with exquisite hand stitchery. The padding on the long window seat is apple green, and the cushions are in primary colors drawn from the quilt. The furniture, in natural maple, lends itself to the bright and airy scheme.

A number of hand-colored botanical copper engravings framed in braided gold leaf are hung in a symmetrical arrangement that stands out on the crisp white walls. When I first glanced at them, I thought they looked familiar. Then, upon closer inspection, I realized that they were original prints by Maria Sibylla Merian, a famous Swiss botanist whose illustrations I use to copy. I researched her for a paper I had to write for a botany class in my first semester at Champlain. She inspired me to continue with my art practice and possibly become a scientific illustrator. She was a trailblazer, the first person – the first woman, to ever collect and observe live insects to illustrate their metamorphosis.

How uncanny that Merian's works are actually hanging here in my room. They give me another clue about Alexander's aesthetic sensibilities. These were not 'staged' pieces picked by a decorator. Like the Audubon and the horse paintings, they have been curated by a connoisseur.

Mrs. O is in the kitchen in the mornings when I come down. She makes coffee, and I'm reluctant to tell her I'd prefer tea. She's not overly talkative, and when she does say anything, it's usually about the mundane routines of the household: laundry is on Thursdays, cleaning staff every other Friday, and so on. Sometimes Hedley comes in to have breakfast, and then the three of us sit together, Alexander having long gone to work.

With Hedley, the mood is very different. I see Mrs. O smile, revealing charming laugh lines around her mouth and eyes as he holds forth in his lackadaisical way. One morning, as we were devouring Mrs. O's fluffy pancakes, they started opening up about Alexander.

"I met him at my dad's summer riding camp when we were fourteen," says Hedley. "We remained in touch through the years while he studied and then built his career. I knew he'd be a huge success. About five years ago, when he bought this place, he asked me if I wanted to help him build up a stable of horses and come to Elderberry to look after them. I jumped at the opportunity, and the next day, we went to Saratoga to buy our beauties."

"Alexander loves the horses, doesn't he?"

"Oh yah, he knows how to treat them, and they love him back." Hedley smiles sheepishly, and I wonder whether he has knowledge of a darker side of Alexander. "He's a real decent guy. He saved my dad from bankruptcy when the Riding Camp business was about to go under. Alex invested in it and turned it into a free riding school for special needs kids, which he funds."

Then Mrs. O pipes in;

"He saved me at a time when I thought I was worthless and was ready to quit my career. He had me stay after his parents died, and when he bought this property, I moved out here. He is generous with his time as well as his money, right Hedley?" Mrs. O and Hedley nod in agreement.

"Alex has enabled me and Mrs. O to become financially independent by setting us up with an online business, a subsidiary of Worldwide Pharmaceuticals that distributes medical equipment." Again, a sheepish glance at Mrs. O that is puzzling. "Mrs. O and I are partners. That's our headquarters," he says, indicating the closed door in the Great Room behind us.

Every tidbit of information I glean about Alexander adds fuel to my growing love and my burning need to know whether there is a darker side to him. I venture to broach the subject.

"What happened with Susan Richards?"

After an awkward silence, Hedley starts talking, and I notice Mrs. O's cautionary glance at him.

"She was a bitch," he says. "She slept with him, spied on him, and even stole some proprietary information." He gestures toward their 'headquarters' and says, "That's why we keep that door locked now."

"But why did she bring charges against him? What did he do?"

Mrs. O gets up abruptly, taking some dishes to the kitchen, obviously uncomfortable with this topic.

"He tied her to the bed and left her there while he went riding. Alexander likes to play rough sometimes, and she was amenable, so he thought he would teach her a lesson. It was Mrs. O who finally heard her screaming and released her."

"He isn't flawless," says Mrs. O as she clears more dishes, "but he has already done more good in the world than most people do in a lifetime. Whatever iniquity may be lurking in his soul, he keeps it under control." She turns her back and closes the subject.

In my solitary days at Elderberry, I hike the trails, observing the beautiful mosses, lichens, and fungi on the rocky bed of the forest; it's as if I have stepped into that old painting hanging in the hall at home. It makes me think of Dad. How did he know the name of everything? I remember being mystified by the disparity between his stoic, philosophical attitude and the expression on his resting face, which presented a furrowed brow and a far-off look. Was he thinking of my mother or Gabrielle? Or Alexander? Was he tortured by the thought that Alexander might be his son? Did he know the truth? I feel a fresh stab of grief because I'll never know.

I don't want his image to fade like my mother's has. I am determined to lock my memory of him onto canvas, and I immediately start sketching studies working only from memory. I draw multiple trials of head and shoulder sketches in full face, profile, three-quarters, and two-thirds views. I discard so many where I've rendered him caught in concentration, or as if in pain, where his mouth is neutral, or where he presents a serious, closed-lip stare. It takes me a long time to land on his truest expression, reflecting his inner essence. I concentrate on his eyes and eyebrows, which can register emotions in infinite variations. I trash them all until I land on that expression of displeasure that was so often directed at me.

Ready and eager to begin, I ask Alexander to drop me in the city to buy materials. It's not hard to find the Blick store in Soho because its façade is made to look like old Greek architecture. Faux columns with ornate capitals run the full length of the building, half a block wide. A continuous line of dentil tops them and features a large pediment over the door.

As soon as I step inside, my senses come alive. I sniff the unique smell of art stores – paint, ink, and raw wood. At Blick, I am awed by the thought that the likes of Andy Warhol, Jean Michel Basquiat, and Keith Haring browsed these very aisles. Famous abstract expressionists at the center of the New York School, like Jackson Pollock, Willem de Kooning, Mark Rothko, and many more, all came here for paint because Blick has an exclusive supply of handcrafted top-quality paint from their original New York mill.

The staff are friendly and knowledgeable; they direct me to where the canvases are. I'm trying to visualize the scale and content of the portrait to decide on a size. Will I seat him in his chair or just paint his stern face close up? I bypass the synthetic canvasses and reach for a cotton duck one when a girl in an apron approaches and asks,

"Are you painting with oil or acrylic?"

"This one will be in oil."

"Then I would suggest a linen canvas. Belgian linen is the ultimate surface for oil painting, and these," she points to the bin with the highest prices, "are already primed with acid-free Titanium gesso. It's more expensive than the cotton duck but offers the smoothest and stiffest painting surface. And this size," she notes I've pulled out an 18" X 24", "is not that much. I'm sure whatever you create is worth the price for the longevity of the piece."

I decide to splurge on a set of Utrecht oils and four of Blick's own brand of red sable brushes. Starting a new painting is exciting, and now I'm impatient to get back to Elderberry. It's still early; maybe I can catch a train to Greenwich.

I haven't had a cigarette in three weeks. Thanks to the concoctions Alexander has made for me, I haven't even had any cravings until just now. The thought of diving into a new painting seems to trigger old compulsions. Instead of buying a pack, I decide to have another of his smoothies when I get home. I don't want to fall back into bad habits. I'm grateful to Alexander for his help and support, and I don't want to disappoint him.

I am totally immersed in my work out on the patio in the shade of the awning, my canvas propped up on a chair and my paints, brushes, and pallets beside me on the table. I don't know how long he's been there, but when I notice Alexander looking at me from the door, my pulse quickens as it usually does in his presence, and I drop my chalk as he approaches me.

"You look so concentrated and content. I hate to disturb you, but I've got news."

My senses become acute as I struggle between the instinct to flee and the need to know. He pulls up a patio chair to face me.

"Manon, I've received the results of the DNA tests, and they clearly show that you and I share a parent."

Blissful oblivion suddenly becomes brutal consciousness. Alexander is holding my hands in his, and the contact still electrifies me.

"Happy to meet you, little sis."

CHAPTER ELEVEN

Gashes of orange and deep purple rip the horizon, and the white walls of my bedroom are aflame with the rising sun. I awake with the knowledge that I have a brother. My longing for family has miraculously been fulfilled with Alexander. However, my more immediate longing, my physical desire for him, along with any dreams of him wanting me, have been dashed because of our consanguinity. Isn't there supposed to be some mysterious reflex that prevents siblings from being attracted to each other? Apparently, he has it, but I don't.

While we waited on the DNA results, I never let this possibility sink in. Never allowed it to interfere with my desire. This morning, as I masturbate in my gold-washed bedroom, I feel even more wicked. Logic dictates that it's time for me to go home.

With each step I take down the stairs, I take special note of everything so that when I'm gone, I'll remember this place that has so quickly come to feel like home. The house is quiet. There is no Mrs. O and no coffee. I wander out into the perfect stillness of the August morning. Mist from evaporating dew lingers low in the meadow, and the foamy white blooms of Queen Anne's lace float above it. I fill my lungs with oxygen-rich air that carries scents of crape myrtle and fresh straw. To leave this idyll and wrench myself away from Alexander makes my stomach hurt, and my heart break. How can I bear to leave his orbit? Yet how can I bear to be around him and resist the urge to touch him? On top of it all, Mrs. O had mentioned that from time to time, Alexander brought his girlfriends here for weekends; how could I deal with that? I couldn't. I must go home.

Walking through the tall grass, my canvas runners are wet with the dew, and my cheeks are wet with tears. I think of Dad, still struggling with the idea that Gabrielle was besotted with him just as I am with Alexander. Is this a genetic flaw?

After a long walk, I return to the house and find Alexander at the trestle table reading the New York Times. Mrs. O. is busy at the stove making oatmeal, her ample behind shaking with the vigorous stirring.

"The Mars Reconnaissance Orbiter is launching from Cape Canaveral today," he says to her. But when he sees me at the door, he bounces up to greet me, "There you are!" and hugs me. The gesture is spontaneous; he seems even more fraternal now. I want to hang on tight, like when we were riding. "Did you sleep well?" He asks. "Come and have some breakfast."

I am enticed by a big bowl of glistening strawberries and a smaller bowl of clotted cream on the table. I take a seat on the bench opposite him. His glowing face is intent on me. This scene is so reminiscent of mornings with Dad sharing the newspaper at the kitchen table that I shift in my seat unconsciously, preparing for some lecture or argument.

"Manon, can you tell me about Gregory?"

Now that he has asked so directly, I try to imagine what Dad might say to him. But I haven't even the tiniest clue of how he might react to an estranged adult son. I search Alexander's face and find that same expression of burning intelligence that Dad had.

"Dad was really smart," I say. "He read a lot and knew about everything. Work was his life. He loved his library." Sometimes, I felt that he loved the library more than he loved me, but I don't say that. Alexander pops a strawberry into his mouth, and I'm distracted for a moment.

"Go on," he says, leaning forward, eager for me to continue.

"He was involved in so many projects that he was constantly running to meetings." Even when I was little, he would leave me at the library under Sage's supervision when I wanted so badly for him to choose me over his other obligations, another thing I don't say. "For years, he worked on switching everything to digital, then developing online educational programs, as well as lobbying the municipality to fund them. He organized everything from toddler story time to adult book clubs. He was a devoted community activist, and everybody respected him." I was flabbergasted by the number of people who showed up at the funeral, a lot of them strangers to me but unanimously full of praise for Dad.

Alexander reaches across the table and touches my hand. He searches my face beseechingly. "That all sounds great, but please tell me what he was really like?"

"He was… philosophical, kept his emotions private, except when I exasperated him. There was a volatile undercurrent in him; occasionally, his anger would burst out in hurtful words. When I quit college, he called me a loser. It still stings."

"That sounds awful. Was he mean to you?"

"No, he tried to be a good parent but didn't always succeed. Despite our quarrels, we were very close in our way; he was my world, and although he never said it much, I know he loved me."

"What did you do together?"

"He didn't really have much time for me. But If I had questions, no matter how silly, he would stop and give me answers." My mind flashes to memories of me trying to get Dad's attention by asking compelling questions. "He always encouraged me to ask if I was unsure of something, even if it meant confronting authority. He would say; Don't be gullible, and don't be a pushover for a sexy argument – ask questions. And he loved music."

"I guess we have that in common."

"Every year, like a ritual, we watched the Grammys together. He especially loved jazz and was very interested in the emerging Jazz Rap Fusion. The rhythms rooted in hip-hop, combined with repetitive jazz instrumentation phrases, excited him. We'd discuss the social relevance of their lyrics. He understood that the sexist and homophobic lyrics were not simply 'throwaway entertainment' but a call to action, like the shocking lyrics of *'Strange Fruit'* written by Abel Meeropol, aka Lewis Allen."

"I agree with that. I have versions sung by Billie Holiday and Nina Simone."

"You do have a lot in common."

"What else?"

"Other than the distinct widow's peak that's slightly left of center in both of you?"

We smile at each other, and I try to put a finger on how it is that he reminds me of Dad. "You both have a quiet confidence about you. Dad never second-guessed himself. You seem as self-assured and in control as he was." I pause and then add, "And he also has a huge collection of vinyl records, like you do – all the jazz greats: John Coltrane, Charlie Parker, Thelonius Monk, Billie Holiday, Nina Simone…"

My grief has been coming in waves. A thought or mention of him inundates me with my loss as it does now, remembering the music that filled our home, and silence descends between us. I get lost in my own thoughts, trying to arrange them in some logical, orderly relationship to one another. It frustrates me that I don't know Dad as well as I should. Would he have become a musician if he didn't have me to look after? So many questions.

Just as I start to say, "I've been thinking…" he also says, "I've been thinking…" and we have to laugh.

"Okay, you first," he says.

"No, you ..."

"Listen, we are the only family we've got, and I think we should stick together. I hate the idea of my little sister going back to a lonely house and struggling to support herself when I have more than I know what to do with. Let me share my good fortune with you. I want to help nurture your talent and give you the freedom to paint; that's what you need to be doing. Come and live here at Elderberry; ride Banjo, paint, and immerse yourself in the New York art scene."

He is so earnestly making this offer that it seems like a no-brainer, but the image of some gorgeous woman coming to Elderberry to share his bed keeps interrupting the blissful fantasy. I need space from him and his brotherly love.

"I was going to say that it's time for me to go home. Don't worry about me. I can manage my life, support myself, and still paint freely."

"But Manon, there is so much opportunity for you here. I want to introduce you to Julian Fisher, my friend and accountant. He is an avid art collector and is on a first-name basis with many of the gallery owners in Chelsea. And he's friends with the dean of Pratt's School of Art. These are people you should meet. You should begin work on a collection to show. You will be noticed. I'll convert the gym into an art studio for you. Nobody ever uses that space."

I remember thinking on my first tour of the house that the upstairs was like a country inn, complete with amenities. There's a huge workout room, the size of the three garages below it, which has two dormers facing east and two large windows facing west. In the late afternoon, filtered light pours in through the trees, giving the room an ocherous glow.

"The studio sounds great; the light in there is perfect."

"So you'll stay," he says, and the subject is closed.

Although his offer is compelling, the looming inevitable encounter with a girlfriend is so repugnant that I feel I have no choice but to go. If I don't go home, I feel like I'd be abandoning Dad at Elmwood Cemetery. After all I have learned, I want to go back to his grave to see if confronting him there will make me feel better. And I miss Sage, the only other constant in my life.

Even when I was little, she treated me like a person, and I knew I could count on her to be a buffer between Dad and me. She was the one who came to the hospital when Dad had the accident. She waited with me through the long hours of surgery, and when he didn't make it, she was the one who held me up. I feel bad for taking her for granted and taking advantage of her whenever it suited me. I owe it to her to fill her in on these developments. I know she must be wondering about me.

So I decide to stay only as long as it takes for me to finish Dad's portrait, which would be my parting gift to Alexander.

CHAPTER TWELVE

I spend the next few days trying to work out the problem of how to render Dad on the canvas. I have already decided it would be a bust and have sketched an outline of the head, tilted right and bent slightly forward. I have done the underpainting in three colors and begin to fill in features. I imagine him looking up through his fair lashes the way he did when trying to figure out what I might be hiding.

Although his hair was thinning in recent years, there was the remnant of a hairline with that signature peak slightly off-center, like Alexander's, which corresponded with the angle of his head when confronting me. I've captured his features accurately, but try as I may, I just can't portray that expression in his eyes, a combination of anger and anguish that used to make me cringe. He always seemed to know whatever it was that I had done.

Once, I had shoplifted some fancy underwear at Zeller's and got caught. I could have bought them. I just wanted to see what I could get away with. I felt no fear, and the idea of carrying it off electrified me. So when I felt a hand on my shoulder, catching me in the act, that electricity galvanized me to talk my way out of getting arrested. I was pretty satisfied with how I convinced them not to call Dad. My satisfaction fizzled when I got home and saw that look. I couldn't shake the feeling that somehow he knew what I had done.

Putting off the most difficult part of the portrait - his likeness, I spend an excessive amount of time detailing the checkered shirt he favored, rendering it in perfect magic realism. I did a good job with that little hollow at the base of his throat and his sinewy neck with the jugular vein that pulsed whenever he thought I was being unreasonable. I painted, then obliterated his likeness over and over again, changing the angle of his head and the position of his jaw with each iteration, the eyes ever elusive. The canvas is so thick with paint that I have to wait for it to dry before I can begin again.

Frustrated, I leave the damn thing and go into the city to distract myself. Instead of a mere distraction, the city inevitably seduces me, and I end up staying at the Colosseum, where George, garrulous as ever, welcomes me with the latest gossip of the city.

"Did you hear the latest from our very own Queen of Mean, Leona Helmsley? She's leaving twelve million dollars in her will to her dog Trouble." Yet again, I am impressed with his wealth of trivia. He accompanies me out the door onto the street, still talking;

"And our current 'It Girl,' Paris, is all over town promoting herself and her new movie."

I've been reading the *New York Times* and contribute to the bantering with some trivia of my own.

"Yes, and there are a lot of musicians in town for the Higher Ground Hurricane Relief Benefit Concert at Lincoln Centre."

"You're right. I saw James Taylor just the other day walking down Broadway."

Alexander seems very busy with some major project he's working on. I hardly see him. Now that we're past Labor Day, the city is more hectic. I've grown accustomed to the velocity of pedestrian traffic and have adjusted my stride, spending days on end walking. I have yet to explore some of the independent galleries in Chelsea where contemporary, avant-garde artists show. Today, I decide to visit the Whitney.

The exhibits vary from floor to floor. My first encounter as I exited the elevator was a birch tree made of paper, paste, paint, and wire. It appears to have taken root somewhere under the building, burst through the floor, and grown into the wall. It isn't strictly representational; it's rather messy, and it seems to fracture the austerity of this cavernous space. Is it meant to question the stability of the foundation? Whatever it means, Valery Hegarty wanted to convey something other than just making a crafty art piece. It's up to me to figure it out. I am awed, puzzled, and inspired by the variety of work on display. The more I see, the more I despair that I can ever produce anything meaningful. I have that haunting feeling that Dad was right: I am a dilettante, and my work is nothing more than an obsessive hobby.

I stay in the city and, the next day, head to midtown with no destination in mind. I am greeted by Patience and Fortitude, the marble lions that guard the majestic Beaux-Arts building of the New York Public Library. On the first floor, I see the Map Room and spend a good two hours indulging my wanderlust. Has Dad ever been here, I wonder? I don't even know if he'd ever been to New York. Did he ever come to visit Gabrielle? How he would love this place.

Ever since Rosalia cried out; Don't tell me this is Gregory's daughter? I have been wondering what she may know about him. Had she ever met him? What had Gabrielle revealed about their relationship, their parents, and grandparents? I know Alexander is not keen to seek her out again after the last time when she gleefully alluded to his parents' kinky sexual relationship, but I really want to pick her brain before I leave. Rosalia and Gabrielle loved having afternoon tea at the Plaza Hotel, so I walk up 5th Avenue to check it out. Who knows? I might bump into her.

I get there too late for the tea service but take a look into the vast Palm Court, where busboys and wait staff are busy preparing for the dinner crowd. I hear the tinkle of crystal and the clatter of silverware. I see the snapping and billowing of fresh white table cloths and the careful setting of tables and am dazzled by the romantic setting.

Huge planters with giant palms that reach the beautiful stained glass laylight dome populate the room—a veritable garden of purple sage crowns the bar at the entrance. White freesias in large vases set in alcoves and in smaller ones on each table lend their sweet, peppery scent to the whole place. Light filters through the airy lace pattern of leaded black lines and stained glass. I imagine Jay Gatsby and his beloved Daisy gazing into each other's eyes in the waning afternoon.

I return the next day and the day after, hoping Cruella will show up. Then, finally, on Thursday, I see her. I arrive just before they start the tea service and see her flounce in as if she owns the place. She looks as if she just stepped off the page of an old Vogue magazine, wearing a vintage afternoon dress in printed pastel green chiffon with a matching scarf at her throat. Immediately, an unctuous Maître D' ushers her to a table by one of the giant pale green ceramic planters, the same shade as her dress. Did she picture herself sitting there when she picked that outfit? I'm so glad I browsed through Gabrielle's closet instead of pulling on my jeans this morning. I'm wearing black satin capris under a turquoise tunic printed with Areca palm leaves, which camouflage me in this room of palms.

I straighten up, square my shoulders, and walk with a deliberate stride toward her table and slow as I approach.

"Rosalia?"

She looks up from the leather-bound menu.

"Yes?"

I must not have made much of a first impression because she can't quite place me. My shoulders begin to sag, and I falter. But she is a living connection to the past that I have an urgent need to explore.

"Remember me? I'm Gregory's daughter."

"Oh, yes, you're Alexander's cousin." Innuendo drips off this last word, and for some reason, I blush – I never blush. "How lovely. Do sit down."

I get straight to the point. "Did you ever meet my Dad?"

"Well, let me think…" she teases. "It was a long time ago. Ye-es, I do feel as if I had met him, if only through Gabrielle's rose-colored lenses."

"What did she tell you about him?"

"Oh, she loved him, truly and completely. He was a god to her. She lived with her grandparents, and when Gregory's father disappeared, he went to live there too. He was her savior."

"Did she ever talk about her parents or Da... Gregory's parents? Did their mothers disappear too?"

"Didn't Gregory ever tell you anything?" Her question sounds like an accusation as if somehow I didn't merit the information that Dad withheld. I look down at my lap, examining paint-encrusted cuticles. She is right. I hadn't earned Dad's trust. I deceived him any chance I could.

"No, I never knew about Gabrielle or his grandparents until Alexander found me."

"Well, I think her dad and Gregory's dad were up to no good. They may have been arrested and imprisoned for some petty crime. Or, possibly, they overdosed and died. She never mentioned her mother or Gregory's mother, for that matter. The grandparents would never speak of them, so I don't know... Gabrielle didn't talk much about her family, just about Gregory."

These revelations generate more questions than answers. Does this clarify anything? Can I have inherited my larcenous behavior from them? Is this why Dad was so disinclined to talk about his family history? Could it explain why he overreacted if I did anything wrong? Could my grandparents still be alive? I will visit Saint-Henri Cemetery to see if there are any Moulands buried there, and I resolve to use my library research skills to see what I can learn about any Moulands arrested in Montreal around the time Dad was a teenager.

"What about her grandparents?"

"I got the sense that the sooner Gaby and Gregory could leave, the better. I gather they weren't loving parental substitutes. Gregory left first, and Gaby was desperate to follow him. He made her stay until he could establish himself and get her out of that oppressive house. She told me he came regularly to check in on her. She remembered how she lived for the days when he'd come back, how she waited for him, and how when she spotted him from a distance, walking down their long block, she thrilled at the sight of his long strides, lanky body, and handsome face. She described her excitement so well that I do feel like I'd seen him."

I try to envision Dad in that reckless relationship, but I just can't reconcile it with the stoic, responsible man I knew.

"Did he ever get her out?"

"Sorry, kiddo, I don't know what more to tell you. All I know is that Gaby used to sneak out of the house and go downtown looking for Gregory. That's how she met Sebastian. Apparently, he fell in love at first sight of her; who wouldn't? She was a beautiful, sweet girl." The waiter arrives with a cocktail that she didn't have to order. "Bring another for my guest," she says without asking me if I'd like one.

"Gaby got pregnant, and Sebastian offered her a chance to give her child a normal life. It was a hard decision. Sebastian was very forceful in getting her to leave with him." Again, her pronunciation of forceful insinuating some underlying nuance that he bent her to his will. "I met her a few years after she came to New York, and she seemed to have adjusted to her life on the Upper West Side, but that look of longing, a sorrow that lay behind pretty blue eyes, was perpetually there. She often teared up talking about Gregory. Her guilt for abandoning him plagued her life."

"Do you know whether she was ever in touch with my father after she moved here?"

"She tried to get in touch secretly because Sebastian would never have allowed it. Gregory's refusal to accept her calls was a painful rejection."

❁❁❁❁

It's twilight, but I can't bring myself to go to the Colosseum. I enter Central Park at 59th St. and start walking north on the paved path by a stream with floating algae and clumps of Goldsturm daisies on the banks. I linger for a moment under the rustic arch of a stone bridge, inhaling the musty smell of mildew, which reminds me of being under the back porch at home. The acrid smell of urine soon urges me along. I like this in-between day and night light when hard edges disappear and colors are muted to pastel grey. Soon, the thick vegetation along the path obliterates the last glimmer of sunlight. I walk without purpose or destination.

I feel tremendous remorse for not being the scholarly, independent person Dad wanted me to be. He never wanted me to have to rely on a man. Now, as I'm getting glimpses of Gabrielle, I think it may be because of her. Gabrielle left him by letting herself be beguiled by Sebastian. It may be why he never approved of any of the guys I dated; he didn't want me to be seduced.

One time, when Gerry the biker drove me home, I invited him to come in. Dad refused him entry and told him to stay away from me for no apparent reason. I was furious. After all, I was eighteen and thought I could do what I wanted. I had never seen him so incensed. Did Gerry, in some way, trigger his wrath at Sebastian? He grounded me and forbade me to date even the local guys, who, in any case, I'd long outgrown. It was a joke. I defied him, of course, and even lied to him, going off on my long weekends of debauchery in Montreal. He knew what I'd been up to. I don't know how he knew, but he avoided me for days when I returned. Did I look different?

Just then, my phone vibrates in my pocket, a text from Alexander. Where are you? Are you okay? I reply instantly; Yes, I'm okay, just walking in Central Park. Instead of a text reply, my phone rings, and he starts talking as soon as I've answered.

"Manon, this is not a good time for you to be walking in the Park. It's not safe. I want you to get a cab and come home." I don't know whether to be touched by his concern or annoyed by his bossiness. Mixed emotions are becoming the norm.

"I'm fine. I'll see you later," I say, and turn my phone off.

Wandering in the dusk, I ask myself: who am I? As Gregory's daughter, I was selfish, petulant, and angry. Who am I to be as Alexander's sister? How would he perceive my promiscuity? Will he begin to avoid me, too, once he realizes what I'm like?

I get home a little after ten to a deserted apartment. I check my phone and see he's texted that he will be out for the night. In the silence of this warren-like apartment, I feel a sense of dread. Is he avoiding me already? Then I hear an unfamiliar chiming in the living room. By the time I find a strange cell phone, clad in a pink glittery case, with the photo of a cute little Bichon Frise as a screen saver, it stops ringing. My roiling emotions and my long walk home have exhausted me. I go to bed and slip into oblivion.

When I get up in the morning, Alexander is already gone, or maybe he never came home. The fancy pink phone remains where it was, dark now. My imagination torments me with images of some sophisticated socialite putting her hands on him, kissing him, caressing him the way I want to. The pain of this impossible love sets my resolve to go home.

CHAPTER THIRTEEN

There are many things I would love to do before I leave New York, but if there's one thing I must do, it's to buy those Katherine Hepburn pants I've coveted since I first saw them. I retrace my steps to the Nolita neighborhood, where I first found Marmalade Vintage. The owner greets me with a friendly;

"Hey, you. Have you come back for the Schiaparelli?"

"You remember me!?"

"Of course, you were wearing a lovely vintage silk blouse."

"Actually, I was wondering if you still have the Hepburn trousers. They were a fawn color..."

"I know the one. Do you want to try them on?"

Slipping into them, the satin lining caresses my thighs and tickles my legs, and I feel like I'm afloat in mercury. The waistband is a bit snug, but the fabric billows from it and moves with me. Also, it's a little long, but it will be just right with boots. I have to have them, so I muster the temerity to offer Hannah half the price on the tag, intending to take advantage of the credit card Alexander gave me to use freely. It's the first and only time I'll use it.

"This garment has a history. It's one of a kind." She looks me up and down and says, "They do look good on you." She proposes a counteroffer, two-thirds of the ticketed price. I can't believe I have the wherewithal to engage in this haggling.

"I'll be back for more if you can let me have them for $800.00; that's my final offer." She smiles and lets me win, and I feel I have conquered the world. Before I leave, I ask her which is the best way to get to Brooklyn.

Oblivious to the tumult of people and cars, I think about the work I saw at the Whitney, which troubles me. What is art? What is an artist? Will I ever produce anything thought-provoking or relevant? Will I ever be a legitimate artist?

I decide that once I get to Brooklyn, I'll take a cab to MoMa's PS1 in Queens, where there is another exhibit of work like Hegarty's. The use of recycled materials to create themes of memory, place, and history intrigues me. I'm haunted by some of the pieces I saw, and I'm getting the idea that I can explore my own history if I could just assemble the right elements.

When I arrive at City Hall Park, I see the Promenade entrance to the Brooklyn Bridge and join the throng headed in that direction. Leaving terra firma, I walk onto the pedestrian deck, and as the buildings of Lower Manhattan recede, the grand expanse of the East River is suddenly before me. The late September sun creates interesting slanting shadows on the deck.

The first tower rises before me, and I see its identical twin through its iconic Gothic arch. I am awed by the beauty of cable wires strung in great loops from one to the other. The rhythm of treading feet and the vibration of cars zipping along the lower deck have a hypnotic effect. My pace is steady, like an automaton, as

I'm drawn toward the vortex of cables. Thoughts about my relationships with Dad and Alexander and about who I am vanish. Joggers and cyclists whiz by in their designated lanes, and pedestrians march past me at their own robotic paces.

When the Manhattan Bridge comes into full view, I sit on a bench to take in the spectacular panorama. I notice a peculiar-looking man buttoned up in a black tailored overcoat from a previous era despite the warmth of this sunny autumn day. He walks with authority and surveys the bridge as if it were his personal turf. I picked him out immediately, like an aberration in one of those puzzle games where you have to find the thing that doesn't belong.

Unlike the other pedestrians who are occupied with gazing at the majestic East River or snapping selfies with the distant Statue of Liberty, this man gets up close to examine the bridge itself, fingering the steel cables as if rating their gauge. With one eye shut, he squints to follow their rise to the apex of the tower. I mimic him, trying to see what he sees. The steel ropes are anchored in perfect symmetry at intervals on the deck and soar to the center point of the tower.

He sits down beside me and produces a little leather notebook in, which he begins to scribble. I sneak a peek. He's drawing diagrams, noting angles and details of the construction. When he notices me prying, I get up hastily, embarrassed at having been caught spying. He gets up, too and follows me.

"Your hair is a halo of sheer energy!"

I am jolted by his deep voice, so close that I can almost feel his breath on my neck. He articulates each word clearly, with a guttural pronunciation and a hint of an accent I can't place. I should bolt, but I'm curious. I turn to him, and now that we are face-to-face, I am mesmerized by his eyes, black as charcoal glinting in the sun. He registers every detail of me. Suddenly self-conscious, my hand automatically reaches up to try and restrain the frizzy mass on my head.

I can't come up with a clever riposte. I am an observer like him. I notice details and store them for use in my art. He must be an engineer. Engineers have an air of assurance about them as if they are supremely in control of the material world. This mysterious man in the ancient frock coat, with the intense gaze, might be from the immaterial world, a ghost as old as the bridge itself.

Perturbed, I walk briskly to the next bench and wait to see if he will pass me by. He sits down beside me.

"Who are you?" He asks the very question I've been asking myself.

"I don't know," I manage.

"What do you do?"

"I'm just visiting."

"That wasn't my question."

His impatience unsettles me, but I feel compelled to satisfy his curiosity because I sense his urgency to know. I inadvertently utter the words. "I paint."

"So you're an artist?"

"Well, I don't know. . ."

"You paint pictures?" I nod silently. "So you're an artist!"

I smile, and he beams a great wide grin, his eyes sparkling with satisfaction. I wonder who he thinks I am. We have reached Brooklyn, and as I head for the stairs, he turns and heads back toward the City. I walk away thinking I have crossed a bridge and become an artist. He's right, good or bad; that is who I am. I mustn't second guess myself anymore. I am an artist.

I feel a sense of urgency to finish Dad's portrait, so instead of going to the gallery, I go back to the Colosseum and pack my stuff. I look in Gabrielle's closet. I want to take something of hers with me. I pick an olive-green cashmere twin set, which will look great with my awesome trousers. Then I head back to Elderberry, determined that when I finish the portrait of Dad, I will go home to Lennoxville, begin my independent life, and devote myself to my calling.

Mrs. O is busy in the kitchen making something that smells scrumptious. I barely greet her and go up to the workout room where I've set up my paints and canvas; the light is perfect here. It takes weeks to get to the point when I think the painting is done, always painting and obliterating Dad's blank expression. I start again with a keener sense of urgency with each iteration. I struggle to capture him in emotional torment, that moment when he banned Gerry and grounded me so many years ago – contorted by anger and anguish. When I finally stop and look at him staring back at me, admonishing me, I begin to sob.

I have accumulated more things than I arrived with. It won't all fit in the small suitcase I came with, and my knapsack is already full, so I search for some luggage I could borrow. I find a suitcase at the bottom of the linen closet, just the right size to fit the extra clothes I bought, including the priceless trousers. The riding boots that Alexander had made for me have just recently arrived. They are gorgeous supple leather and will complete my Hepburn look. I wrap up my new paintbrushes and grab what's left of the luscious oil paints. Finally, I place my old Audubon on top and zip it up.

It's getting dark, and Mrs. O is on the patio sitting by the fire in the chimenea; an open book that she can no longer read in this light sits on her lap. I want to go out to the barn to see the horses, but it will mean having to say goodbye to her and to Hedley, who is visible in the distance grooming Cassie. Instead, I just call out to her from inside.

"I'm leaving!"

"Will you be back for dinner? I've made a beef stroganoff." She stuffs another log into the belly of the fireplace.

On the train to New Haven, I finally send Alexander a text, knowing that he is attending some function in the city and probably won't see it until later. Had I called him earlier and heard his voice, he would have convinced me to stay. Like Dad, he really wants me to follow the plan he has laid out, his vision of what my future should be. He wants me to be his little sister, and I just don't know how to be that.

Alexander, I am on the train on my way home to Lennoxville. I'll call you tomorrow when I'm settled. I have finished the portrait of Dad and left it for you in the workout room. I hope you like it. Thanks for everything.

As soon as I press send, I regret the feeble phrase, thanks for everything. What a paltry statement for the gratitude I feel for his generosity. Ten minutes later, my phone rings. Even though I expected it, my heart beats like a snare drum with each *brrng, brrng*. I can't speak with this huge lump in my throat. I feel like shit, but I turn my phone off.

By the time I get to New Haven from Greenwich, it's almost 10:00 p.m., and I have three hours to kill before boarding the overnight train to Montreal. The terminal is virtually deserted; its limestone walls and ornate ceilings echo with my footsteps. I choose a spot opposite the Dunkin Donuts shop. The wooden benches are polished to a smooth, silky sheen by the bottoms of travelers that have passed through over the decades. I resign myself to the wait and pull out the book I have been trying to read for weeks, The Last Painting of Sara De Vos by Dominic Smith.

It's a story about a seventeenth-century artist named Sara who defiantly paints landscapes despite it being forbidden for women to do so, possibly because, in Dutch guilds, men made their living by painting landscapes. If women produced any such work, it would have been attributed to their husbands. However, women were permitted to paint still lifes. Thus, tulips bloomed on canvasses as much as in the fields. I brood about the obstacles women artists have to contend with. I understand the injustice of having to suppress creative urges and how that feeds our self-doubt.

A young guy enters and heads toward the Dunkin' Donuts. He slumps on the bench opposite me when he realizes the shop is closed. He is unkempt, his unwashed hair sticking out from under a trucker hat, and his clothes are a mish-mash of urban street clothes: skinny jeans in an unfortunate burgundy color. He looks at me from under his greasy bangs, nonchalantly displaying a joint and cocking his head toward the door by way of invitation. I accept.

He says his name is Johnny. He's on his way back to Corning, taking courses in Automotive Technology at SUNY. He becomes animated when talking about cars, or maybe he's just cold because he constantly moves from one foot to the other. We pass the joint back and forth, and without any other authority, I admonish myself for being so reckless.

Talking about cars reminds me that I will have to deal with the wreck of Dad's totaled car. It is one of the many realities I will have to address when I get home.

CHAPTER FOURTEEN

When I exit the Gare Centrale in Montreal the next morning, the sky is the color of steel, and the heavy clouds look ready to drop their load of freezing rain. I hurry up Metcalfe Street, hoping to get into the Metro before I get drenched. However, the odors emanating from Dunn's as I pass remind me that I haven't eaten since last night in New Haven when I filled up on Fritos and KitKats and coke after having smoked that joint with Johnny.

The steamy warmth and the smell of deli food is comforting, and even though it's early, I order their famous platter. The bulging smoked meat sandwich arrives wearing a tiny slice of rye like a jaunty beret, inadequate to cover the mountain of meat. Fries, fresh from the fryer, never tasted so good. I savor every bite, balancing the salty goodness with vinegary coleslaw and a juicy dill pickle.

I like being here. Montreal is a quaint version of New York – a miniature metropolis, complete with all the benefits of a cosmopolitan city with fewer of its disadvantages, and there is the bonus of a European influence. People here still dress up when they go downtown. Whether you're in the West Anglo end or the East Franco end, there is a multicultural atmosphere. It has bridges, although none as magnificent as the Brooklyn Bridge. Being here gives me some clarity. I could settle here, maybe rent a studio space, and work at being an artist.

Sage is the only person in Lennoxville I feel the need to call. I reach her at the library.

"Hi, Sage, it's me."

"Manon! I haven't heard from you in ages. Are you okay?"

Why does everyone keep asking me if I'm okay? Do I seem unstable? Fragile?

"I'm on the bus on my way home. I'll come and see you later."

The trees whizzing by have already lost their leaves and look like smudged charcoal skeletons through the rain-streaked windows. I can only deal with one dramatic emotion at a time and a new sense of dread of re-entering my old world forces Alexander from my thoughts until the phone vibrates in my pocket. It will be him, but I'm still not ready to hear his voice, so I ignore it. A minute later, I get a text.

Manon, I'm worried about you. Please call me.

I reply immediately; I'm fine. Just need a little time.

I feel that familiar sense of guilt in the pit of my stomach for leaving without as much as a personal goodbye. He's been nothing but good and generous to me. I still long for his touch and the thought of hearing his smooth baritone and his seductive assurances that he will look after me, that we are family now. It all makes me queasy.

The emptiness of our house looms as the bus approaches the terminal. Then I spot Sage in her Burberry trench coat and tartan tam, scanning the platform for me, and the knot in my belly is replaced with something warm and pleasant.

In less time than it has taken for me to get from Montreal to Lennoxville, Sage has managed to get away from the library, shop for groceries, and arrive at the station to pick me up. She has always cared for me in her quiet, pragmatic way, but I never showed her the affection I now realize I feel for her. Once again, she is here for me, and I'm grateful for not having to enter the deserted house by myself.

Driving down Massawippi brings back memories of my long solitary walks to school. As we pull up in the driveway, our clapboard bungalow looks even smaller and more rundown after Alexander's 'Martha Stuart' house. The siding needs paint, and the concrete steps leading up to the front door are crumbling. By contrast, the Richardsons house next door looks immaculate. Mr. Richardson is always working on some improvement or other. Even in November, his lawn is greener than ours ever was in June. His eaves troughs are clean of debris, while ours are overflowing with leaves and pine cones. His shrubs are neatly bundled in burlap for the winter, ours have already turned brown.

I can't believe six months have passed since Dad died. I feel like I've been missing him for much longer than that, and four months since I've stepped foot in the place he had made home. I drop my bag and glance left into the living room. Nothing's changed except the lone philodendron in the corner is now dead. There are still books everywhere, and Dad's chair still needs mending. Sage removes her coat and heads to the kitchen.

"I'll put these groceries away and make some tea."

While she is busy in the kitchen, I take my luggage to my room. The good thing about my bedroom is that it is isolated at the back of the house and looks onto the river; the bad thing is that I have to pass Dad's room to get to it, which meant that he always knew when I came in late. This small rectangular space was my refuge. I flop down on the dreadful floral comforter that Dad chose and close my eyes. I used to console myself here, hands between my legs, innocently grinding into the mattress while my stuffed animals watched.

"Lunch is ready!"

We sit opposite each other at the table, Sage taking Dad's chair. Dad and I spent a lot of our time here sharing thoughts and ideas if not feelings. I was always fascinated by the patterns of light and shade as the sun moved from its zenith to finally set behind the trees. What comes to mind now is how Dad showed me how to make shadow puppets with just my own hands and fingers. When the sun was framed in the window in the afternoon, I became a puppeteer, creating all manner of odd-shaped creatures that flew, skulked, and leapt on the whitewashed wall. As the sun lowered in the sky, I became the puppet and would dance and twirl until I disappeared. I have a vivid memory of a violent storm when silhouettes of flailing branches, backlit by flashes of light, sent me cowering under the table. Dad pulled me out and reassured me that thunder and lightning could not hurt me.

A steaming pot of tea sits steeping between plates of cream cheese and watercress sandwiches, evidence of Sage's British roots, and I see that there is a box on the third chair, where newspapers used to pile up.

"What's this?" I ask.

"I collected Gregory's personal stuff when I moved into his office. I thought you might want to have it."

We chat for a bit about the discovery that Alexander and I are half-siblings, but I withhold sharing my attraction to him.

"That's wonderful news! I think Gregory would be comforted to know that he didn't leave you alone in the world, and it sounds like Alexander is happy to have found you. What's he like?"

"Oh, I hardly know where to begin. He's a pharmacologist, a great philanthropist, and a talented musician. He's very wealthy, and although he must have had a substantial inheritance, his great financial success is self-made. He is brilliant and accomplished at everything he touches. People around him hold him in such high regard that I can't help but admire him."

"I'm sure Gregory would have been proud that his son became such a great success."

"I'm not sure how he would have felt if he had known about Alexander. The fact is he never mentioned the possibility of it to me, so I don't know if he would be happy at all. Imagine having missed the opportunity to know his son."

We fall silent, thinking about the tragedy of it. If he had known Alexander, would he have been proud of him? I never made him proud. In fact, he always berated me for not living up to my potential. Sage takes a glance at the clock and makes ready to leave.

"I want to hear more about him and your time in New York, but I've got to get back to the library. Shall we have dinner tonight?"

After New York, I have no desire to go to any of the mediocre restaurants in Lennoxville and going to some better place in Sherbrooke doesn't warrant the effort. Memories of potluck dinners and picnics for library staff remind me that Sage's cooking is best avoided.

"Why don't you come back after work, and I'll see what I can scrounge up."

When she's gone, I go into the living room, taking the box with me. I look at the array of knowledge my father had accumulated on these shelves. I fondly touch my favorite volumes: the exquisitely illustrated volume of Grimm's Fairy Tales with rich color plates of Rumpelstiltskin and Hansel and Gretl, and the classic Russians, including Tolstoy's short stories. My art supplies are still in their basket beside the turntable. I look through Dad's jazz collection and pick out my favorite, a Billie Holiday. The portrait of her with a stunning white gardenia in her dark hair looks like a watercolor painting.

Inside the banker's box, I find file folders with heartfelt letters from library clients thanking Dad for his help, including one from Sherry Hyland, who spoke at the memorial. There are certificates and plaques that he was awarded for various achievements. There is the rock I had painted for him when I was small, which he used as a paperweight. There are several of my early drawings, even one that I must have done when I was very little because it's in crayon, and I had only used green ones; it looks like a jumble of bushes. The idea that he had kept any of my creations despite his lack of support for my artistic ambitions is surprising and heartbreaking.

At the bottom, there is a large brown inter-office envelope, the kind that has a string wound around a button, marked personal in Dad's handwriting. In it, there are another two envelopes, one with a note and the other with three postcards. I open the envelope that contains a terse note in childish block letters, misspelled and passionless, ridiculously signed as Olive and Arthur Mouland, your grandparents as if Dad might not recognize them by their names alone.

Gregory,

Tell Gaby that Stuart is ded in prison. We dunt know how to reech her. Some postcards from Alice are hear for you.

Olive and Arthur Mouland, your grandeparents

Just as I wonder where my grandmother was during this time, I look at the postcards addressed to Gregory Mouland, 733 Rue Lenoir, Montreal 3, Quebec, and postmarked in Calgary, San Francisco, and Brasilia, respectively. The postmarks dated from 1955 to 1957. They were written in a kind of shorthand as if full sentences weren't meant for postcards.

Dear Greggy,

Tim left me. Got job in restaurant. Will right when I can.

Love

Your Mom

In another, she wrote:

Greggy,

Am in San Francisco with Lester.

California is like paradise.

Be a good boy.

Love,

Your Mom

In the last one, postmarked in Brazil and dated December 1957:

The winter is summer here. It's very hot.

No work yet, but maybe soon.

Love

Your Mom

I retrieve a newspaper clipping from the Montreal Gazette, dated March 4, 1963. The headline reads;

Bandit Cut Down as Violence Continues

The first victim was a 69-year-old woman who was hit by a stray bullet in the North End. Two QPP constables spotted a car in a snowbank and began searching the bush. Gunshots flashed through the bush and one suspect was wounded.

They held Mrs. Andre Lebrun, the manager's wife, at gunpoint while they stole $4,500. from the safe.

When the bandits left, Mrs. Lebrun ran to a neighbour's to telephone police and a long chase began. In the meantime the bandits stole the police car, and then abandoned it when it got stuck in another snowbank.

Then they commandeered a passing pickup truck driven by Jean Cabana, 25, of La Macaza. Cabana was made to drive until they reached a house owned by Frank di Francisco. They stole his car.

They had to abandon his car when it too, went off the road. By this time QPP reinforcements were closing in.

The bandits were forced to surrender and the wounded man, identified as Stuart Mouland, 37, came out with his hands up.

Ed Mouland tried to fire his machine gun, but it jammed. A police slug struck him in the chest. He died on route to hospital.

I read it through once, and then again, my heart rate quickening as I try to put the words into context – my grandfather, a bandit, killed during the commission of a crime! I begin to understand why Dad didn't ever mention him; he wanted to protect me and possibly himself from being tainted by this villainous family history. My heart pounds, and I feel an ache in my chest thinking of what he had to overcome. I feel a tremendous desire to forgive him for his deception, but it's too late.

I am numb trying to process all this. In my lifelong yearning for family, it never occurred to me that I would discover such nefarious roots. My overwhelming emotion is utter sadness for Dad. There is a schism in our family history, one that Dad has crossed over into a world of his own by sheer force of his will and intellect. As I contemplate the challenges of his life, the ache in my chest descends to my stomach, and it begins to heave. I make it to the kitchen sink just as bile and watercress erupts from my gullet.

Oh, Dad, where are you? Why have I been such a difficult daughter, adding to your grief? How can I ever forgive myself?

Despite the nasty November chill, I feel the need to visit the cemetery. The earth covering my parents' graves is frozen hard as a rock. The headstones declare they were loving parents. I try to feel a connection to them being here, but all I feel is bitterness.

I still remember when I was little, and Dad had brought me here. "We are going to visit Mommy," he would say, and I tingled with the anticipation of seeing her – I missed her so much. I was heartbroken every time when she didn't appear. "Where is she, Daddy? Where is Mommy?" I would cry, and in response, he would simply point at the grave, speechless, suggesting that she was there.

My four-year-old mind could not associate that hardened mound of earth and that cold stone slab with my mother. I kicked at the pebbles around the grave, scuffing my pretty patent leather shoes, which I had insisted on wearing because Mommy said they were special. I picked up a handful of stones and threw them at the headstone. Daddy pulled on my arm and said, "Stop that! Don't be disrespectful."

I didn't know what disrespectful meant. I just knew he was angry. I was angry, too. He promised I would see my mother, and he had lied. I threw more stones in defiance, and he was at a loss for what to do with me. It was then that I understood I had power over him and could hurt him, and I wanted to. When we left, I could feel the weight of those pebbles sitting in my chest, and I cried from a tremendous longing that I couldn't understand. I felt abandoned and all alone.

I must call Alexander. He needs to know of these new insights into our parentage. Since we share this history, he is the only one who can understand how I feel.

"Oh, Manon, I'm so glad you called. You left so suddenly I wasn't sure I'd hear from you again. I worried that somehow I had driven you away."

"I have some news."

Once I recount my discovery, we both fall silent. The void that was our history is now filling with a legacy of criminality, cruelty, deception, and desertion. What can we make of it? How can we reconcile the life we live now with the one our parents were born into?

"Shall I come to you?"

As much as I want to be cradled in his arms, I need to deal with these revelations on my own. Now that I have an address and some names to follow up on, I need to go and see for myself where Dad came from. It's not likely that I'll find my great-grandparents alive, but I will try to learn what I can. Whatever happened to our grandmothers?

"No. I'm fine. I'll see what more I can learn and call you soon."

"Listen, Manon, I want to hire a private detective to see if he can track down Gregory's mother. If she is living and we can find her, she may be able to fill in some gaps."

"I'm not sure I want to know why Dad's mother abandoned him; it's too cruel."

"Never mind, leave it with me. Just send copies of what you've found. Oh, and Manon, the portrait is amazing."

"It is? I'm glad you think so."

"When I first laid eyes on it, it was as if Gregory was communicating with me. I was taken aback by the intensity of feeling it evoked. You are very talented. You should concentrate on creating art. I wish you'd let me help you."

"I'm working things out on my own. I promise to call soon."

CHAPTER FIFTEEN

I search the freezer and find six-month-old shepherd's pie from Mrs. Richardson and tortière from her neighbor Mme. Beaudoin. Sage has stocked my fridge with fresh produce, so I make a watercress and tomato salad.

She arrives after work with a bottle of Shiraz, which will go well with the tortière. I'm glad for her company after the shock of learning that my grandfather was a criminal and my grandmother a lowlife who abandoned her son. Sage is a good listener, never judgmental, so I always felt I could confide in her. However, I won't share this latest news; it's too raw. I haven't yet unraveled the complexity of emotions coursing through me. Anger, loss... shame?

Sitting at the table, Sage gives the false impression of being tall and slim because her face is long, ending in a pointed chin, and her shoulders are narrow. Her round, deep-set eyes droop downwards. Despite their sorrowful aspect, her lips seem always on the verge of a smile. Her get-on-with-it approach to life and her no-nonsense attitude reminds me of Mrs. O.

"So tell me everything. What was New York like? You know, I've been meaning to go and experience the city as it should be experienced, not like the one and only time I was there on my paltry long weekend, in the dead of summer, over a decade ago.

"I remember that. Your excitement in planning the trip was contagious, and I wanted so badly to go with you."

Sage plants her elbows on the table and clasps her hands together under her chin.

"Well, now you've actually lived there, and you can tell me much more about it than I ever experienced."

I tell her about the Colosseum and all the people I got to know: Alexander first and foremost, then Mrs. O and Hedley, George the concierge, and Rosalia. I recount my outings in Soho, Noho, Greenwich Village, and Chelsea and my walk across the Brooklyn Bridge. She makes me go and get the Katherine Hepburn pants, and she's absolutely green with envy. Of course, they would never fit her, she being pear-shaped, belying her seated impression. We laugh and enjoy my coup – only eight hundred U. S. dollars!

The tortière is surprisingly scrumptious despite its sojourn in the freezer. The crust is flaky, and the meat filling is aromatic with sage, thyme, and cloves. I'll have to thank Mme. Beaudoin.

"Did you get to the New York Public Library? It's one of the places I managed to get to that weekend I was there."

"Yes, it's like a museum with all the portraits in the various halls. I was lost in the Map Room for hours, fascinated by the beautifully illustrated maps. I thought about how Dad might have liked it."

"Oh, he certainly would have loved that library."

I begin to tell her about Elderberry, describing the house, the grounds, and the barn.

"The barn is home to four horses: Artemis, Cassandra, Banjo, and Fred. Banjo was designated my horse. He is sweet and has the most beautiful big brown eyes – how I will miss him!"

"It reminds me of the Nottinghamshire of Lady Chatterley's Lover," she says.

She is totally engrossed in my story until I begin going off on a tangent about all the art I saw. MoMA's New York School collection especially intrigued me; Rothko, Rauschenberg, Motherwell, and others, who are equally exciting if not as well known, how I became enamored of the kaleidoscopic canvases of Lee Krasner.

"Manon, what will you do now? Do you have a plan?"

"I had this idea to rent out the house and find a place in Montreal. People often inquire about leasing here for the summer; maybe I could find someone who would like to move in year-round. With that and the insurance money, I could concentrate on my art. I am brimming with inspiration."

Only when she leaves do I descend into the depths of my new reality. I remember a time that I shoplifted just for the thrill of it. Is that a genetic tendency? How would Dad have reacted had he known what I'd done? I marvel at the life he carved out from what must have been a very difficult childhood. How hard it must have been for him, his losses and his sacrifices, the burden of being a single Dad, losing Gabrielle whom he loved, and my mother who was, in the grand scheme of things, only a brief companion in his life. I wonder if my mother knew his history or did he protect her from it, too. Was she a consolation to him? Did he even love her? These are things I will never know.

The very next day, I head back to Montreal. I have no trouble finding 733 Rue Lenoir. The row housing has mostly been replaced by townhouses, and # 733 is in the middle of a block of cheap brick dwellings. Walking to the end of the block, I see a Dépanneur on the corner. I go in and address the old couple behind the counter; they might have been here in the sixties. I pull out the photos I've brought with me and show them.

"There was a family named Mouland at number 733. Do you recognize these people?"

The old woman holds out her hand, palm facing down, and waves her fingers inwards. I think she's shooing me away, but actually, she's beckoning me to come closer. She takes the pictures and flips through them, talking in a joual dialect with a few words of English mixed in. Her monotone stream of words are incomprehensible to me, but I get the general gist that, yes, she remembers them.

"Ouais," the old woman nods her head and then hands the photos to the man, "Check-moé le don."

He nods too and says, "Le gar toujours en bécik, la 'tite court à pied après."

Then the woman wrinkles her nose and, tapping her finger on Dad's grandfather, just says,

"Botare." I'm thinking she means to say bâtard.

I think of Dad as a young boy inhabiting these streets. At the end of Rue Lenoir, there is a park, no playground, but lots of space for kids to run around. Certainly, Dad would have hung around here. I walk through, touching the bark of the same maple trees he may have played hide and seek against. I cross the park and end up on a footpath by a train track that takes me to Courcelle St.

The streets here are littered with the dross of overfull trash cans, and the metal shutters of closed businesses bloom with colorful graffiti. In fact, there is graffiti everywhere; one building is covered entirely in ghoulish caricatures of screaming monsters in military khakis. There are many other murals, less disturbing than this one, surprising you at every turn with splashes of brilliant color.

When I get to Notre Dame Avenue, I see a public library. This is a place I'm sure Dad would have visited. Maybe it even inspired him to become a librarian. I go in to see if I can find anyone who has worked here for a long time. The young woman at the desk says there have been many staff changes over the years. I ask her where the nearest elementary school is, and she directs me to St. Zotique Elementary, just around the corner. As it turns out, it's the nearest school to Rue Lenoir. I feel certain that this is where Dad must have attended, and my heart pounds as I retrace the steps he may have taken.

I snap some pictures to share with Alexander. He's been calling me regularly to see how I'm doing and to try to convince me to go back and live at Elderberry. Each time I hear his voice, something flutters in my belly, and I long to be with him. I'm determined to overcome this sexual reaction to him, to keep away until I can embrace him as my brother. Sometimes, because I'm so susceptible to him, I don't answer when he calls and just reply with brusque messages.

Sage happens to be in Montreal today to do her Christmas shopping, so we agree to meet for lunch at a bistro on Rue de la Montagne. She arrives with shopping bags from Ogilvy's, which is her go-to department store. I tell her that Mrs. O is actually Mrs. Ogilvy but that surely there is no connection to be drawn.

She offers to drive me home after she's visited with a friend of hers. In the meantime, I go to the Plateau to look at the spaces for rent I found in the Gazette. They sound reasonable and are available on December 1st. I waste no time, and before we head back to Lennoxville, I secure a 1 ½ bedroom in a building directly opposite Park Square St. Louis on Henri Julien Avenue. It's a third-floor walk-up with good morning light. I can't believe my luck to have found this place. Maybe I could just use the insurance money and not have to lease out the house. There is barely enough room for a futon, a worktable, and an easel. French doors open onto a Juliette balcony, just big enough to step out on and see a bit of the park. I'm feeling very accomplished and excited to move in.

The first real snowfall of the year arrives on my move-in day. The accumulation clings to the tree branches and makes everything look pristine—a fresh start to my new life.

CHAPTER SIXTEEN

M. Fournier, the super at my new building, let the delivery guys bring the futon up. When Sage and I arrive with a carload of my stuff, it's already there in the apartment. Having climbed three flights of stairs, Sage is glad to be able to plop herself down on it. I get busy setting up my easel and the trestles for my plywood table top and begin unpacking all my supplies.

It's almost dark when Sage leaves for a long drive home. Since I've been back, we've managed to spend a lot more time together. She has been a great support, not dictating what I should do but rather taking cues from me and pitching in without discussion. She's happy for me to have discovered family.

There's a soft, benign snowfall. Wide papery flakes, with no wind to impede their gentle drift downwards, float through the air, deadening the sounds of the street. By five o'clock, it's dark, and with the street lamps at my window level, I realize I'll need curtains. But then I'll need more light to work in the evenings, so I'll also need lamps.

Keen to get painting, I prep a canvas with underpainting and try a few chalk markings, but I have to be patient for it to dry. Thwarted from starting the painting, I set out to discover what my new neighborhood has to offer.

The featherweight of snowflakes on my eyelashes contrasts with the heaviness in my heart. Paradoxes are becoming a theme. My face is frozen, and my body is aflame. My spirits soar, then crash. How can I be happy and sad and excited and scared all at the same time? Something is happening to me, and I'm not sure if it's good or bad.

My new independence is exciting and it's also a little scary without the safety net that was Dad. The responsibilities of adulthood are now all mine. The mundane things that life requires, things I never had to think about, make it hard to focus on my art. I must learn to compartmentalize my life and organize my time.

St. Denis Street is lined with bistros, brasseries, and patisseries. I note the location of a handy dépanneur for future reference. Despite the snowy night, people stomp about snug in their Sorels and knit tuques emblazoned with Canadiens logos. They're unfazed by the cold and the steady snowfall.

I pass a bar and hear the soft silvery sound of John Mayer's voice pouring out onto the street. My heart squeezes with memories of last February when Dad and I watched the Grammys together. John Mayer won for his song *Daughters,* which both of us loved. Now, it is a bittersweet memory for me. I decide to go in and celebrate my move with a glass of wine.

Sitting at the bar, mellowed by Mayer and alcohol, I feel the familiar tug of my libido, so when a smooth-talking guy takes the stool next to me, I lean into the flirtation.

"The house Chardonnay is not bad," he says, indicating the small carafe and my solitary glass, "but if you'd allow me to treat you, they have a very decent Pinot Noir."

"I do enjoy a good Pinot."

"Good," he says to me and then to the bartender "Une bouteille de Trapiche Rèserve Pinot Grigio à la table s'il vous plait." He takes my elbow and leads me to a quiet corner table, where he proceeds to bore me with stories about people that I don't know or care about. By the time he pours the last bit of Pinot, I'm yawning.

"Thanks for the wine. I really must go home now."

"It's still early. My place is just around the corner. I have a great sound system and all of John Mayer's albums. If I promise not to ply you with more booze, will you come up?"

Marvin smells sooooo good – I succumb to the scent of sandalwood and citrus. His flat is on The Esplanade, where I spend the night with him but am not satisfied by him. I'll never be satisfied since all I want is Alexander.

Walking home the next morning, I feel awful about my self-indulgence. I hope I don't bump into Marvin again any time soon.

Ensconced in my cozy pied-à-terre, I decided to abandon the painting that would have been a street scene with my own graffiti on the buildings. My thoughts are of Dad. How did he manage to avoid being traumatized by his mother's abandonment? How did he overcome the criminality and violence of his father? The inequity of it makes me so angry that I want to scream. At the same time, it makes me incredibly sad. Deep down, despite our confrontations, Dad was a man of integrity, and now more than ever, I see how heroic that was.

Anger is like a splinter working its way into my palm – I must paint. I begin working in a frenzy, lashing paint on top of the beginnings of my street scene. My arms move up and down and side to side, a broad brush in each hand creating a riot of movement. I don't even bother to mix a pallet. Instead, I apply color over color until I see something taking shape. It feels like I've been fighting with phantoms, and the image that is emerging is a nightmare. Suddenly, my confidence collapses. I drop the brushes and quickly turn the canvas to the wall, my arms aching and my heart pounding.

Something has happened to me. I have crossed a chasm and let my feelings fly onto the canvas. It's not confidence I've lost; it's the lack of it that is gone.

For the next couple of weeks, I spent hours experimenting with different brushstrokes and subjects, emphasizing form and color in nonrepresentational expressions. I abandon the techniques I used for the arabesque florals and the precision required for painting birds. I feel freer to express more conceptual, abstract themes – love, loss, longing – manifested in vibrant colors and strong, bold images. I fall onto the futon, almost unconscious with fatigue most nights. All the while fending off the well-meaning exhortations from Alexander to come back, at least to spend Christmas together. I'm just getting used to my solitary life, and I've never liked holidays. There's no escape from the season's aggressive cheerfulness, and it only emphasizes the loneliness of a two-person family.

"I'm sorry, Alexander," I say during one of these phone calls, "I have promised to spend the holiday with Sage."

"Bring her to Elderberry! Mrs. O will be so delighted to make a feast. Hedley's fiancée Stephanie will be here, and you'll meet some of the other people in my life."

That's news. I am intrigued by any woman who has won Hedley's heart. He always seems so aloof. I've never thought of him being romantically attached.

"Okay, I'll ask her."

When I propose the trip to Sage, she is thrilled at the opportunity to go to Connecticut and experience Christmas in New York, so it's settled. Her excitement infects me, and I begin to feel the happy anticipation of my two worlds meeting.

꩜꩜꩜꩜

I go to Ogilvy's to shop for a few gifts. For Mrs. O, I get an Edinburgh lamb's wool stole. It's a Stewart Tartan in camel, which I think will look good with her auburn hair and pale complexion. There is a pewter kilt pin in the shape of a bagpipe that I can't resist. I pin it to the stole. For Hedley, I find a Shetland wool sweater with a shawl collar to keep him warm in the barn. I buy tins of shortbread cookies, toffee, maple sugar candies, and a bottle of maple syrup to make a gift basket.

It's hard to come up with something meaningful for Alexander, so I decide to create a piece of art just for him. Researching my grandparents led me to the library, where I was surprised to find a Mouland family crest in the Dutch section of a book on family crests. The duotone crest has a knight's helmet at its center crowned with five grey and yellow plumes sitting on top of curlicues of oak leaves with a shield-shaped plaque at its center. I traced it.

I have the idea to do a collage using Lee Krasner's method of cutting up rejected canvases. I had painted a leafy maple tree once that I didn't like and now cut it into strips, which I mount onto a Masonite board. One of the branches sprouts the pen and ink reproduction of the family crest, and another has cut-outs from the pictures of Dad and Gabrielle dangling from it with bits of actual rope. St. Zotique Elementary is juxtaposed at the end of a strip of bark-painted canvas, partially hidden beneath some oak leaves I've drawn in pen and ink. I hope he'll like it.

CHAPTER SEVENTEEN

We take an early flight on Saturday the 24th. Alexander has organized everything for us, including flying first class and a black car to pick us up at LaGuardia and take us to Greenwich. We are both as excited as schoolgirls on an adventure. At the airport's arrivals I am, once again, greeted by a placard with my name on it. This time, a uniformed driver, complete with a chauffeur's cap, is waving it up high.

"This sure is different from my first trip to New York when I arrived at the smelly bus terminal in the sweltering heat. This I could get used to," says Sage.

"Me too. New York is much nicer when you have money." We laugh, once again, at the outrageous amount I spent on my beautiful trousers, which I'm wearing now with Gabrielle's olive green twin set.

Since it's still early, we make a little detour to midtown to see the magnificent 84-foot Norway spruce set up in Rockefeller Centre. After the holiday, it will be harvested by Habitat and hewed into two-by-fours to build a home to replace one that Hurricane Katrina destroyed. There is also an 18th-century menorah on display, which will be lit tomorrow for the first night of Hanukkah.

We watch the skaters glide below the towering Christmas tree. Then, as if to enhance our experience, grey clouds release their load, sprinkling snowflakes, like icing sugar over the whole scene, as classic Christmas music provides a soundtrack to the experience.

"Not to sound cliché," says Sage, a prodigious reader who balks at hackneyed phraseology, "but this is like being inside a snow globe. It's magical!"

"It's as if we've stepped onto the set of 'Miracle on 34th Street,' and my belief in Santa has been restored," I reply in awe of the setting.

"This experience alone would have been worth the trip," she says.

"I agree. I'm really glad we decided to come."

We gaze at the gold statue of Prometheus and lift our faces to the sky, where the top of the Christmas tree ends with a shining golden star. The twinkling lights, the colorful skaters, and the sprinkling of snowflakes, Sage is correct, we are suspended inside a snow globe. I have to pull us away as we have an hour's drive ahead of us, and we want to arrive before dinner.

Alexander greets us at the door. The sight of him, his face lit by a beatific glow, increases my heart rate, and my cheeks feel hot. He immediately envelops me in his arms and holds on for a moment longer than needed, transferring his feeling of warmth to me. When we look into each other's eyes, I see a glimmer of what might be love, like I used to see in Dad's eyes when the veil protecting complicated emotions lifted momentarily. It changes the dynamic between us. When we look into each other's eyes now, we see the shared sordid history of our grandfathers, and it curiously bonds us with a sense of solidarity.

Released from his arms, I falter for a moment and then recover to make introductions.

"This is my friend Sage Hume." She smiles broadly and extends her hand.

"So good to finally meet you, Alexander."

"And so nice to meet you. I am happy that I can tell you in person how eloquently you spoke at Gregory's funeral. It was eye-opening for me." Mrs. O comes out of the kitchen, and Alexander introduces her to Sage. "And this is our own Mrs. O, without whom we would suffer some catered holiday meal."

The two women shake hands, and I'm surprised to see their immediate connection. Mrs. O, contrary to her stoic, detached demeanor, is focused on Sage so that as they look each other in the eye, she actually blushes. The image of a yin and yang circle comes to my mind in which Mrs. O's broad shoulders, large bosom, and narrow hips fill in the space left by Sage's narrow shoulders, flat chest, and wide hips. To my surprise, Mrs. O says,

"Hello, Sage, please call me Peg."

Alexander and I share a moment of incredulity – Mrs. O has a given name! Then she moves in and surprises me with a little hug.

"Welcome home, Manon." I've never seen her in such a good mood.

It's only six weeks that I've been gone, but it does feel like a homecoming. The place smells of the same woodsy leather and suede, and now there is the added scent of pine from the large fir tree by the window. It is lit up with tiny white lights that twinkle.

There are some out-of-the-ordinary ornaments; painted birds and children's mittens, tiny harps, real flutes, and metallic kazoos. The odors wafting from the kitchen hint at roasted meat, garlic, and cloves, and there is the intoxicating smell of mulled wine. The dining room is set for eight with gold-trimmed dinnerware, crystal goblets, and a gorgeous spruce and holly centerpiece with red candles.

"Let me show you your room," says Mrs. O. She leads Sage and our little delegation up the stairs, Alexander trailing with our bags.

"Hedley and his fiancée, Stephanie, will be coming in soon, and I've also invited my friend Julian Fisher, WWP's CFO, and his niece Nicole, who recently moved here from upstate. She's doing an internship with me at the lab. Manon, I've told you that Julian is a knowledgeable art collector. He's seen the portrait of Gregory, and he thought the work was masterful. I'm sure you'll have a lot to talk about."

At around five o'clock, Hedley and Stephanie come in through the French doors, their arms around each other's waists. They stomp the snow off their boots and fill the room with their radiance. I can hardly recognize Hedley, his face so openly happy. He and Stephanie make a handsome couple, both tall and lithe. They move like synchronized swimmers. Their dark hair is almost the same shade. His is wild around his ears and neck, and her soft waves are shoulder-length. When they put their heads together, it's hard to tell where he ends and she begins. Hedley leans into me for a little hug.

"Manon, I'm so glad you came back. Banjo misses you."

"I was just about to go out to the barn and visit him. I'm so happy to see you."

"This is Stephanie Kelsey, my fiancée. Stephanie is a medic in the army and is home on a well-deserved two-week leave."

"Steph," Alexander buts in, "this is my little sister, Manon." It's as if he takes pleasure in showing off our relationship. I feel a little tingle up my spine, too, when I'm reminded that I am a sister and that Alexander is my brother. The warmth it generates is not so much in my belly but higher up, in my heart.

I immediately like Stephanie. Her beautiful hazel eyes meet mine, and I can tell that she has seen things and knows things that I have no concept of. I fall into a kind of awe of her. Instead of shaking my hand, she hugs me too.

"I've heard so much about you," she says. "How extraordinary that you and Alexander have found each other."

We hear a car in the driveway, and Alexander goes to open the door for Julian and Nicole. When all the introductions are made, Mrs. O starts filling glasses with mulled wine, and Sage makes herself useful by passing the glasses around. They move in concert as if they had always collaborated.

I watch Alexander small-talking his way about the room, smiling. He's in his element, hosting, taking care of everyone's needs, and engaging each person with a comment or compliment. I can see why people gravitate to him – he's not just handsome, smart and talented, but he also has that special quality that men don't often have, a kind of empathy that makes people trust him and strive to please him. I want to please him, too. When he looks at me with the loving warmth of a doting older brother, my heart sinks and soars. When he grabs me around the shoulders and pulls me to him, I melt on so many levels. What kind of love is this?

Aromas emanating from the kitchen make us salivate. Christmas dinner is delicious. Mrs. O has outdone herself, creating a veritable feast. The table is laden with a colorful array of dishes. Burgundy and gold roasted beets gleam in a silver chafing dish; green Brussels sprouts peek out between orange sweet potatoes; little jewels of pomegranate seeds shine in the saffron-laced dressing; and a curl of steam rises from a bowl of glistening green peas. When Alexander brings in the golden brown turkey and places it on the table, appreciative oohs and ahs are directed at Mrs. O.

During our leisurely meal, the conversation drifts from animated cheerfulness to quiet remembrance of the horrible event of just a few years ago, with many topics covered.

"I think that autonomous cars will definitely become ubiquitous transportation in the very near future," says Julian.

"Yah, I read about the DARPA Grand Challenge in October." Hedley adds, "They raced them through three narrow tunnels and navigated more than 100 sharp left and right turns. It's unbelievable. But if you ask me, horses are still the best mode of transportation."

Nicole pipes up shyly, trying to make a joke in her high-pitched voice, "It might be good for Lindsay Lohan, though. She can drink and drive without causing an accident." Everybody laughs, and then Alexander adds,

"Robotic technology is getting quite advanced with nano circuitry, but I fear we aren't ready for it until they can figure out how to circumvent virtual crime sprees."

"What worries me," says Sage, "is the technology they're using to spy on Americans by listening to their phone calls and reading their emails. They're probably doing it in Canada as well. Who knows?" Mrs. O responds by adding, "Privacy has always been an issue. Long ago, only a small segment of the population could afford a house, and even they didn't have private bedrooms for all. Now, the bedrooms are private, but our lives are out there for all to witness."

"You're right, Peg," says Sage. "They've just launched something called YouTube where people post their stories and another site called Reddit where they air their personal lives for everyone. Privacy has been an issue, even in Canada, when our charismatic Prime Minister Pierre Trudeau, made his famous proclamation as Justice Minister in 1967 that '*There's no place for the state in the bedrooms of the nation*'."

"I wish the esoteric debate about privacy was our greatest concern." Alexander becomes serious and continues, "Doctors Without Borders reports a plethora of humanitarian crises around the world, not the least of which is the ongoing fallout of the Tsunami that happened exactly a year ago. A staggering 200,000 lives were lost. How do you recover from that? The loss of 3,000 lives on 9/11 is still raw after four years." Conversation stops briefly for a quiet remembrance of that horrible event.

Then, to break the spell of gloom on what should be a joyous night, Alexander gets up and circles the table, topping up wine glasses and humming as his iPod shuffles to a jazzy version of Silent Night.

Hedley and Stephanie are engrossed in each other, and Mrs. O and Sage share their mutual interest in Anglophilia, especially the British monarchy. Nicole's apple-like cheeks blush whenever Alexander offers her anything; more peas, more wine, more attention than she's used to getting from him at the lab – she's obviously smitten hard. I understand this infatuation. The more he reveals of himself, the more my sense of pride in him grows.

Julian asks about my art, how long I've been painting, what my preferred medium is, and whether portraiture is a specialty; have I 'shown' anywhere? Focusing in this way on my passion is daunting. His evident depth of knowledge is intimidating, and it makes me feel like an imposter on the verge of exposure. I hardly know what to say, so I change the subject. Since everyone engaged in their own conversations, I shift in my chair to face him better.

"How long have you known Alexander?"

"Long enough to recognize him as a uniquely talented and brilliant man, a visionary who can see a better world and is capable of creating it."

"I'm beginning to see that."

"Alexander is undaunted by obstacles. He just methodically works through them to achieve his goals. He is a master of the art of the possible." Echoes of Dad, I think.

"Alright, Julian, stop boring Manon. Let me propose a toast," and raising his glass, he says, "This is for Manon, a sister I never knew I had, and for Gregory, the father I will never know. Let's drink to family." We all lift our glasses, and I take a small sip to toast Dad.

Then Julian exhorts Alexander to play for us, and we move into the Great Room. He starts with a piece by Bach, which he introduces as the Prelude for Lute Suite 4. It sounds like rain spattering relentlessly on leaves, and I'm awed by the strength of his fingers dexterously plucking and pressing the strings. We applaud him and beg for more, so he plays a challenging piece by Paganini, Caprice No. 24. his hands stretched to incredible limits, moving swiftly up and down the neck of the instrument, playing hard and soft in swift succession. When he stops, we are all silenced and in awe of him. Then Hedley, a huge Jimi Hendrix fan, asks for something contemporary.

"I won't compete with Jimi," Alexander says, "but here's something for our ladies from Quebec."

He begins strumming and plucking and tapping out a slow beat on the hollow body. His mellow baritone imitates Leonard Cohen's raspy rendition of Anthem;

The birds they sang

At the break of day

Start again

I heard them say

Don't dwell on what has passed away

Or what is yet to be

We all sit mesmerized by the lyrics and his voice, which soars to a crescendo.

Ring the bells that still can ring

Forget your perfect offering

There is a crack, a crack in everything

That's how the light gets in.

By the time the party breaks up, it is already past midnight. The horses are resting, and I'll have to wait until the morning to visit the barn.

Through the bay window of my bedroom, I look at the silver crescent of the moon against the dark sky freckled with stars. It is so quiet. I am filled with wonder at what Alexander has accomplished from what might have been a very different life had Gabrielle stayed in Montreal, not to mention that I may never have come into existence if that had happened. She did what was best for her son. If she had stayed with Gregory, the stigma of their affair would surely have had a negative effect on Alexander, along with the stigma of his grandfather's ignominious demise. Her sacrifice was for Alexander, even though it meant separating him from his father.

CHAPTER EIGHTEEN

I can't wait to go riding with Alexander. I dress quickly in layers and head out without even a sip of coffee. He is already in the barn with Hedley. I hear them talking about the vet's last visit and the amount of feed they'll need to order. Alexander is looking up into Arty's face and stroking his neck. Expecting me, both Arty and Banjo are saddled up, their snorts creating clouds at their nostrils in the frigid air.

My legs are cold, and I can't wait to be astride Banjo's warm body. I trail behind Alexander to the path into the forest. He's mounted with such a calm, assured elegance, his body moving rhythmically as he rides. I, on the other hand, still feel hesitant and amateurish atop Banjo. The path widens, and we plod along side by side. Alexander begins talking about the private detective he's hired.

"The chances of him finding your grandmother are slim. However, he may turn up some information, maybe find someone who may have known her, someone who she might have confided in."

My interest in Alice is nil. When I think of her, my stomach churns, imagining the hurt she must have caused my Dad. I hate her for it. Nevertheless, I can see that Alexander is keen on unearthing whatever may come to light. I don't say anything, so he drops it. The more I get to know him, the more I'm reminded of

Dad's quiet concern for me. It's comforting. My feeling for him is shifting. Although I am still affected by his exquisite looks, now I feel something more like pride than lust for him.

"Manon, I don't know about you, but since you've come into my life, I feel generally more at ease, less guarded, as if being moored to family has freed me somehow. Even though you've decided to live in Montreal, I feel a really close connection to you. You are precious to me, and I have a strong desire to protect you. I hope you will let me be your brother. You must promise that we will try to spend the holidays together."

"I want that too," I say

Banjo's body heat and Alexander's proximity have warmed me. I too, feel that some of the tension I always carried has eased by being linked to him. It's more than a sense of solidarity. It's a special kind of love, one that I could never articulate, one that I longed for all my life. We begin to gallop faster, grinning as the cold air rushes over us. I'm happy.

When we reach the frozen pond where the horses usually like to drink, we slow again.

"I've managed to get four tickets for Balanchine's Nutcracker at Lincoln Centre tonight. It's an annual spectacle not to be missed. I'd like to take you and Sage along with my friend Juliette. She's dying to meet you."

"Oh, that sounds great," I say with less enthusiasm than is warranted. Why does the existence of Juliette shock me, and why do I feel immediately antagonistic toward her? Suddenly, I feel cold again.

Dad used to bring home video tapes of full ballet performances from the library, and I became fascinated and enchanted by the movement of dancers' bodies. I remember how he used to get annoyed with me for begging him to pause the tape while I sketched the dancers in various poses. I went through a period where all I sketched were bodies; lying, leaping, sleeping, dancing. But I have never been to a live ballet.

Back at the house, Sage and Mrs. O are sitting having coffee.

"Sage, guess where we're going tonight?"

"Are we going to the city?"

"Better yet, Alexander is taking us to the ballet! At Lincoln Centre. To see The Nutcracker!"

"Really?" she literally shrieks in delight. "That's my favorite ballet," she says and then immediately adds, "But I've brought nothing to wear to the theatre."

Alexander suggests we leave for the city right after lunch and rummage through Gabrielle's closet.

We arrive at the theatre dressed to the nines: Alexander in a dark suit and white shirt open at the collar; Sage in a loose caftan with colorful panels of silk shot through with silver threads, and me in a little black cocktail dress under a grey and silver Boucle box coat. As the patrons start filling the lobby, my anxiety heightens. I look around nervously, wondering if I can guess who Juliette is. Abruptly, she appears from behind me and moves in to kiss Alexander chastely on the lips.

"Juliette!" He slips his arm around her slim waist, happy at the sight of her. "I want you to meet my sister, Manon, and this is Sage Hume, visiting from Quebec."

When she turns her head to us, the precise edges of her geometric haircut swing momentarily at her jawline and then fall back into place perfectly.

"Manon, what a pleasure." A delicate hand with short French-manicured nails envelops mine and squeezes it gently. I'm all flustered and tongue-tied in the face of her gorgeous green eyes, sculpted cheekbones, and flawless makeup. This cannot be the owner of the pink glittery cellphone case I saw in the apartment last summer. This woman looks worthy of Alexander.

"Hi," I manage finally, thankful that we have no time for chatting as the flickering lights summon the audience to enter the theatre.

When the show ends, I find myself on my feet with the rest of the audience, shouting *Bravo!* I'm clapping so hard my hands hurt. I don't want it to end. I don't want to have to face Juliette *with* Alexander; I just want to disappear. But he's proposing drinks at The Iroquois Hotel.

"You ladies will love it," he says. "They don't take reservations, but I know the manager."

For the ten-minute cab ride, I am wedged between Sage's ample hip and the softness of Juliette's cashmere coat, close enough that I can smell her perfume, a magnificent floral bouquet of jasmine with notes of citrus. Alexander, in the front seat, keeps turning back to meet Juliette's eyes. Sage is ebulliently recounting her delight in the Dance of the Sugar Plum Fairies, her favorite part. I'm quietly miserable.

Alexander greets the host at the door of Lantern's Keep, saying something confidentially in his ear. After that, we are ushered right into a mahogany paneled room appropriately decorated with reproductions of Renoir's ballerina paintings in gilt frames. The lighting is dim. There are little lanterns that create intimate spheres of light on all the white marble tabletops.

Sage is grinning and then looks at me quizzically. "What's wrong?" she whispers. "You look like your dog just died. Didn't you love the ballet?"

On Boxing Day, we awake at the Colosseum, where Alexander had dropped us off and went off with Juliette for the night. Sage is already busy making tea and plans for the day. She wants to see the Rockettes Christmas Spectacular. I want to stay in bed and tend to my aching heart. I should be happy that Alexander has found his perfect match, but I mourn the loss of the final glimmer of hope of ever being with him, and all I want to do is go home.

CHAPTER NINETEEN

January is almost gone before I even realize that a new year has arrived. Sage has returned to Lennoxville, sparing me her rapturous re-living of our brief holiday, and I revert to my solitary life in my little studio. It feels cramped, cold and gloomy.

Moving away from Lennoxville has given me independence from both Dad and Alexander. I have my own schedule, with no one to remind me of chores or to tell me that painting rectangles of color over and over is a waste of time. I trudge through the days of February as if wearing the dirty overcoat of a sweaty old man. It's heavy, yet it doesn't keep me warm, and I can't ever take it off. I feel like a beggar – for inspiration, for sunny days, for sparks of insight. My mind is blank, my body is sluggish, and none of my self-gratifying tricks and occupations work to improve my mood.

As a countermeasure to the unrelenting dreariness of the month, I bring home an amaryllis to brighten the place. However, even this splendid plant makes me heavy-hearted because I know of its imminent demise. It stands like royalty, tall, straight, and proud, a promise of spring. It is a cruel deception. Far too quickly, the spectacular bloom loses opacity as it begins its rapid decline, which I document in daily sketches. The impressive fan of leaves at its base becomes limp and wrinkly. Then, finally, for pity's sake, I sever the bare stem. It yields easily to the shears, oozing drops of slime like tears.

The wind howls and sends ice pellets, clattering against my window. Daylight is miserly and has a murky quality as if the sun were shrouded in a smoggy veil. February daylight is forever twilight. Outside my window, I hear the cacophony of a flock of hungry sparrows gathered on the branches of the bare maple. Their energetic chirping prompts me to get busy. I start to work, painting in the half-light. I work maniacally through the long, dark nights.

Ever since I stood in front of Mark Rothko's paintings at MoMa, I have been trying to understand why his abstract expressionist color fields, which seem to disintegrate into pure light, are capable of making me cry. They wound me. Confronted by them, I feel dislocated. I feel compelled to re-evaluate myself. How does he evoke such fundamental human emotions as tragedy, ecstasy, and doom? How has he tapped into my own complicated emotions: rage at having been left in the dark all my life, the shame of my despicable ancestors, the pain of missing Dad, more poignant because I can't confront him? And now, with Alexander in my life, fear. I'm afraid of losing him so soon to Dr. Juliette Badour. I hate myself for not wanting to share him. Even knowing that he cannot be with me the way I want doesn't change the constant fluttering and flushing of my physical responses to him.

I begin exploring the limitless possibilities of layering rectangles onto fields of color, pouring my emotions onto the canvas. By March, I'm doing this so obsessively that the sheer volume of paint, turpentine, and canvas I consume costs more than groceries. I need additional income to keep myself in art supplies, so I sign on to a temp agency and spend half days in drab office towers.

All this while I keep in touch with Alexander, or rather he keeps in touch with me because I'm so immersed in my work that if staying in touch depended on me, days could turn to weeks. One day, when he calls, I let slip that I'm at work and can't talk. He admonishes me for not having reached out to him for help. I think he's decided that it is his duty, as a brother, to look after me. It's hard for me to accept his generosity because, even though Dad was my support, I always maintained a certain self-sufficiency by having some job or other. Temping has given me enough to buy what I need. I'm doing okay.

I've removed my table to make space for the large canvases leaning against the walls. Giddy with the smell of paint and turpentine, I live inside the rectangles of color I've created; blue over black, orange over purple, red on top of red. Large flat blocks squeeze narrow ones, their soft edges making them look misty. The rich red hues pulsate and seem to glow even in the dark. Occasionally, slivers of white creep onto a canvas only to be obliterated by black.

Sometimes, I get claustrophobic and dream of the studio above the garage at Elderberry. Then I think of Alexander. As time passes, my feelings toward him are becoming more sisterly. I'm happy that he's found Juliette. He mentions her often. My antagonism toward her has changed to a cautious wariness, more of a protective instinct than jealousy. He seems less guarded than when I first met him. As much as I'd like to think that it's because we are moored to family, such as it is, it's really because of Juliette, and so I reconcile my feelings about her. She is good for him.

Shortly after I let slip that I'm working, Alexander calls back.

"Listen, Manon, Julian, and I are coming to Montreal. I'm setting up a trust fund for you that will relieve you of having to work for a wage. You'll be able to devote your time to painting. We'll have some papers for you to sign, and then we're going to the bank.

"That's really not necessary. I'm doing fine."

"There's no need for a discussion. It's all set up."

I know him well enough by now that any discussion would be futile. Once he's made up his mind, I can't change it. I realize I don't want to.

"When are you coming?"

"Nicole will text you when she's organized it. We'll be staying at the Ritz."

The Ritz! Just last week, on a drizzly March day, after spending the morning in an office tower pushing paper around, I went to the Musée des Beaux Arts to see the Jean-Paul Riopelle exhibit. When I stepped out into the damp cold, lashed by frigid winds, my mind reeling with Riopelle's jagged images, I crossed Sherbrooke Street to seek refuge at The Ritz Carlton. They offer an afternoon 'tea experience' in their Palm Court, just like at The Plaza. Huddled under the fur trim of my hood, deprived of peripheral vision, I squished into a wedge of the revolving door that was already occupied by a man who smelled like bergamot and peppermint.

"Ah, pardon," he said in French without a French accent.

"No, sorry, it's my fault. I wasn't looking," I replied. That's bilingualism in Montreal, people just switch to whichever language works best in the circumstance - it's an instinct.

He wasted no time in asking, with an extended hand and slightly bent toward me;

"My name is Jack Webb. May I invite you to tea?"

Like Alexander, he was tall, fair-haired, and carried himself with assurance. He wore a grey overcoat with a burgundy scarf and a tweed flat cap. On the surface, he was a sedate, good-looking man, about ten years my senior, not usually my type, but I found him very appealing.

He said he's a Union organizer. Not likely. He's dressed more like a banker in his elegant cashmere coat and impeccably tailored suit. Wanting to appear smart and worldly, I told him I'm a writer. In no time at all, we were in his room, and without many words uttered, he had me quivering with desire. He knew what to do and was cool about it all. In my mind, he could be whoever I conjured, and he obliged me by never interrupting my fantasies, instinctively following the script in my mind, knowing exactly what I wanted. After two days on a sexual odyssey in his luxury suite, he sent me on my way without any promises, without even an exchange of phone numbers. Perfect.

They arrive on a Thursday and come straight to my little studio. There is hardly space for two grown men and me. I have only one chair and one stool beside the futon, so we stand around awkwardly while Julian eyes the paintings that clutter the room in various stages of completion. Alexander finally pulls up the chair, and he takes my hand. The warmth of it makes me tingle.

"How're you doing, Sis?" He smiles at his own pleasure in addressing me this way. "You look a little tired."

"Fine. I like to work late into the night, so I don't sleep too much."

"When did you start smoking again?" His look is penetrating and accusatory.

Not wanting to make eye contact, I turn to Julian, who is busy flipping through a stack of drawings on the futon.

"Oh, these are just sketches," I say, taking them from him. He turns his attention to the canvases stacked together by the French doors. "And those aren't finished." I turn them to the wall one by one, feeling a little annoyed at his invasion of my privacy. He ignores me and pulls out one of the rectangle studies, the dark one that I'm not happy with, black and blue rectangles on a royal blue field.

"Some of these are really good," he says.

I'm shy about having my work scrutinized by a connoisseur, worried about being exposed as an amateur. I begin to tidy away the jars of tinted water with dirty brushes in it.

"I told you she's talented – you saw the portrait she did of Gregory."

"Yes, but these …these are… moving, even if they are just experimental," he says, looking at me.

֍֍֍֍

At the Bank of America branch on René-Lévesque Blvd W., where we are expected and greeted with extreme deference, we sign some papers and open an account in my name. The trust enables me to draw funds freely, only requiring a sign-off from the Executor, Julian if the amount is over $10,000. I'll be able to buy the most expensive oil paints. I'm going to get a whole new set of sable brushes and pre-stretched linen canvases. On the shopping spree in my mind, I stopped at Holt Renfrew, where I saw a Canada Goose down parka in the window. It has an oversized fur-trimmed hood, side vents, and four exterior pockets, so I won't need to carry a purse and even backpack straps for hands-free carrying when I'm inside a mall. I want the red one.

We go for dinner at Maison Boulud at the Ritz. Over shared appetizers, I tell them about the Riopelle exhibit across the street. They both know the artist, and Julian reschedules their morning flight so that they can see it before heading back to New York.

"So, Manon," Julian says. "Where did you learn to do such sophisticated work?"

I tell him that I didn't have any training beyond my high school art classes and that I've been doing art in some form or other since I could remember. I described my feelings upon seeing into the 'forest' painting in our hallway, how it affected me, and gave me shivers. The more I examined it, the more I was fascinated by the phenomenon of being able to elicit emotions such as fear and wonderment with brushstrokes on a canvas.

"My Dad didn't want me to go to art school,"

"Didn't he see how talented you are?"

"He worried I'd become an aimless idler; he wanted me to have a more well-rounded education so that I would have options." I stop folding the linen napkin when it becomes too small to fold again and begin gesturing with my hands as I describe how I practiced on my own. "I had a whole library of books on art at my disposal. I did a lot of copying and studying perspective, composition, and technique."

"That's remarkable," says Julian, "but you have a great sense of color that can't really be learned from a book."

"Well, I spent hours of trial and error mixing colors to find the right pallet for whatever the subject. I loved the sensual effect of the various hues. I wanted to swim in them, drown in them."

Before I know it, we are halfway through our entrees, and I feel like I've been talking the whole time, in between mouthfuls of daurade in a rosé sauce with blanched almonds and baked red onion. I've never had such succulent fish. Between sips of champagne, we talk of art, and then Julian asks as if the idea just occurred to him,

"Would you permit me to present some of your work to a gallery owner friend of mine?"

"Splendid idea!" says Alexander. "You could come back to New York. I've renovated the gym into a studio. It's ready for you. If you wanted to, you could take some classes at Pratt – or maybe teach some!" He smiles admiringly. I think he's proud of me. I never realized how liberating a bit of encouragement can be. Once again, I feel happy until he adds, "And once you're back, we'll deal with the smoking issue."

࿇࿇࿇࿇

A little worm in my brain is plumbing the possibilities of going back to New York at the expense of abandoning the life I've begun in Montreal. Living out the fantasy of attending Pratt, of devoting my life to art without a care, is seductive. But the idea of showing my work and entering the commercial art world is daunting. Critical acclaim is one thing, but exposing my soul and then failing to sell is scary. And although I'm coming to accept Juliette as someone who is suitable for Alexander, I can't shake the image of that casual kiss she gave him at the theater. It still gives me an unpleasant sensation in the pit of my stomach.

I decided to spend the weekend in Lennoxville. I have a longing to explore the woods around our house, where the first hint of spring in March is fascinating. The redolence of the warming earth is irresistible. Delicate shoots emerge. Even as early as this, I might come upon a Yellow Trout Lily bud dangling atop a pair of mottled purply-brown leaves, about to flower. It's a bit early for my favorite fiddleheads. I also feel like talking to Sage.

While she is more of Dad's generation than mine, she's not as rigid in her ideas as he was. She has a way of reflecting my thoughts to me in a more coherent way.

I stop by the library first to see her. On Saturdays, when the reception staff is off, instead of working at her desk, she spends the time reading in one of the armchairs with an eye on the entrance, just in case anyone needs her.

"Manon, I'm so glad to see you. How are things in Montreal?"

"Alexander came in with Julian on Thursday, and they're urging me to go back to New York. I'm really not sure what to do."

"What exactly is your dilemma?" This is the way she manages to get me to nail down my thoughts instead of jumping from one thing to another.

"I'm not sure."

"Your Dad liked the Ben Franklin method of decision-making. Have you tried that?" Sage gets up to put the kettle on in the kitchen and comes back with a pad and pen. "Here," she says. "Start with the pros and cons of going and then do the same for the 'staying' option."

It seems ridiculous to list the positive reasons for going to New York. Who wouldn't want to be there?

"What intrigues me is the possibility of taking classes at Pratt."

"You'd have to apply. Do they have a summer semester?"

"Julian is good friends with the Dean of Visual Arts there. He might be able to get me in midterm."

"Okay, that's good," she says. "What else? What about Alexander?"

The lifestyle my generous brother affords me is more than anyone could dream of. In the four months that I spent there, I barely scratched the surface of what the city has to offer. The high caliber of art at every turn is inspirational. So much to see and learn. And then there's Elderberry Lane to retreat to when the stimulation gets overwhelming. It should be a no-brainer, but my brain is not ruled by logic.

There's plenty to be apprehensive about. Julian's involvement in my career should be welcome, but it is the opposite. I'm not ready. I don't know if I'll ever be. I don't know whether commercial success is even what I want. Although Alexander's belief in me is gratifying, the expectations it places on me are daunting. I'm not sure I could live up to it.

That night, I dream of horses and feel the exhilaration of galloping through fields of daisies. When I awake, with my heart racing, my mind is made up.

CHAPTER TWENTY

When I left Montreal early this morning, the trees were still bare and grey. Here in Connecticut, they have already sprouted those soft green halos of early spring leaf. Gentle April rains have resulted in stunning bursts of yellow daffodils and red tulips. Baby-blue puddles of forget-me-nots cover the ground under shade trees, and foamflowers stick their cone-shaped white heads up through the detritus of winter.

Arriving at Elderberry at twilight, I notice a little Lexus coupe in the driveway, and my heart sinks to think that Juliette might be here. It's just the kind of car she would drive – in white, no less. I expect to see vanity plates declaring the owner as DocJB or some such moniker, but they are simply the regular gold and blue New York state ones. When Alexander hands me the keys that night, I hardly know what to say.

"I got this for you because you'll need a car to get back and forth once you start your classes, and I hate the idea of you carting those big portfolios on the trains."

His generosity is so natural that I can't even make a polite objection, so I simply say,

"Thank you."

"Take a look inside. I'll point out some of its features."

He opens the driver's side door for me, and I am inundated by that 'new car' smell with overtones of fine leather. Everything from the soft-touch dash and door panels to the supple leather seats exudes high quality. "It has a keyless entry and ignition system. You just have to have the key with you, and the doors will unlock as you approach. Just put your foot on the break and push this button to start the engine. The gear shift is here in the middle. It's pretty peppy with a 2.5-liter V6 engine. But in case you get a little carried away with its power, it's also got some state-of-the-art safety features, including airbags, front seat-mounted side airbags, traction control, and four-wheel antilock disc brakes. Then, for fun, I've added some options like the moonroof and the 13-speaker premium audio system with an in-dash six-disc CD changer. I've even put in some CDs for you."

"It's amazing," I say, "I love it," but I don't tell him that, as far as I'm concerned, white is not a color for cars.

I resume my idyllic life at Elderberry, only now I'm driving into Manhattan instead of taking the train. Mrs. O, Hedley, and the horses seem to be pleased that I'm back, and we settle into the same routine as we left off. Riding at dawn, then, famished from the air and exercise, we have a hearty breakfast together and then go our separate ways. Alone but together, like a family, with Alexander as the head.

֍֍֍֍

The spring session at Pratt is already underway, yet I've ambitiously enrolled in some classes as a mature student. I'll have to work hard to catch up through the semester. Life Drawing is no problem; Color Theory will be interesting but Graphic Design will be hard. I'm also beginning to tackle the reading list for an Art History class I want to take next semester. It's a heavy load for someone no longer used to the rigors of academic performance. In spite of that, I am very excited.

My Life Drawing class is on the second floor of the Manhattan Campus, where privileged alumni also have studios. One evening, as I was leaving, I accidentally bumped into a tall, dark-haired man coming out of an adjacent studio. He stared at me like a blind man suddenly struck with vision, and I became rooted to the spot by his magnetism.

"I'm sorry; I hope I haven't injured you." He says with exaggerated concern, considering it was only a slight bump. Is he mocking me for being clumsy? His beautiful almond-shaped eyes are a stunning shade of jade mixed with sapphire. He boldly takes my hand, grabs my arm, and says, "Are you alright?" His exaggerated expression is clearly facetious.

"Yes, I'm fine!" My reply is emphatic. I try to move, but he seems unwilling to let go of my arm, so I add, "Really."

"I'm William Stein. I work in this studio," he indicates the large sculpture studio that is reserved for artists in residence. It is usually locked. Now, it's open enough for me to glimpse a large block of marble beginning to take the shape of some kind of animal. "How is it that I've not seen you before?" There is a glint of something wild and dangerous in his eyes, something that is unrelated to the gentle expression of his smiling mouth. I pull my arm away and start to move without responding. I need to free myself from the shock of those eyes. He persists, walking alongside me down the long corridor.

"What's your name?"

He reaches for my hand again, and, unable to ignore him, I stop and face him bravely. I'm on the verge of rebuking him for his audacity. However, to my surprise, I hear myself saying,

"My name is Manon."

"Mmmanon." He tests the sound of it with his lips pursed, pronouncing it as if tasting something delicious, and then he grins and looks so delighted with the sound that I have to smile.

"You must come for coffee with me. Now!" He is lit by such an irrepressible energy that it affects the atmosphere around him, and he is so earnest in his request that I can't refuse him. He takes me by the hand again, and we cross the street to Tom's Diner. I've lost control of the situation, letting him lead me this way. It feels oddly comforting, this letting go. In the booth, I sit quietly opposite him, wondering what on earth I'm doing here, while he orders coffee and pie.

"You do like pie, don't you? Everybody likes pie." He is so exuberant, excited, and happy. His energetic gestures are like an adolescent's, yet his eyes burn with a fever that alludes to some deeper, more mature emotion. He doesn't stop talking long enough to let me reply. I actually giggle when he takes my hand again and pulls it to his chest. "Mmmanon, feel my heart. You're making it skip beats." His gorgeous eyes twinkle mischievously as he bats his thick, dark lashes. "What are you doing to me?"

My heart is also aflutter – clearly the effect of his touch. When the coffee arrives, I manage to pull my hand away, trying to regain my composure. He tells me about his work and his passion for sculpting. I'm impressed. It makes sense that he's a sculptor, given his build and his sturdy hands. Although he is tall, his body is stocky and muscular, with forearms that bulge beneath the sleeve of his waffle weave Henley, its frayed cuffs encircling thick wrists. He must be very good to have achieved 'Artist in Residence' status at Pratt and merit a studio of his own. He doesn't look much older than me, and he's already accomplished so much.

He coaxes information from me as well. I tell him that this is my first year at school and how overwhelmed I am by the volume and complexity of the work. I find it easy to talk to him, and as we get acquainted, afternoon turns to evening. I panic when I remember that I'm expected back for Stephanie's homecoming dinner. I'll never make it.

"I've got to go!"

"No, don't go yet. What's your rush? Stay with me."

"William, I'm sorry I can't stay."

"Then let's meet tomorrow, after your classes, for dinner. Anything, anywhere. Say yes, Mmmanon!"

"No. I can't. I am with someone," I lie. It's my standard line when I am trying to fend off unwanted advances, in this case, not so much unwanted as scary because of the strong feelings he's already awoken in me.

"You are?" Stretching his neck to look over my shoulder, he teases, "I don't see anyone." and he holds my hand again.

"Please, William, let me go," I plead.

"Your hands are so beautiful." Trapped in his grip, my hand is turned over and over again while he examines both the palm and back. He caresses my palm with his fingers – long, thick fingers with jagged nails and chafed knuckles. His hands are tanned and rough from the materials he works with. His touch sets off a tremor that travels from the point of contact straight to my belly, which clenches with the sensation. I snap my hand back just as my cell phone rings.

"Oh, hi George, no, that's okay; I'm just getting a cab. Thank you. See you in a bit."

"Is that the one you're with?" William asks, gesturing air quotes to let me know he knows I was lying.

"Bye, William. Thanks for the coffee and pie."

"I'll be here, waiting for you." He grins, and his mane of wavy black hair is caught up in a sudden gust as he flags a cab for me.

֍֍֍֍

I quickly text Alexander to tell him I won't be able to get home until later. They should start dinner without me. By the time I get into my car, it's after nine.

I love driving my car! It's surprising how relaxed I am behind the wheel, considering I've never really driven much. It gives me a wonderful sense of being in control, which is comforting after my experience with William. The drive from Manhattan to Greenwich can be accomplished in no time if you take I95. I usually prefer the more scenic US1, even though it takes a bit longer. Often, feeling adventurous, I take alternate routes on the smaller roads, confident that I won't get lost because of the handy GPS device that Alexander bought for me.

This time, I race up I95, and by the time I get back to Elderberry, Hedley, and Stephanie have retreated, and Mrs. O has retired to her quarters on the lower level. I poke my head into the library to find Alexander working on his laptop.

"I'm sorry I missed dinner."

"Mrs. O left a plate for you in the oven. What's up? You look a bit frazzled."

"I was immersed in a complicated project for Quark. I'm not sure I'll ever conquer that program." Making excuses has become a method of dealing with my inadequacies, especially in the face of Alexander's perfectionism.

"I can get Simon, our graphic designer at WWP, to help you if you like."

He has a solution for everything, so much like Dad. I decline this offer because, really, I am getting to understand the layout program quite well. I 'get' the way you can flow text and images into an organized, coherent vision. I just need to perfect the shortcuts.

"Okay, let me know if you change your mind," he says, and then adds, "By the way, I'm going on a business trip for a couple of weeks."

"Where to?"

"You remember me telling you that I've been trying to get authorization to establish a drug dispensing facility in Central African Republic?"

"Yes, you mentioned it."

"I've been working toward this for several years but could never get near enough to President Bozizé. Then, a few weeks ago, by sheer coincidence, I met Monique Bozizé, the President's wife, at that charity function I went to with Juliette. I gave her a synopsis of my idea, and now I've finally got a meeting with the president."

"That's wonderful, when do you leave?"

"Tomorrow."

"Can I come with you?" I ask, only half-jokingly. I would die to go to Africa. I've never been anywhere.

"Manon, CAR is not the place for your first trip abroad. You would be left on your own much of the time while I attend to business, and it's not safe for a woman to wander around alone." He actually took me seriously, so maybe he'll take me on another trip abroad.

CHAPTER TWENTY-ONE

That night, I had the most vivid dream. I'm running frantically on the savannah toward the shelter of a tent in the distance. I keep stumbling on the rough spikes of dried grasses. My shins and ankles are bleeding, and a sense of danger nipping at my heels. I must reach the safety of the tent, which keeps moving further away the closer I get. Suddenly, my wrist is grabbed from behind, and I am yanked backward. Losing my balance, I fall against a big barrel chest. When I whip around, I see that I'm up against a tall, dark-haired man with Alexander's grey eyes, only now they are shot through with sparks of green and blue. He maneuvers me into the tent and, with one of his large hands, traps both of mine behind me. His rough fingertips chafe my nipples through my gauzy chemise while he forces his tongue into my mouth, weakening me with desire. He tastes like wine-soaked cherries. I succumb to the flavor and feel drunk with it.

I awake at twilight in that strange interval just before daybreak, when wild, lusty fantasies abound. William fills my head. I move to the window seat without breaking the spell and await my fate.

The house is silent. My thoughts meander from William to Alexander and my grandparents, faceless and evil. I think of the Dad I never knew, how his need for love must have been so great that he fell into it with Gabrielle, and how Alexander came out of that love. I wonder if I was created out of the love between my parents. I think of my colored rectangles. How can I imbue them with a Rothko-like power? I think of William the Sculptor, and all other thoughts vanish. His exuberant lust for life excites me. I realize I want him in a way I've never experienced before. I feel strangely guilty for my attraction to him, as if I were betraying Alexander.

I've never revealed my 'liaisons' to Alexander, just as I never let Dad know what I was up to, and after his initial question when I first arrived, whether I had a boyfriend, he's never asked about it. I suspect he doesn't want to think of me as a sexual being, and I fear he would be disappointed in learning of my wantonness. I wonder what he would think of William.

I can never ride on the first day of my period. The jolting up and down motion is too much for my already throbbing pelvis, so I take a blanket and sketchbook to the meadow. The air is humid and infused with the scent of wild poppies, hay, and horses. The mist is just dissipating. Looking up at the flawless blue sky, I give in to the ache in my belly and lower back as carnal desire, preoccupied with William Stein. My next Life Drawing class isn't until Monday afternoon. I agonize over whether I'll see him or not. I've never met anyone like him; so warm, so exuberant, so tactile as if he wants to experience everything first hand.

I hear Bobby and Macy barking and yelping in play, and when I turn to look for them, I see them running alongside Stephanie, who has come out for an early morning jog. When she sees me, she changes her path and comes over to where I am stretched out on my blanket.

"Hi, Manon, I'm glad to see you. We missed you at dinner last night."

"I'm so sorry I was late getting back. This whole school thing is a huge adjustment for me."

"Adjustments are what life is about. I'm trying to adjust to life post-service."

The dogs keep nudging Stephanie, whimpering and whining. They want to get on with the romp in the woods they had set out on.

"Want to go for a walk?"

"Sure. So, are you done with the military?"

"I was discharged after ten years of service as planned."

"That *is* a big adjustment. What will you do now?"

"I thought I would take a job as a paramedic in the city, but Hedley and I are having a disagreement about it. He is adamant that we should get married and start the family we planned to have."

When we enter the shade of the forest, we slow our pace and I look up at a sun-dappled Stephanie as we talk. She is tall and has strong features, prominent cheekbones, a large straight nose, and full lips, an excellent subject for sculpting. The dogs explore the forest floor and sniff in the mounds of leaves blown like drifts of snow against the tree trunks. Bobby has found something and is on his back writhing deliriously.

"Bobby! Come!" Stephanie laughs, "He's going to stink like hell from whatever that was."

"How long have you and Hedley been together?"

"A long time. I met him and Alexander at the same time at Hedley's Dad's riding school when we were young teenagers. I guess you could say we were 'childhood sweethearts,' although it wasn't always 'sweet.' We had very different ideas about the world, but we loved each other and stuck it out. Now, I can't see myself living without him."

"What were your differences about?"

"Oh, Manon, so many I wouldn't know where to begin. Suffice it to say that at one point, I went off to join the army. That was ten years ago, and now that I'm out, we can begin to build the life we both want." We follow the dogs, veering off the riding path onto a small trail that is a shortcut to a little brook.

"Alexander always played a role in supporting our relationship. He often acted as the mediator in our arguments. Among his many talents, he's quite accomplished at dispute resolution."

"I guess you know him pretty well. What was he like when he was younger?"

"Everybody wanted to be Alexander's friend. He has that particular quality, a certain empathy that makes people trust him instinctively and want to please him."

I couch my curiosity about his girlfriends by asking,

"Did he have many close friends?"

"He did have a lot of acquaintances, but other than Hedley, I don't know how many were *close*. His friendships often fizzled because he demanded a lot from people. The lack of competence that was normal for most kids his age frustrated him. He still gets impatient with incompetence, only now he's become more diplomatic about it."

"How about girlfriends?" I have to ask.

"By the time he was a teenager, when I got to know him, girls swooned and vied for his attention. Believe me, he took full advantage. Hedley told me that he gave as good as he got. He had a gift for pleasing women. He left many broken hearts in his wake because, being busy building his empire, he didn't have time for long-term relationships."

"What about Juliette?"

"Hedley tells me he thinks she's a match." Despite having reconciled my amorous feelings for him, I cringe a little to think I will lose him. "He might love her, I really don't know. What I do know is that he is really happy to have you in his life. Growing up as an only child, he really longed for family. He hit the jackpot when he found you."

CHAPTER TWENTY-TWO

I'm always up early at Elderberry. In Lennoxville, the shaded dimness of our house was conducive to sleeping. The west-facing window of my room kept it dark until the sun was directly overhead. Here, my bay window faces east, letting in the first light of day. At this time of year, the air is so crisp I could take bites of it and feel the energy it generates in me.

This Monday morning, I leave for Manhattan before rush hour traffic so that I can rummage through Gabrielle's closet before going to school. I want to find something nice to wear just in case I bump into William. I pick out a long-sleeved tailored shirt in pale blue Egyptian cotton, which fits as though it were made for me. There is a burgundy and blue paisley worsted vest with a burgundy satin back. These two items dress up my comfy old jeans. I plaster my frizzy mess of hair back into a tight ponytail at the base of my scalp, foolishly thinking it would remain neat all day.

I spend the morning in the computer lab on the fourth floor, unable to concentrate on my Quark project because my head is on the second floor. I need coffee. I go down the west stairwell to the second floor so I can cross the long hall to the east stairwell and pass the sculpture studio. A few kids are sitting on the old linoleum tiles, defying the new 'No Smoking Indoors' law. I inhale the second-hand smoke as I walk by and feel a craving, which I quickly suppress. The sculpture studio is locked, and I'm disappointed, like a child who's been denied a promised treat. Will I ever see William again? Was he just toying with me?

Hot coffee in hand, I enter the Life Drawing class and see that today's model is a wiry Asian man, slight of stature with shapely limbs. He is wrestling with the prop he's bought with him – a twenty-foot length of thick red rope. In preparation for his first pose, he is busy creating visually intricate patterns on his body. The bright red rope contrasts his warm ivory skin. He has coiled it twice around his neck, pulled it down the center of his torso to his waist, wound it around several times like a belt, then down beneath his testicles, around his flaccid penis, looped it to the back and up between his buttocks to join the back of the belt he's created. He finally settles into the pose that he will hold for fifteen minutes while we sketch the beauty of the tight binding that accentuates his human form.

My hands tremble as I try to focus on the shape of his torso while ignoring the rough rope, which is very challenging to draw. At the break, I go out into the hall, aroused by the model's body and the anticipation of seeing William. I'm desperate for a smoke. When I go back for another set, I see the model has hogtied himself like a magician, and he is lying on his side, his penis jutting perpendicularly from the restraint around his groin. I sketch furiously, trying to capture the straining curve of his body. The man's face is a picture of serenity in contrast to the tension of his body.

When the class is over, I feel completely drained. My mind is so muddled that I startle when I hear the low murmur of my name.

"Mmmanon, there you are."

"William!"

"How was your class?"

"Um, it was . . . challenging."

"Mmmanon, you look flushed, and you have these yellow flecks in your eyes that sparkle. You are positively lit up. You must have had the Shibari model today."

"The what?"

"Hmm, it looks like you could use a drink. I have some wine in my studio." He takes my hand and flings open the door to the mysterious sculpture studio. I notice that some of the young women sitting about on the floor whisper to each other and have the dreamy look of groupies, having been blessed with a sighting of their idol.

Inside the large studio, a wall of windows illuminates the well-organized space. There are open shelves stocked with supplies and equipment and closed cupboards along one wall. The wide open floor space has a large square pedestal with a jagged chunk of marble from which some feral creature is about to leap. There's a counter with tools and stools. It has a coffee maker, a collection of mismatched mugs, and smudged drinking glasses. Under it is a small fridge from which William pulls a bottle of Chardonnay.

"Sit," he says, and I obey, settling on one of the stools. I want to ask what he's working on, but I'm like those starstruck groupies, all tongue-tied and titillated. "So, will you show me your sketches of the Shibari model?"

"Um, I'd rather not. I didn't really get very much. I couldn't do the ropes, and his flesh looks like it's been gouged by a machete." I laugh, trying to make light of my frustrating incompetence. "What is Shibari?"

"It's the Japanese art of rope knotting with the artistic aesthetic of sexual bondage. Our friend Haruto is a master at Kinbaku, the practice of effective bondage with an emotional element – pain and pleasure. You seem to be quite affected by the art of it."

William has his hand on my arm, absently petting it. I feel the heat of his touch through the thin cotton of my sleeve, elevating my blood pressure to dizzying heights. He places a large hand on my hot cheek and strokes it. I am lit up by his touch and feel my lips puckering of their own accord, pulled by some sort of magnetism toward him. He leans in, looking into my eyes, raising a thick eyebrow as if asking to kiss me, and then he does. I've only had a sip of wine, yet I feel as if I had guzzled the whole bottle. The stool seems suddenly very high, and I feel vertiginous. His lips and tongue fill me with such a powerful need that I hear myself moaning.

"Mmmanon, you are so delicious. I want to savor you properly, but unfortunately, I have to go now to sit shiva for my great-aunt this afternoon."

"Sit where?"

"Oh, it's a Jewish custom where family and friends of the deceased gather together for seven days to share memories and support the loved ones."

"Oh, I'm sorry to hear of your loss."

"My great aunt Goldie was a force of nature. She had just turned ninety-five and was quite ready to go, but she will be missed. After I make an appearance tonight, I won't go again until Wednesday. May I take you to dinner tomorrow night? We'll go somewhere special, make it our official first date. I'll pick you up at eight."

The next evening, William arrives at the Colosseum. He's obviously made a special effort to clean up his plaster-studded wardrobe and looks fresh in khaki trousers and a bright white polo that contrasts his olive complexion. Under thick dark eyebrows, his teal blue eyes shine as if backlit.

I'm wearing a hippie-style maxi wrap-around skirt made of Indian cotton that I found in Gabrielle's closet. It must be from the seventies, with its silkscreened swirls of indigo, black, and white. A white V-neck Angora sweater is perfect for a cool spring evening, and a silk camisole under it frees me from having to wear a bra. The swaying fabric of the skirt makes me feel sexy. Feeling sexy suddenly makes me think of Alexander, and then I feel ashamed. What would he think if he knew what I was up to? Does he think about Gabrielle when he sees me in her clothes?

I am surprised when we arrive at Daniel, a high-end French restaurant on E 65th St. where the rich and famous are known to dine. It boasts an haute cuisine experience where each dish is a work of sculpted art. How appropriate. William knows how to impress. He's a real New Yorker.

We seem to have so much to share that we talk through the whole three-hour meal. I haven't been as engaged or smiled this much since dinner at the Ritz with Alexander and Julian.

He talks about his tumultuous life, his family, and growing up in Brooklyn.

"I must confess I was a hell-raiser when I was a kid."

"Me too. What did you get up to?"

"Once, in grade school, I had this great idea to pile disparate objects precariously on top of each other, creating a wobbly structure, a sculpture of sorts, twice my height. It ultimately came crashing down on Tommy Winter and broke his nose.

"Tell me, what did you do?" he smiles and raises his eyebrows expectantly.

"Oh, just stuff to annoy my Dad. Once, when I was seventeen, I went off to Montreal, and by the time I got back, Dad had the police looking for me."

"Ouch! Grounded much?"

I press him to talk about himself some more, and he tells me how, as a child, he often got into trouble because he practiced passionately jumping in with both feet to experience things firsthand.

"My parents couldn't discipline me. However, they were great with diversion tactics, making me work on something constructive and channeling my energy. Their tactic worked so well that by the time I was in High School, I was involved in pioneering art projects, which the school board ultimately adopted into the curriculum."

All I can say is, "Wow. How did you discover that sculpting was your calling?"

"I had an innate understanding of the language of art. Compared to other kids, I was weird." Me too, I thought. "I would be joyous at having observed something beautiful or weep when I saw the underlying pain that inspired a piece of art. When I was about twelve, I saw a Moore sculpture on a family trip to Chicago. I couldn't keep my hands off it. I climbed, caressed, and cuddled it like a lover. It was a revelation for my parents as well. They recognized my need to create art. I was lucky that they supported me unconditionally." Not like my Dad, I think bitterly.

"I envy you for that. My Dad never supported my passion to make art."

"And yet you are an artist, support or not. I understand the drive to create."

I am completely starstruck.

After I have been wined, dined, and sated, William takes me back to his loft in Chelsea. We ride up to the 6th floor in an antique Otis freight elevator. Once he pulls up the gate, we are right inside his loft. It must be over five thousand square feet, with a thirty-foot ceiling and a long wall of multi-paned windows facing west. Its wide-planked hardwood floors are distressed and polished by wear.

He steers me toward the living room area of this enormous, eclectic place.

"Make yourself comfortable," he says, gesturing to a variety of seating options.

I plop down on one of several oversized cushions in jewel tones in the middle of the large Persian rug, from where I can survey the whole place.

"How long have you lived here?" I ask, wondering how much time was needed to collect all this stuff.

"It used to be my grandfather's factory and had been sitting empty in escrow for a long time. I begged my parents to let me use it, and I've kind of moved in over the last ten years or so."

The majority of the space is devoted to works of art in various stages of completion. There are wood carvings, plaster casts, and smaller bronzes. Various other objects are placed in strange juxtapositions on available horizontal surfaces. There are mannequins awkwardly leaning against each other in odd stances, some draped in fabric.

A potbellied stove sits in the middle of the enormous space, with a long exhaust pipe leading out through one of the many panes.

There is an area like a stage set where a model might pose on a chaise longue in front of a big black drape. It doesn't have the ornately carved wood frame as the one at the Colosseum but is so lushly overstuffed that the edges are rounded and poufy. It's upholstered in a puce-colored mohair with bald spots where the sturdy fabric has been rubbed away by years of use. To the right of the studio section, there is a set of wooden steps leading to a loft that overlooks the whole space.

William busies himself with opening a bottle of champagne, his eyes only leaving me when some fine motor skill requires him to tear them away. His scrutiny of me is like a physical touch. I see him eyeing me from top to bottom, watching me as I explore the 'studio' part of the space. I imagine him noting every detail of me: my shape, my colors, my locomotion. He inhales deeply as if he can smell the secretions of my excitement from where he stands.

"Manon, come sit here with me. Have some champagne."

"I'm not much of a drinker, and I've had so much wine already. Thank you for a lovely dinner." I saunter back toward him from the studio area thirty feet away, self-conscious, feeling naked under his gaze.

"Yes, but this is an exceptional day, and you must celebrate with me. You are the birthday gift of my dreams."

"Oh, happy birthday, William!"

"What, no kiss for the birthday boy?" His arms open in a welcoming gesture as I approach, and he pouts like an adorable little boy.

As I move closer to oblige him, he pulls me into his arms, his lips hovering above mine. I kiss him, and he tightens his hold on me. My body ignites as he slips his tongue into my mouth.

William adroitly moves me toward the sofa. He slips his hand under my skirt and runs it up the inside of my leg. I am cooing like a pigeon, and my hips are moving of their own accord.

"I can't wait. You must say you want me."

"Yes, William, yes, please…!"

Reassured, his urgency abates, and he starts to take his time.

"Manon, you are so beautiful. I want to see all of you."

His masterful hands make quick work of pulling my sweater over my head.

"Stand up," he says and skillfully peels my skirt away. Finally, he slips off my camisole and underwear, all the while multitasking, with his mouth planting kisses on my face, neck, and each newly exposed part of my skin. "Now, walk over to the settee."

He prods me lightly with a hand at the small of my back.

"William, please, I…" His mouth closes over mine again and stifles my protest. I'm shy of my nakedness in this big open space while he is still fully dressed.

"Go now. I want to watch you walking. Go slowly." He gives me another little push, and I reluctantly start the ten-yard walk to the other end of the large space.

I am conscious of him behind me and feel like I'm in one of those nightmares where you are walking down a crowded street stark naked, only this excites me differently. I hurry toward my destination.

"Slow down, Manon, and walk with your entire body. I want to observe the movement of your back, your buttocks, and your calves as you walk." Seriously? I am mortified, under his scrutiny, conscious of my heel-toe steps and my swinging hips.

"You know, Leonardo noted that the function of muscle is to pull, not to push, except in the case of the genitals and the tongue." Oh, genitals and tongue!

When I reach the settee, I turn my head and look over my shoulder, too self-conscious to show my front. He moves toward me. He's shirtless, exposing broad shoulders and a compact, muscular upper body, which is patterned with tight dark curls of hair across his chest, down his abdomen, a trail continuing down to where there is a visible bulge in his pants. He reaches me while shedding socks and dropping his pants. I can't look.

"Turn around, Manon, let me see you. Put your hands together above your head," he commands. "Yes, like this. Ssss..." He makes sibilant sounds as he watches my breasts perk upward with this posture. "Are you on birth control?" I shake my head. "Never mind, Baby, I'm a good boy scout."

With a boyish grin, he produces a couple of silver pouches. He holds my hands behind my back while his other hand encases my nape and firmly pulls my face to his, our eyes locking in recognition of the passion smoldering there. My chest is heaving, and he turns his attention to my breasts and nipples.

"Ahh!" I cry out as the sensitive knobs are fingered and pulled. "Ahhh!" again as his large, rough hand surrounds my breast and kneads it.

His hand trails down my abdomen, owning wherever it touches, and I can barely contain myself. I'm moaning, mewling, whining as I push my body against him insistently. In a seemingly single motion, he puts the condom on and pushes me onto the settee.

CHAPTER TWENTY-THREE

As the weather begins to heat the New York pavement in May, William heats my soul. In a short time, we have become inseparable. Mostly we are on the cushioned pallet that serves as his bed on the upper-level loft, our carnal cries echoing through the cavernous space. I feel like I have broken out of a chrysalis and am floating above the ground on air. If William loves me, then all things are possible.

He introduces me to his art world, and I am electrified by the creative energy surrounding me. We're forever going to a gallery opening or some other art event that he wants to attend, and my head is spinning with color, sound, art, and art lovers. He takes me to Motherwell's Place, a garage converted to gallery space around the corner from his loft. The ambiance is reminiscent of Andy Warhol's Factory, serving as a gathering place for some of the avant-garde of New York's art scene.

I'm surprised when he presents me as his girlfriend, and although I'm welcomed into his social sphere, I distinctly feel that some of the women are suspicious of my intentions. Everybody loves William, and they seem intent on saving him from predatory women - there must be many. There is one girl in the group, Adrianna, who is obviously in love with him; her enormous sad eyes glaze over with unshed tears when she looks at him, devastated that he has someone new. I feel bad for causing her heartache.

All this while William is prolific as ever, keeping up a fevered pitch of creativity. He has an opening coming up, an installation of thirteen pieces, which I haven't seen because they're at the foundry. He sleeps little, thriving more on his work than on the sleep required by regular people.

I am a seedling in a greenhouse, watered and fed in this passionate milieu. I'm painting more enthusiastically than ever, using larger and larger canvases, devoting myself to labor-intensive paintings mimicking Lee Krasner's gestural style – paintings of patterns with infinite shards of color, using bold black to underscore their shapes. In fact, I'm so busy that I almost forgot that Alexander will be back tomorrow. As reluctant as I am to leave the city, I head back to Elderberry for his homecoming.

֍֍֍֍

I arrive on Friday evening just as Mrs. O, Stephanie, and Hedley are finishing dinner.

"Hey, Manon, we've missed you," says Hedley.

"Have you eaten?" asks Mrs. O. "There's roast chicken and those fingerling potatoes you like." She serves me some asparagus salad and places a chicken leg on my plate.

"What have you been up to?" asks Stephanie. "You look great."

"Oh, I've been really busy with school; the term is almost over, and I'm still just catching up. Also, I'm painting a lot." And then, to change the subject, I ask, "When does Alexander arrive?"

Hedley says, "I'm picking him up at Kennedy at six in the morning."

My city energy keeps me awake that night, and I miss William's presence next to me . . . on top of me . . . under me. . . However, I must have gotten some sleep because I'm up early on Saturday and keen to go riding. I'm excited to see Alexander again. And I want to hear all about his amazing trip to the heart of Africa.

He arrives just as I'm taking Banjo to the stable. When I see him at the patio door, I run to greet him. He is grinning, his teeth gleaming white in his darkly tanned face.

"Manon, I've missed you." He holds me in a tight hug and kisses both my cheeks. "You look different. You've let your hair go wild. You look positively leonine. I love it." It's true, my hair has gone wild; I don't care, it manifests how I feel these days.

We gather on the patio for coffee and a light breakfast, the sun and Alexander warming us all. And even though he must be wiped after his long journey, we pepper him with questions.

"What was the city like? Was it crowded with people and cars?" Hedley wants to know.

"It wasn't crowded around the Renaissance Palace, where I was honored as a guest of the president."

"Did you notice much military presence in the streets?" Stephanie asks, and Mrs. O wants to know about the food.

"The city was relatively calm. The population, about the size of San Francisco, went about their business normally; I even saw a boat race taking place on the Ubangi River. There are palm trees and traffic on the dusty streets, and yes, I did spot a few armed soldiers." He nods at Stephanie. "But you can't imagine the hospitality! Michele Bozizé arranged for a musical presentation by a Broto orchestra with bongo drums and a xylophone-like instrument made of wood planks." Alexander launches into his typical tutorial style. "The Broto horn is a traditional instrument, making deep, kazoo-like sounds. It's made of tree roots and is really heavy."

Listening to him speak, I am overwhelmed by a new kind of love for Alexander: admiration, respect, and familial pride.

"Mrs. O, there was a feast of national dishes including cassava, rice, squash, pumpkins, okra, some grilled meat, a selection of fresh water fish, and plantains served in peanut butter sauces. In fact, there were peanuts in everything.

With the President's blessing, I was able to travel to Kabo, a town in northern CAR, a bumpy six-hour drive by Jeep, to the proposed site of our distribution center. Once I secured a location and met with some local builders, I took a four-hour flight in a small twin-engine plane to Abuja, Nigeria. That was a thrilling flight – my heart and stomach were in my throat the whole time. Although I would have loved to explore Abuja, I only spent the night because Juliette happened to be in Paris, and I took the ten-hour flight there so I could spend a couple of days with her before coming back." This little surprise sets me wondering how serious he is about her. Will he still have room for me in his life if he marries her?

"How was Paris?" Stephanie asks.

"Hot and full of tourists. But great." That he had a great time with Juliette rankles. I hate that I'm jealous. "Now I must get busy solidifying plans for building and stocking the facility. I plan to go back in July or August to oversee the first shipments of vaccines and begin distribution throughout the region." He beams with satisfaction.

After a long nap, Alexander emerges fresh and handsome as ever. Heading for the library, he puts an arm around my shoulder and pulls me along with him. He wants to chat.

"I've had some news from Pete Hunt, the PI," multitasking on his laptop as he talks. "He located Alice, living in a favela in Brasilia. He went to see her and found your grandmother to be a wizened old woman with dementia."

I have a living grandmother! I can hardly believe my life-long dream has come true.

"He said she spoke English, sometimes breaking into French or Portuguese when trying to capture a thought. She didn't really understand who Pete was and what he wanted. When he asked her questions about her life in Montreal and her husband Edward, she simply gazed at him vacantly. When he mentioned the name Gregory, she began to howl like a wounded animal. He couldn't get any information from her. He did manage to snap a photo before her neighbors chased him away."

Alexander turns the computer to face me. He has pulled up the picture of my grandmother, a disheveled, shriveled old woman, sitting on a stool, arms crossed and held tight across her chest. She's bent slightly forward, as if she may have been rocking. Her wispy grey hair frames a deeply creviced face with wild grey eyes. I try to find some resemblance to Dad, but just can't connect this woman to him in any way. She could not have given birth to my big, strong, intelligent Dad – my heart breaks for him and for the loss of an idealized Granny. Tears fill my eyes as I think of how she abandoned my dad.

"I hate her!"

"Don't cry. We don't know the circumstances under which Alice took off. She obviously lives with the guilt of abandoning her child."

"Is there ever a justification for that?"

"Listen, Manon, don't dwell on her motivations. Gregory survived and thrived, and now we have each other. Look at where we are; regardless of the sketchiness of our grandparents, *we* are the family, and we belong together forever." Alexander knows how I feel; he understands the pain of discovering that my dad's parents abandoned him, just as his beloved mother's parents left her to her own fate.

After a few more minutes of commiseration, he closes his laptop and changes the subject.

"Now tell me what you have been up to. How's school? Have you mastered Quark yet? Do you have any work you can show me?" All I can think of is William. Instead of answering any of his questions, I blurt out, "I've met someone," then immediately feel stupid for having mentioned it.

"Who is he? What does he do?" Echoes of Dad on the offensive whenever he found out I was seeing someone.

"His name is William. He's a sculptor. I met him at school." I offer up the minimum, hoping it will suffice.

"William Stein, the sculptor?"

"You know him?"

"He has quite a reputation. He's been written about in Page Six, *The New York Post's* celebrity rag. He's a wild child, not someone I would want you to be around."

"He isn't wild; he just loves life. What have you read?" Getting annoyed, I feel like a teenager again, defending William.

"I recall reading a piece several years ago about this wunderkind of the art world. A prolific prodigy of a sculptor, with such promise that the art world was abuzz with him. Suddenly, he stopped working altogether."

"What happened to him?"

"Apparently, he had a bad breakup. The tabloids shadowed him as he went on a promiscuous odyssey for months on end in which he indulged his darker side. They reported his sordid liaison with an older woman named Alma, who was known to host the most Bacchanalian underground parties in the city. They reported how she took ownership of him and involved him in every imaginable depravity the city offered. He became kind of a legend, and one of his sculptures has become a mecca for the lowlifes of the city."

"What sculpture?

"The one in front of the IBM Building at East 57th Street and Madison." Alexander emits a cynical snort; "Ironically, it is one that depicts the innocence of youth."

"What does it look like?"

"I'm sure you must have seen it in your travels; you can't miss it. The installation is about eight feet by eight feet and features a wrought iron park bench with three life-size children made of bronze. Two little girls are sitting on the bench; one with pigtails licking a dripping ice cream cone, the other holding an open book, looking up at a boy standing in front of her. His arm is extended, offering her a rose."

I am astounded. I *have* seen that sculpture. I even waited to sit beside the little girls on the bench while tourists took turns taking selfies with them. The cherubic children are irresistible. In fact, the bronze has become so polished by the stroking of passersby that their chubby bronze cheeks coruscate in the sun. William did that?

"Be careful, Manon; don't be fooled into falling for him."

"We have a genuine connection."

Alexander shifts in his seat and straightens his back. "Alright, if you say so. Just bring him here so I can meet him. C'mon, now let's go riding. It's a beautiful day."

The following week, Alexander and I are like ships passing in the night. He is up early and gone before I've even fallen into REM sleep. Now that he's back, I don't stay overnight with William; I don't want Alexander to know how besotted I really am.

CHAPTER TWENTY-FOUR

Since finding out about William's sordid past, I've become suspicious of his true feelings for me, although that hasn't kept me from his bed. It's clear that he's had many women. He's said so himself, bragging that women think he is a great lover. This I also know. In fact, he told me that his very first girlfriend nicknamed him 'Billy the Mechanic' because he knew women's bodies so well. The moniker stuck with subsequent lovers. Am I just one of them?

The week proves to be a grueling one. I have a final in Art History and my graphic design project is due. My life has become so complicated. I can hardly believe all that's happened to me since Dad died a little over a year ago. His birthday is coming up on June 20th. I'm so sad that his life was cut short and that I can't share this new world I'm living in with him. What would he make of it all?

I want to confront William to satisfy myself that I'm not just another in a string of lovers. But honestly, I don't want to find out whether he is stringing me along, so I keep my questions to myself.

At the end of an exhausting day, we mount the wooden stairs to lie down and rest. However, resting in bed is not William's style. The large, cushioned pallet is his playground, and he's continually devising new erotic games to play. Once we are divested of our clothes, I lie down and await his caresses, but William pulls me up so that we sit cross-legged opposite each other. On this summer solstice, I can see the last hint of orange on the horizon over the

Hudson through the multi-paned windows. Then all goes black. William has conjured two strips of black satin from somewhere and ties one around my head covering my eyes.

"What are you doing? I don't like being blindfolded." I whine, feeling panicked.

"I'm blindfolding myself too, so I can concentrate all my senses on feeling you, and I want you to concentrate all your senses on my hands, feeling you. I want to explore your contours to feel every pore and follicle of you, memorize your body so I can call it up any time I wish."

He touches my skin and tests my flesh with his expert sculptor's hands. Those talented hands travel slowly from my face to my neck, collar bones, breasts and ribs, tracing each rib from side to sternum with two thick fingers, caressing the curve of them, outlining how they shape me. Reaching behind me, he runs his hands across my shoulder blades and scrapes his fingers down my spine, touching each vertebra. He pulls and presses my flesh inciting excruciating sensations in my whole body. I feel like fresh clay being sculpted, becoming the Manon that he sees, a version of me that is beautiful.

❀❀❀❀

On Wednesday, I get a text from Alexander: *I'll be home earlier today. Can we have dinner?*

After my last class, I rush out of the building lest I bump into William and succumb to his pleas for me to stay. I quickly head back to the Colosseum and find Alexander is already there. He's brought our favorites from Zabar's and we sit, happy in each other's company, eating cheese and drinking a chilled Chablis.

"I'm sorry I've been so preoccupied with CAR, and now, with the earthquake in Java..."

"Don't apologize. It's amazing that you are able to help. What are you doing for them?"

"At this acute phase, we're sending meds for the prevention and treatment of diseases like malaria, leptospirosis, meningitis, encephalitis, acute respiratory infections and diarrhea, which are all real threats at this critical juncture." I should have expected the systematic, detailed listing. I asked for it. "We have to act fast." His altruism contrasts my hedonism and I feel ashamed. "It's pretty well in the works now. What I want is to hear about what you've been up to. I've hardly seen you at all since I'm back."

Before he has a chance to delve into my activities, I use a diversion tactic that worked well with Dad, asking about something vitally important to him;

"When are you going back to CAR?"

"Probably in a couple of weeks. July is very hot there but the heat is mitigated by the rainy season. They get a lot of rain, which presents challenges for the stable storage of vaccines and certain drugs." He thrives on challenges. And speaking of challenges, he asks, "So, are you seeing this William Stein?"

"I've been quite busy gearing up for final presentations," I deflect.

"Yes, I imagine, and I want to see your work, but that doesn't answer my question."

"He's taken me to some amazing art events. We went to see the Whitney Biennial – Day for Night – and we saw a new exhibit of recent acquisitions in the New York Public Library Print Gallery. I learned about aspects of printmaking that I was totally ignorant of.

I've never done printmaking, but I'm going to try my hand at it. He even took me to the Yeshiva University Museum to see an exhibition of history and art relating to Jewish culture. It was eye-opening for me. He's introduced me to a lot of people."

"Listen, why don't you invite him to Elderberry for the weekend? I'd like to meet him and make sure he knows how to treat my little sister." I balk at the thought of that. Even so, I would love to bring William to Elderberry. I've told him about the horses and he's really keen to photograph them, even film them to capture their movement. I imagine a statue of Banjo.

CHAPTER TWENTY-FIVE

William is busy gearing up for his huge public installation, so I've been spending nights at the Colosseum. The city is hot and I long to escape to my studio at Elderberry. I can see that William could use a break, so one steamy night, I finally invite him to Connecticut for the weekend. He is delighted and we plan to leave early Saturday morning.

"Dress warm and wear leather if you've got any. I'll pick you up at eight."

"Why? It's July; it's hot even in Connecticut."

"Just trust me, baby, I'm going to give you the ride of your life."

There is a motorcycle tucked into a corner of his loft. I've never actually seen it because it's covered by a tarp, and now a little worm of excitement starts to wriggle around my belly. I search Gabrielle's closet and find a pair of leather pants. I try them on even though it's not something I would normally wear. They're a little tight around my hips and the waist is a bit snug, but I like how they contain me and I love the smooth suppleness of it against my skin. I can't bear to wear anything 'warm,' so I pull on a tank top and grab the black leather bomber jacket I've been eyeing for the fall.

When I emerge from the building, William is there astride a big black Harley Davidson. He is the image of Marlon Brando mounted on his Triumph in the classic film appropriately named The Wild One. I have a fleeting pang of anxiety that Alexander will have his suspicions confirmed at first sight of him. William is grinning so hard his face nearly splits and looks so hot in his own bomber jacket and leather over pants that I'm immediately distracted.

The motorcycle gleams with all its chrome detailing and sleek black body. The cruiser handle bars rise elegantly above the bike, making it look as if it might take flight. The seat, William informs me, is a vintage one-piece Mustang in saddle leather. The back seat is slightly higher than the driver's, giving the passenger a good view of the road ahead over his shoulder. As it idles, it put-puts and purrs – not like a kitten, but like a deep-throated lion.

He's sooooo happy, and I'm sooooo excited.

We weave through the streets on our way up to U.S. 1, me clinging to William for dear life. I love this mode of transportation for the mere fact that I must have my arms around him at all times. People notice us; they smile, and some of them wave and offer peace signs or thumbs up. This bike is a statement.

Rather than taking the Thruway, we drive along the city streets through Harlem, Fleetwood, The Bronx, and Pelham Gardens, where we stop at City Island Lobster House for a bite to eat. The 'bite' turns out to be a huge portion of crab cakes and the best fried shrimp either of us have ever had. We eat with gusto and lick the salt off each other's oily fingers.

We ride through Pelham Bay Park, a huge area of parkland and lagoons with diverse flora and fauna. There's a vast tract of pristine salt marsh dotted by rock outcroppings inhabited by red-tailed hawks, long-eared owls, and even harbor seals. I see herons and egrets in the cordgrass. As we slow around a curve, I spot a red-backed salamander dart off the road.

The brilliant sunshine warms my back as we drive along the scenic parkway. We see the crescent of a sandy beach in the distance and views of City Island, Pelham Bay, and Long Island Sound. I am thrilled by this ride. The rush of air around us; the heady sensation of speed and freedom; and the headier feel of William's flexing muscles as he maneuvers the bike with casual ease.

We enter the drive at Elderberry and rattle and crunch our way up the gravel driveway. Just as William cuts the engine, Alexander strides around the Mulberry tree at the side of the house, the axe he's been using to chop firewood hanging at his side, exuding all his powerful Alpha maleness. William also makes his Alpha maleness apparent as he swings his body off the bike, sets the heavy beast to rest on its stand, and stands tall with his legs wide apart. He helps me unfasten the strap and pulls the sleek black helmet off me. I'm self-conscious of this intimate gesture and look to Alexander to see if he senses it.

"Alexander," I say, "meet William." Both men extend their hands straight out, making direct eye contact, and with head nods, they open their palms to engage in a firm handshake.

"That's quite the bike you have there," says Alexander. "What model is it?"

William rhymes off its pedigree with obvious pride.

"It's the Fat Boy Lo, air-cooled twin cam 103B."

"She looks the beast, how many CCs?" It seems Alexander knows something about motorcycles.

"You won't believe me if I tell you," says William, beaming.

"What, like 1200?"

"No, this baby has 1690 CC's and rides like the wind." William laughs as the information registers on Alexander's face, and he whistles a long note. "I've only had her since last fall and haven't had too much opportunity to ride. Taking Manon out today was a trip." He looks at me and smiles at our shared experience.

"Well, welcome to Elderberry. I bet you could use a cold beer. Manon will get you settled and bring you down to the patio."

With beer bottles in hand, William and Alexander exchange, in a somewhat braggadocious way, their accomplishments. I think Alexander is impressed when William describes the upcoming permanent installation of no less than thirteen bronze children at play in a park in Chelsea.

"I have been working on these kids for years. Now they'll get to be together in the park, leapfrogging, swinging on a bronze tire, playing tag, throwing a pitch, wielding a baseball bat, roller skating, and one peeking over a wall, watching the goings on. You should come to the opening. Mayor Bloomberg will be there to mark the occasion."

Then Alexander tells him about WWP. He talks as passionately about his creation as William does about his. When I go into the kitchen for some snacks, Alexander is explaining his work in CAR. I watch them from the kitchen window, and Alexander is leaning forward, gesturing with his hands, and speaking with a serious expression. I can't hear what he's saying, but he looks as if he's reading out the Riot Act. William moves back in his chair to maintain a distance between them and nods in compliance.

The weekend was a success. Everybody likes William, and Stephanie in particular can't take her eyes off him. He's infatuated with the horses, which ingratiates him with Hedley. Even Mrs. O is affected by his flirtatious attention to her. When he heads back to the city on Sunday after dinner, literally riding off into the sunset, we are all out front, waving him goodbye.

CHAPTER TWENTY-SIX

With school commitments completed, I am free to paint nonstop. Working at William's loft is difficult because I am so distracted by wanting him, so I stay in Greenwich and hunker down in my very own atelier. My experimental rectangles are taunting me from where they're stashed in the corner; I just can't revisit them now. Instead, I have a slew of figure drawings from my classes that I want to paint from. Somehow the song *'It's Raining Men'* is stuck in my head, and I move around the studio with the rhythm and pace of it, fired up and eager to begin working on a piece that is forming in my mind.

First, I begin outlining various bodies from my big sketchbook: bodies standing, walking, sitting, and lying down juxtaposed against a sky-blue background. I'm not sure what it will be. I imagine Seurat's Picnic and then Dali's stick figures, but it's Chagall's flying lovers that are dominant in my brain. I run down to the library and retrieve an art book with sumptuous reproductions of his paintings. They give me that sense of lightness, of floating in the air, and I begin to imagine the composition.

Choosing a small, hard, flat-ended brush, I begin working the background until it is filled with a myriad of tiny, distinct multi-colored dots, patterning the canvas in windy waves. This process is surprisingly satisfying, despite my aching wrist, so I keep at it until all my outlines have disappeared and the floor beneath the easel blends with the painting. I enter this phantasmagoria as if in a dream.

Large sheets of charcoal drawings from the class litter the floor. My eyes land on the series of Haruto. I sketch out several of the poses and paint them in a solid black silhouette on top of the colorful static background. Finally, I draw the ropes and have the figures dangling from the top of the canvas like raining men. After hours of work, I stand back to survey what I've done, thinking it's finished, but then I decide to enlarge the jutting penises. It makes the piece more comical than I intended, but I'm smiling so it's finished.

Over the next few weeks, I have such a spurt of creativity that I run out of supplies. William and I haven't been together in a week, and so when Alexander is ready to leave for the airport on his way back to CAR, I offer to drive him. On the way, we talk about our parents. The mystery of Gabrielle's mother festers in Alexander, and he is constantly pushing Pete Hunt to discover who she is or was.

Pete is currently in Montreal, tracking down more information on Edward and Stuart and searching for marriage records. Although there are no clues about his grandmother, he has found the name of the owner who leased out the property on Rue Lenoir to our great-grandparents, Arthur and Olive Mouland. He will have another report to us in a week or so. Alexander and I are united in our need to know and also in our apprehension of finding more bad news about these people who are family and yet so foreign to us.

We say our goodbyes at the airport and hug. I bury my head in his neck, and he kisses the top of it. I watch him go into the terminal and stay until he is out of sight.

It's five o'clock, and William will likely be going to Motherwell's. I drop the car off at the Colosseum and head to Chelsea to meet up with him there. When I walk in, I see the regulars standing around. Some of William's friends, upon seeing me, stop talking and turn their heads in unison over to where William is seated. They look back at me expectantly. He's at a small table, deeply engaged with a woman, their elbows on the table, hands intertwined, their eyes locked. When he senses my presence, he turns to see me wide-eyed, frozen to the spot. He continues to hold the woman's hands absentmindedly as his eyes meet mine.

"Manon, y-you're here."

Now the woman turns toward me, and we look at each other. She has sparkling green eyes, a genuine smile, complete with dimples and perfect white teeth. A mane of curly auburn hair spills over her shoulders and cascades down her back. She's dressed casually in what I recognize as very expensive designer sportswear. The scent of Nina Ricci wafts around her and makes me feel suddenly nauseous. I'm on the edge of an abyss and rapidly spiraling downward. I feel a sharp knock in my chest that makes me want to cry out, but I swallow the cry, and it becomes a persistent ache that causes my eyes to water and renders me inarticulate.

All I can do is turn around and start toward the door. Just as I step onto W. 25th St., William catches up with me and grabs my wrist.

"Manon, please don't go. Let me explain. Please Manon!"

"William, I am tired. I'm very, very tired and I'm going home. Let me go." I gather the strength to yank my arm from him just in time to hail a passing cab, which I get into, leaving him standing in the street.

Alexander was right. William Stein is too much for me to handle, and I wish he were here to protect me now as messages and missed calls from William hound me. I try to eradicate him from my mind by riding Banjo harder than he's used to. We race through the field and gallop on the trails until we are both exhausted and I let Banjo lead me back to the barn.

Back at the house, I retrieve my phone and see a missed call from Gertie Stein, William's sister. I met Gertie (named for Gertrude Stein as their parents' little joke) and his parents, Leslie and Ruth Stein, when William took us all out for dinner to introduce us. We went to Delmonico's, the famous steak house that occupies the large triangle at the tip of the flatiron building down in the Financial District. Ruth and Gertie monopolized me throughout the whole meal, regaling me with William's virtues and tales of his mischief, all the while quietly evaluating me. They seem to want to protect him from potential slippery slopes with inappropriate women. He and his dad bantered easily. They were all smart and interesting, and they doted on William the whole time as if he were still their little boy. "William, try some of this zucchini," his mother had mothered. "Spoken to the Mayor lately?" his father had asked proudly. I liked them all instantly. Now I can't ignore Gertie, so I return her call.

"Manon, I'm so glad you called. William is so miserable without you. Can we talk? Will you meet me for lunch?"

"I would be happy to meet you for lunch, but William and I are done."

"Listen, I'll take the ferry from Long Island and meet you in Bridgeport. There's a great little Ecuadorian restaurant that makes the best empanadas. You're going to love it." Gertie is in charge and full of enthusiasm, just like her brother. She's hard to resist.

When I get to the restaurant, I see that Gertie is already there, instructing the waitress on how she likes her tea (herbal, bag on the side). Her mass of curls, frizzed by the humidity, bounce as she jumps up to throw her arms around me.

"I'm so glad to see you, Manon. It's such a treat for me to have an afternoon outing now that the kids are away at camp. Come, I want to tell you about Sarah."

Gertie is garrulous and proceeds to relate the story of William and Sarah. She talks without pausing for my reaction or input.

"Sarah Feinstein and William were high school sweethearts. They were the popular kids that everyone wanted to hang with. They were matched in good looks, intellect, and temperament, and they adored each other." Bile rises in my digestive tract, and I lay aside my empanada. "Their dream was to be together forever. William never had any other future in mind. Sarah, on the other hand, was gifted and very ambitious. She wanted big things, big money, and accolades."

It sounds like one of those predatory women that his friends want to protect him from.

"When she graduated, Summa Cum Laude by the way, from Columbia University, she got her Masters in Marketing and embarked on what has become an illustrious career. At that point, William was still a struggling artist trying to establish himself. His future was uncertain at best." Gertie purses her lips derisively. "She left William and broke his heart. Shortly after she left him, seven years ago now, she met and married one of the rising stars of Wall Street, thus fulfilling her desire for the high life that money could buy. Recently, she divorced and came to William looking for consolation."

I don't really want to hear any more, but Gertie takes my hand, and in an earnest, almost beseeching voice, she says,

"Listen, Manon, William loves you. I've never seen him happier than when he's with you. I know that he will not jeopardize your relationship by allowing Sarah to cry on his shoulder. He told me so."

"They looked like lovers." My voice is a whisper, so soft that it hangs like gossamer in the air. The echoes of its meaning and the hurt it causes me refuse to sink or disappear. "I felt as though I was intruding on their intimacy. I couldn't bear it. I can't share him; I would rather suffer the pain of being without him."

"He loves you so much; he has no room for any other love – not even Sarah's. He told me that he has cautioned her to stay away. He will not see her again. I promise you, Manon. You are too important to him."

CHAPTER TWENTY-SEVEN

On August 31, we get the news that Alexander's small charter flight to Abuja has crashed in CAR.

It was Julian who took the call, and he immediately called Hedley, who is now walking toward the house, not with his usual long strides but slowly, lifting each leg as if he were stuck in quicksand. Mrs. O and I are on the patio, chatting about Sage. I'm amazed to learn that they have formed a friendship and have been constantly in touch. In fact, Mrs. O has invited her for the Labor Day weekend, and she's arriving on Friday, the day after tomorrow.

I barely have time to get excited about this news when Hedley slumps down on one of the chairs, looking so grim that both of us are alarmed. My first thought is that maybe Steph has lost the baby; for loss is all over his face. His eyes to the ground, hands hanging limply between his legs, he finally says, "Alexander's plane has crashed." Then silence. Neither Mrs. O nor I can catch a breath to speak. "Julian just got a call from the WWP rep in Kabo who had only the sketchy information that the plane, which left Kabo at 9:45 this morning, their time, enroute to Abuja, fell from the sky near the border with Nigeria."

I leap from my chair and grab his arm more forcefully than I intend to.

"But is Alexander okay?" I finally manage, anxious for confirmation. Hedley takes his time in responding.

"There were no survivors."

"That's not possible." I freeze; my mind is incapable of processing this. No survivors? But surely Alexander has survived. He is a vital person; there must be a mistake. He is as alive as we are.

Mrs. O puts her arms around me and hangs on as if I'm her life raft, and I cling to her for strength to keep from collapsing. Her large, pillowy bosom pressing against me is comforting. I see Stephanie running toward us, cradling her belly and protecting the baby inside her. The four of us huddle and cling to each other for support.

The next couple of days are a chaotic haze. The phone keeps ringing with calls from reporters trying to get interviews. People are arriving unexpectedly at the house like lost sheep: Julian and Nicole Fisher in shock; Gerry Abrams, Alexander's lawyer, trying in vain to take charge, talking next steps while no one listens; Juliette Badour, pale and grief-stricken; Dr. Bruce Lampard, Head of Médecins Sans Frontière, a friend of Alexander's who collaborated on the CAR project and who just came back from Africa himself; others from WWP in disbelief.

I escape to my studio, where time stands still. I watch the light rise and fade on the walls. The reality is simply too big to absorb. My body is numb, and although my mind screams, I remain dumb. Meaningless charcoal scribbles blacken my hands, reflecting my state of mind.

On Friday, Sage arrives. Seeing her finally opens the floodgate of tears I had tried to contain, to be strong. Sage has been there for all the tragic losses in my life; she is a constant, and with her, I can be the vulnerable little girl she once knew me as. Mrs. O is grateful for her company too. I'm amazed to see them joining hands, and I watch as Sage comforts her with hugs.

At dinner, Hedley lashes out at the airline, the pilot, the weather – anything that he can grasp on to vent his anger. Stephanie has her arm around his shoulder, the center of her forehead is creased, and her mouth is slightly open, as if she is about to let out a sob. She lets him rant while we all listen patiently as he expresses our mutual feelings.

"I'm going to send Pete Hunt over there to get to the bottom of what happened." Hedley finally says as Stephanie rubs his back.

"You're right, Babe, it's just what Alexander would do."

Then Mrs. O looks up with puffy eyes and says, "It's good that Devin Mehta went with him to supervise the start-up; he will see to getting Alexander home."

At the mention of his name and the image of him being 'shipped' home, we revert to our stunned silence, and nobody finishes their meal. My head hangs low over my plate, my elbows on the table, my fingers digging into my scalp, and my mouth is open as if I'm gasping for air but can't catch my breath. Tears drop into a little crevice on the top of my untouched shepherd's pie. Sage, in her even-tempered way, is the calming influence we desperately need. It's good she's here.

The personal loss of Alexander is made worse by what the world has lost with his death. Even though the CAR project will go on under Devin's supervision, the potential of what he might yet have done to improve people's lives is staggering. Our communal grief is so different from my grief after Dad died. This 'family' that Alexander has bequeathed me is united in our love of him.

When the New York Times obituary appears, the phone rings constantly with curiosity seekers and calls from Alexander's many acquaintances. We listen as they leave their heartfelt messages and pleas to call them back to tell them what happened. One, from Wynton Marsalis, his good friend from Berklee, expresses condolences and pleads for someone to contact him if there is anything he can do. There's a call from Rosalia Menendez, whose high-pitched voice and affectations make me want to slap her. Ultimately, Mrs. O unplugs the phone altogether.

I can't sleep at all so in the eerie early hours of the night, I step outside in the pitch dark just as a flash of lightning illuminates the meadow. There is a loud clap of thunder, so close that it pounds both in my ears and my heart. Stupidly, I run out into the field just as huge drops begin to splatter the ground and instantly drench me. The cold and my rapid heartbeat keep me running until I reach the pond, where I finally allow myself to collapse and scream at the inky sky.

I am an expert at loss. I experienced the loss of my mother every day growing up. Losing Dad left me unmoored until Alexander appeared in my life. Losing him is more than I can bear.

I sketch obsessively through the solitary night, my fingers fidgety as if something were trying to escape through them. They produce countless sheets of frightful drawings. Dark and ominous landscapes with jagged daggers of lightning; grey wilted daisies in a cracked pottery jar; a toppled coffee mug spilling its black contents, all evoking a sense of dread. I sit on the floor in my studio. Painting is what makes me happy, but I can't let go of my pain long enough to indulge in the pleasure.

If I can't bask in my brother's love or fall into my true love's arms – if I can't paint, then what is there?

CHAPTER TWENTY-EIGHT

On Sunday afternoon, I hear the unmistakable thrum of the Harley, crunching and rattling its way up the driveway. I can see the whole length of the pebbled path from the window of my studio. There's William getting larger as he nears, finally stopping under my window. He cuts the engine and looks up at me. He doesn't smile. His wind-burned face looks pained, the crow's feet etch his stunning eyes, and his lips are pursed as if struggling with what to do next. Looking at him, I feel as though Haruto's ropes are wound tightly around my waist.

Muffled voices float upward. Condolences. I imagine heartfelt hugs, and then as they enter the vestibule, the odd word in Mrs. O's guttural tones, "Upstairs ... coffee?"

I imagine his progress up each stair, then past the two guest rooms, then rounding the corner to the hall leading to my studio. I hear his steps in the hall, and with each step, my belly clenches and my body betrays me with such a palpable physical need that I jump when he reaches the entrance to the studio.

"I had to come when I heard," he says. He steps closer, and I back away, into the corner with the remainder of the gym equipment. "Please let me in, Manon. Let me help you through this."

Already, tears are running down my face. It seems I have no control over them, just as I have no control over his effect on me. I'm weak. I want him. He knows it. I become a puddle in his arms. Something's broken in me, and Billy the Mechanic hones in on where and how to fix me.

Although his ministrations are soothing, they don't eradicate the hurt he's caused. I can't deal with it now, so after a night of passion, I send him away.

There is a pall of sadness over the whole house. Even the horses are unusually quiet. The absence of Alexander and the knowledge that he is never coming back suffocates us. We are in a state of shock, wraiths floating around each other, mute, unable to speak his name.

The end of September brings a change in atmosphere. Suddenly, the heat of summer turns into the cool, sunny days that augur autumn. Already, the tops of some trees, where they are kissed by the sun, have begun their colorful transition toward death. The leaves will make a great show of brilliance, a kaleidoscopic display of reds, oranges, yellows, and browns. Then, in one unexpected gust of wind, they will fly away.

Canadian Thanksgiving is early this year, and Sage returns to spend the first week of October with us. She is a blessing to have around. She gives Mrs. O strength, and Mrs. O in turn, is able to look after everyone's needs. It is phenomenal to me that two women, at this stage of their lives, could fall in love, for there is no mistaking what they feel for each other. In the midst of all this sorrow, it is this new love and the imminent arrival of Stephanie and Hedley's baby that sustain us.

Weeks of bleak days and lonely nights drag on. Grief keeps me sequestered in my room, watching falling leaves from the window seat. They leave the skeletons of trees with their branches reaching skyward like supplicants to a higher authority, begging for a miracle.

Manhattan holds no allure for me now. None-the-less, I can't ignore William's pleas to attend the official opening of his 'Kids in the Park', so I agree to go. Mayor Bloomberg is scheduled to be there to officially open the exhibit on October 11th; however, it has been postponed to Sunday, October 15th because the mayor had to make the sad announcement to the city that New York Yankees pitcher Cory Lidle was killed along with his flight instructor when his plane crashed into a building on the Upper East Side. The mayor didn't think it appropriate to attend an art event right after that.

Planes flying into buildings make New Yorkers fretful. I see the furrowed brows of pedestrians, and despite their rushing around, the city seems quieter, as if out of respect for yet another tragedy. News of that plane crash has ripped open the slowly healing wounds in my own heart. I can't eradicate the image of Alexander plummeting to the ground, aware of his imminent death. What was he thinking, then?

I arrive at the loft before the ceremony at noon. There will be press there and of course the mavens of the city's art world as well as family and friends. It is a big deal.

I've taken to wearing black lately and show up in a black leather skirt that clings to my hips and hugs my legs, restricting my stride. I like the discomfort of being forced to walk slowly, mindful that walking on this earth is precarious. The cowl neck of a black angora sweater creates a Goya-esque hood for me to hide under, and I've been wearing Gabrielle's full-length black leather coat this fall, which covers me to below my knees, where it meets my black boots. I wish to be a dark phantom.

There are people milling about the loft, drinking mimosas, and engaging in conversation. When they see me at the entrance, they all stop and gawk. Apparently, the gossip about me and William is still an amusing distraction. William ushers me around, introducing me to the artists and critics in attendance, as well as to his agent, Martin Sheridan. His parents, his sister and her husband, David Silkoff, are here too. They greet me warmly.

At the appointed hour, the whole group takes the elevator down, and we traipse across the street to the little park, where there are reporters, cameramen, and spectators already waiting. News vehicles are parked along 11th Avenue, and about a dozen people are gathered in front of the gate. Just then, a limo pulls up, and Mayor Bloomberg steps out to greet the small crowd. William welcomes the mayor and begins to usher him through the little park. As they chat in front of each of the bronze kids in action, he holds on to my hand possessively, as if he doesn't want to lose me. Everyone is smiling as the sun suddenly pierces the steely grey October sky to reflect off the angelic faces of William's bronzes.

Mayor Bloomberg stands up on the pedestal alongside the bronze statue of a little girl drinking from a working bronze fountain and begins:

> *"It is my privilege and most cherished task as Mayor to officially open this delightful exhibit of sculpture by one of New York's favorite sons.*
>
> *William Stein's work reflects the family values held to be of utmost importance: that of cherishing our children and of our duty to provide safe environments for their carefree growth and*

happiness. For such a young man, with no children of his own as yet," he smiles at William and notes how he has not let my hand go all this time. "It is phenomenally insightful to focus on them – our future. His 'kids' are installed around our city and continue to delight residents and tourists alike.

They remind us that, as our illustrious Senator from New York noted, "It really does take a village to raise a child," and we must make it our personal responsibility to nurture and cherish each and every one to help them grow into happy, productive members of our communities.

William, I congratulate you and New York thanks you for giving us another symbol of the treasures this city holds."

Everyone applauds, and William looks embarrassed, his thick lashes pointing groundward, his toes shuffling the gravel on the path. He is adorable.

After enthusiastic handshakes, the crowd disperses, and we go to one of the galleries in the neighborhood that is hosting a little party in William's honor. There is much lively discussion about William's work and success, and topics range from art and politics to aestheticism and commercialism. I've missed this.

The next few weeks fly by in a haze of lust. William's ingenuity in bed keeps me in a fog, so that I'm unable to concentrate on anything else. Sometimes Alexander's death intrudes and rudely yanks me back into the world without him. Then my body methodically shuts down, leaving me cold, and like a starving woman who over-indulged, I feel sick. Guilt consumes me for my self-indulgence while the world still mourns the loss of my brother.

William is patient, but I know he's frustrated. He is struggling to create a balance in the highs and lows of my moods by alternately giving me space and trying to distract me with new games. When he leaves me with my demons, I wonder where he's gone and who he's with. When he returns, I am starved for his attention.

On one cold December afternoon, when we are once again interrupted by my sudden change of mood, William stomps down the stairs and gets busy stuffing the potbellied stove. He puts on a disc, and the subtle harmonies of Debussy float up to where I am trying to compose myself. When I go down to join him, I see he is whittling a piece of wood. He is a magician whose talented fingers are capable of shaping all manner of media to his vision – including me.

In a playful, teasing manner, he offers me the piece of wood from which a little leprechaun creature has emerged. He holds it out and then snatches it back, his magnificent teal blue eyes twinkling impishly. How easily he can get me to smile. Then, out of the blue, he says,

"Manon, I never tire of looking at you, your lovely face, your sensuous body, and your graceful movements. I love your hands and how, when you talk, your fingers seem to dance to a silent score, outlining angles and negative spaces. Sometimes, when you're sleeping, I catch a glimpse of a single buttock creating a moon-like crescent. Your cheeks, shoulders, ankles, every curve and dip of you move me. I want to sculpt you."

I don't know whether to laugh or cry. The idea of being scrutinized the way my life drawing models were, exposing all their flaws, and the thought of him eyeing me so closely makes me quiver like a leaf. Inevitably, I relent and agree to be his muse.

He adds more fuel to the stove, making the place comfortably warm as I pose nude in front of the black drape on the chaise longue at the end of the studio. He directs me to sit with my feet up, my knees bent, my arms resting on top of them, and my hands dangling loosely from my wrists. He manipulates me as if I were a mannequin.

"Here, bend forward, turn your head, and look up at the windows." he runs his hand down my spine, giving me shivers. "There, a beautiful curvature." He pulls off the elastic band that holds my ponytail, gathers all the wayward strands flat against my scalp, and tightens the band to reveal the shape of my cranium. "Now spread your legs a little more, for support," and saying so, he reaches between my thighs, pushing them apart until he achieves the exact position he wants. I am exposed and want him again, but he is dead serious about his mission and ignores my signals. He sketches me quickly and then takes a tape measure to note the distances between head and torso, legs and arms. Eyes, ears, and nose are also plotted with measurements.

"What are you doing?"

"I'm using 8Hu as my gauge to make the piece at one-third scale."

"What's 8Hu?" I learn so much from him.

"It's the scale of the human figure, which is 8 heads tall. Now don't move," he says and goes to the cupboard to get a Polaroid camera. He begins snapping shots as he circles at a distance around me.

"Okay, Babe, you can relax; I can do the next bit on my own."

He begins working immediately, ignoring me for the rest of the afternoon. He rummages through his toolbox and selects a hacksaw, some bolts, and a length of steel pipe. His meaty hands grip the steel and he cuts it as easily as if it were soft cheese. He connects the pipes with bolted elbows at ninety and forty-five degree angles, creating a crooked structure, which will be my 'spine' and 'neck.' He secures it to a wooden base.

William's face in concentration is animated and expressive. His tongue, teeth, and mouth work together with his hands and body. He moves deliberately and gracefully around the studio. He lays out his tools carefully, as if setting the table for a sumptuous meal. Loop tools, cutting wires, coils, toothed scrapers, wood skewers, and a spray bottle are neatly placed beside the turntable with the pipe already screwed onto it. His biceps bulge as he lifts a two-foot square, one-inch thick slab of clay from a cupboard and places it onto the worktable with a thump. He cuts into it with a confidence I admire and envy. When I start on a new piece, I am uncertain what it will end up looking like. I plod along while he progresses professionally, setting to his task efficiently, knowing exactly what the outcome of his labors will be.

He seems infatuated with the material as he starts compounding the piece. He begins to shape the mass into a rough representation of my pose. He works quickly with muddy hands and, sweaty brow; the serenity of his expression reveals his sheer joy in the work. He is truly a master of this malleable material, shaping it with his wet fingers, smoothing his hands over it, and caressing the clay. As he pulls, presses, and pinches the grey mass, I begin to see my arms and legs emerge. He shapes my breasts and pinches the ends into pointy nipples, his face glowing with the pleasure of it. He works on it obsessively until there is an eerie two-foot-tall statue of me, nude for all to see. I never saw myself so beautiful.

CHAPTER TWENTY-NINE

Four months to the day after Alexander's death, Mrs. O, Hedley, and I are summoned to the WWP boardroom for the reading of his will. It's Sunday, the last day of 2006. The air is crisp, and Elderberry is blanketed with snow that glistens in the sunshine. Everyone feels optimistic for the New Year. They are glad to leave behind the year in which Alexander died and embrace the New Year in which Stephanie will give birth. My optimism is tepid at best.

Alexander has made me the beneficiary of his estate after generously bequeathing staggering sums to Mrs. O and Hedley and making provisions for the care of his aunt in Albany. I am terrified by this wealth and have been ignoring requests from Gerry Abrams and Julian Fisher to meet with them to plan for the future.

WWP has been carrying on under the direction of its board, which includes Gerry, Julian, Devin, and Dr. Lampard as a non-executive director. Julian has been calling me weekly to see how I'm doing. He needs to settle the estate and gently pressures me to attend a board meeting because Alexander's wishes were to have me on the board, and they need my vote to accomplish their agendas. I have no idea what it means to be on a Board of Directors and have no interest in the business of pharmaceuticals or in business at all.

On New Year's Eve, the 'Elderberry family' gathers in the Great Room, drinking champagne (except for Stephanie, who toasts the beginning of the New Year with ginger ale). There is no Christmas tree this year. The scent of pine is absent, but the redolence of birch bark and wood smoke still fill the room, the same smoky masculine smell that made me heady when I first entered here. It smelled like Alexander. Now his scent is fading, and my memory of him is restricted to the brief time we had together. There is no future to create any more. His absence is a presence. I wish we'd had more time.

Nobody waits up until midnight except me. Alone in my room, I study the arrangement of botanical prints and contemplate the events of the past two years. I don't even resemble the person I was back then. Alexander has changed my life. How is it that we could have bonded so tightly that now I feel even more alone than when Dad died?

At the stroke of midnight, I am startled by my phone ringing.

"Happy New Year, Babe!" William shouts to be heard over the raucous revelers at whatever party I had declined to go to.

My eyes fill with tears. Even with William in my life again, I feel so alone.

❀❀❀❀

Through January and February, I spent most of my time at Elderberry. The city is much too alive for me, and William's energy exhausts me. I need to hunker in Alexander's world, to feel his presence, and to try to envision the life ahead of me. All things are possible except the thing I want the most – to have Alexander back.

Julian and I have been talking a lot. He and Alexander were good friends. It comforts me that we share the grief of losing him.

He's wise beyond his years and has intimate knowledge of Alexander's dreams and goals. He explains that having me on the Board would give him an ally in executing Alexander's vision.

He pays a visit one afternoon with some documents to be signed. Sitting in the library, he takes the opportunity to encourage me to consider all the possibilities ahead.

"Manon, you could do some serious good work in whatever field your heart leads you to. Alexander believed in philanthropy and supported various charitable organizations as well as other initiatives."

"You mean like Hedley's dad's riding school for special needs kids?"

"Yes, that one continues to be supported by his estate. I'd be happy to take you there and explain the operations side of it. See for yourself how a foundation can be put to good use."

Sitting on the tufted sofa with my legs tucked under me, I look at the saddle atop the pommel horse, and am intrigued by the idea of a 'field trip' to where Alexander had fallen in love with horses.

"I'd like that."

"He had a lot of other undertakings." Julian leans back in the big leather chair and regales me with more of Alexander's philanthropy. "Alexander was keenly aware that science is surpassing our ability to cope ethically with its advancement. He had a sense of urgency about solving that particular problem and set up trust funds to foster multidisciplinary think tanks. They incubate ideas about the philosophical, legal, and sociological ramifications of scientific innovations, ideas that will initiate research into genetics, bioethics, human biomaterials, human enhancement, and reproduction."

He sounds just like Alexander, and my mind boggles at the detail-laden language I can barely keep up with. So much to think about...

"So you think I could start something like the riding school?"

"Yes. There is plenty of money for you to set up a foundation of your choosing."

On one of those days in March, when it looks as if it's going to rain any minute, I see Hedley rushing toward the house. It's too early for baby Alexa's arrival, but I immediately think that something has happened with Stephanie's pregnancy. I've become so anxious lately.

Hedley tells me that he's had a call from Pete Hunt. He has some information he's uncovered about Gabrielle's mother and is on his way to Elderberry as we speak. When he arrives, we usher him into the dining area and seat him at the trestle table by the French doors. Hedley and I sit on the bench opposite him.

Meeting him face-to-face for the first time, I'm surprised by his unassuming appearance. He's not at all the romantic image of the dogged gumshoe I imagined. He's short, middle-aged, and balding. The oblique light of the afternoon creates shadows on the right side of his face, accentuating deep eye sockets and a large nose. By contrast, the left side of his face, in full light, has no visible cheekbones.

He pulls a stack of file folders from his briefcase. The summary of his findings about the plane crash is the thinnest. Others are over-full with reports, receipts, and his invoices for the last month. I glance at it and am shocked at what this sleuthing endeavor costs, but then I'm quickly distracted by some photographs he pulls from a thick folder.

He spreads them out on the trestle table, and I see pictures of gravestones and others of unfamiliar people. There is the one of Alice that he had sent electronically. It has more impact when printed as a glossy 8″ x 10″. My grandmother's eyes seem even wilder than on that first impression. Thankfully, I still don't see any resemblance to Dad. There are mugshots of Stuart and Edward Mouland. Even in these unflattering photos, taken in 1951 when they were first arrested, they are both good-looking with mischievous eyes and smirking expressions.

Then Pete hands me another 8″ x 10″ of a sophisticated, older woman who might have been Gabrielle had she lived to be that old. The delicately aging woman, sitting in a wingback chair with legs demurely crossed, looks straight into Pete's camera. There is a depth of sorrow in her sky blue eyes that she is unable to mask with her stoic posture.

"This is Sondra Whitehead Cameron, heiress of the Maple Leaf Cotton Company. I explained to her that I was contacting her on behalf of her grandson's estate. She didn't seem the least bit surprised, as if she'd been waiting patiently for contact from the child she had given up. I asked if I could record our conversation. She agreed." Pete turned on the tape.

"I always believed that someday my daughter would make contact."

"I'm sorry to tell you that Gabrielle died in 2003."

"Oh." We hear Sondra weeping softly in genuine grief. *"I'm sorry. Every day, I think I'll be with her again, and now, suddenly, I've truly lost her. . . Where is my grandson?"*

"Alexander is also gone. He died recently in a plane crash."

There is a long pause in the recording during which Pete tells us that she crumpled up and wept quietly.

"Although she's in her eighties, her memory is remarkably clear about those indelible events in her youth. She talked candidly about her brief affair with Stuart Mouland as if it had happened only yesterday."

"Stuie was a very charismatic guy. He didn't have to seduce me because I wanted to be with him more than anything. Of course, my parents disapproved of a Westmount girl dating a boy from Saint-Henri. When I got pregnant, they forbade me from ever seeing him again, and in their piety, they wouldn't let me have an abortion. They insisted that I give the baby away." (long pause) *"I cried oceans of tears. I loved the baby Stuie and I created. When Gabrielle was born and the adoption was about to be finalized, Stuie showed up and took custody of her. He had a new girlfriend, and they were going to raise my baby."*

"Did you ever see Gabrielle after that?" Another long pause...

"I let the tape run and watched her as she massaged her throat and forcefully swallowed her sobs. She didn't speak for a few minutes. Then..."

"I had several clandestine visits with Stuart and the baby in her first year. She was a beautiful baby with light blue eyes and the golden fuzz of hair just beginning to grow out. After that, Stuart and his brother Edward got into a lot of trouble, and we lost touch. Later, I learned that Gabrielle was taken in by her grandparents."

It's a cruel twist of fate that Alexander missed meeting his grandmother and that Dad did not live to know of his mother's existence. I am amazed at the congruence of life events in our family, even though we've been estranged. Are we destined to repeat the mistakes our parents made? Are we doomed to this eternal recurrence? Sondra had Gabrielle out of wedlock, and

Gabrielle had Alexander without his father's participation. She fell in love with her own cousin, as did I, only to learn that he was my brother. What is my destiny? Will I ever be a mother, or will I be content to give birth only to works of art?

CHAPTER THIRTY

I can't believe it's been a year since my first dinner with William. I was his birthday present that night, and he has been my gift ever since. Motherwell's is filled to capacity for his birthday celebration. Dozens of balloons shaped as threes and zeros hover above about fifty celebrants, his closest friends and admirers. Their conversation buzzes like an electric current, and occasionally there is a loud burst of laughter.

The ceiling is covered with twinkle lights that bounce off the top of mingling heads. How is William able to spread himself so thin, engage with all these people, and still work maniacally on his art? Although I am growing in this incubator of William's world, it saps my energy. How can I ever keep up with him? Will he ultimately leave me behind?

My head spins with the excitement in the room. Champagne is abundant and is served continually by white-gloved servers dressed in black.

William's agent, Marty Sheridan, corners me by a small bronze statue depicting a seated boy, wincing as he concentrates on removing a splinter from his sole.

"I've seen some of your work up at William's loft," he says. "I think it would do well on the market."

Marty's focus is not so much on unique talent but on marketability. The thought of my work as a commodity makes me cringe. Does he even like any of those trial-and-error pieces I've abandoned at William's? Talking to him makes me feel as if the seated boy's splinter is in *my* foot. I move agitatedly from one to the other, wanting to escape.

"I could put you in a group show I'm organizing for a few young artists, just to see what kind of reaction they'd get."

Put me? Show me? Sell me? Rothko would never allow his paintings to be juxtaposed with another artist's work nearby; he wouldn't sell his work as decoration, he couldn't care less whether people liked his work. I've been to enough openings to know what nerve-racking experiences they are for the artists. I've overheard cruel criticisms by the aesthetes of New York, denigrating works that bare the artist's soul. I couldn't bear that. Putting a price on my art seems perverse.

I manage to free myself from Marty and wander around, looking for William. As I slide through the crowd, hoping to be unnoticed, I catch snippets of conversations; *Dada is all the rage again. Where are all the mid-career female artists? Design fetishism and radical conceptualism appeal only to the bourgeois. Did you hear they moved into a neo-Bauhaus co-op on the upper east side?* Then somebody delivers a joke: *Pavlov is sitting at a pub enjoying a pint, the phone rings, and he jumps up shouting, "Oh shit, I forgot to feed the dog!"* A roar of laughter rises, adding to the din.

֍֍֍֍

Back at his loft, in the wee hours before dawn, the excitement of the evening has left me rattled. Finally, prone on the pallet in the loft, I get that feeling of calm before a storm. I have a strange sense that things are about to change.

After a quickie, William straddles me again but doesn't make a move. In a way, I'm relieved because I'm still recovering from my recent trip to bliss. Poised above me, his dark hair flopping over his glowing face, he delivers this simple imperative:

"Let's get married."

"What? Why?"

"I love you. I want to have children with you. I want us to be a family."

I am stunned into silence. I love William, and I can't imagine being without him, and yet I'm filled with uncertainty. He starts to move slowly, rhythmically repeating,

"Say yes, say yes, say yes!"

Marriage? What do I know about marriage, or motherhood, for that matter? I've had no model for either role. How would I fit into William's life, his loving family, and the intellectual aesthetes who surround him?

Would being a wife to William cancel the artist in me? What would our marriage be like? Would I be the Lee Krasner to William's Jackson Pollock or the Françoise Gilot to his Picasso? Would we feed off each other's inspiration, or would his talent suck all the energy away from my work the way Pollock and Picasso did? Lee Krasner burst out of the confines of her unending collages and began crafting her enormous paintings only after Pollock's death. Françoise Gilot had to put an ocean between herself and the love of her life to be able to create. Will I lurk in the shadow of William's great success, or must I break away to grow as an independent artist? So many questions.

I suddenly yearn to retreat to my studio above the garage.

֍֍֍֍

The time I spend alone in my studio at Elderberry is my most creative. I finally feel like I am making great strides artistically. This is where I need to be, what I am meant to be doing, just as Alexander said.

Lately, I've been working on a large, unstretched canvas laid on the floor, freeing it of boundaries. I can work all around it and see it from all angles. But unlike Pollock's drip technique, I dance around the floor, painting intersecting 'roads' of color using large brushes with extension poles, like a housepainter. With the adrenalin-pumping music of a Hungarian Rhapsody blasting, I feel the sense of speed on my 'highways' to unknown destinations. I realize I cannot be stalled by marriage.

William's proposal is left hanging, but he's unrelenting in his effort to get me to commit to his vision of a family life. In mid-April, he invites me to his family's Passover seder.

"A lot of my relatives will be there," he says. "I want to introduce you to them so you'll see what you'd be marrying into. Will you come?"

"Do you really want me there?" I ask, a little unsure about the protocol for the Jewish holiday. My exposure to Jewish culture is limited to what I have gleaned from people I've met in New York, and what I know of Jewish traditions is only what I learned at the Yeshiva University Museum William had taken me to.

"I want to share every aspect of my life with you. I don't want to be anywhere without you."

Having already met his parents and his sister Gertie, I thought I'd be comfortable enough; they were lovely and warm and funny. But I wasn't prepared for the huge gathering. There is a celebratory atmosphere, rich with ritual and animated discussion, not only about the holiday but about any topic that comes up and how it relates to the Jewish experience. Everyone is relaxed, and everyone talks – often all at once.

I sit next to William, who sits at his father's side as he conducts the seder. Everyone dotes on William; he is their golden boy. It makes me both happy to see him amidst his adoring family and sad because I never experienced such familial love.

Before the meal begins, they recite special prayers, then there is a sampling of symbolic offerings on the Seder tray, and throughout these rituals, we drink four ceremonial glasses of wine. The youngest cousin, a precocious four-year-old, recites the Ma Nishtana, posing the eternal question of why this night is different from all other nights. He's so cute and so proud of himself when everyone applauds his good job. People provide answers at will, even the kids, who giggle at having spoken at once. An enthusiastic discussion about the liberation of the Jewish people from slavery ensues, which in turn generates lots of discussion about the history of antisemitism. Everyone has an opinion, even the kids.

Next to me, Gertie's husband, David, pokes me gently with his elbow and asks, with a nod of his head indicating the verbose family,

"What do you make of all this?"

I'm not sure if he means what I think of the family or of antisemitism. Either way, I am shy and feel I have nothing to contribute. I'm saved when Gertie raises her glass for a toast to Great-Aunt Goldie, who survived the Holocaust, which makes me think about how one person's life experience can affect subsequent generations. This family, living a middle-class lifestyle in the most cosmopolitan city in the world, carries the trauma of that horror as well as all the previous horrors their ancestors endured.

Everyone feels quite at home amid the clatter of plates and the jangle of cutlery, the din of concurrent conversations, and the shrill voices of excited children who, having tasted the super-sweet kosher wine, run around making mischief. Meanwhile, Adam, Gertie's eldest, takes advantage of the distraction to abscond with the afikomen, the special piece of matzo that William's dad will need to conclude the Seder.

This family feast is so warm, happy, and noisy. After the ceremonial part of the seder is over, Ruth and some of the aunts start bringing out the food – there is so much food! There are hard-boiled eggs, chicken soup with enormous matzo balls, then brisket and roast chicken, and parsley potatoes, and roasted vegetables, and pickled beets with horseradish, and wine, and more wine, and Passover cakes, and macaroons, and coffee and tea and fruit, and matzo with everything.

I witness the important negotiation between William's dad and his nine-year-old grandson for the return of the afikomen. It takes a good half hour for Adam to wangle movie tickets from his grandfather for all the kids, making him their hero, while the adults groan at having to wait for the final prayers to finish the meal because it's already way past the kids' bedtimes. Then there is the singing of melodic, joyful songs to end the seder.

The bonds and rituals of this loving family make me sad for what I never had. I really don't know how I would fit in.

CHAPTER THIRTY-ONE

My 'family' is growing. On April 17th, I get a text message announcing the arrival of Alexa Louise Pritchard in the midst of a raging storm. A nor'easter, with winds sustaining up to 100 mph, is blowing through parts of eastern North America. Major highways in Westchester County, as well as parts of Connecticut, are closed due to extreme flooding. I'm unable to get to Elderberry, where Alexa came into the world at the civilized hour of 6:00 p.m. with the help of Mrs. O and a midwife.

Stuck at the Colosseum without power, without William, with only my thoughts, which whirl like a nor'easter in my brain, I sit by the fireplace toasting my toes. Candlelight illuminates a small sphere around me, a little womb of muted light in which my heart alternately soars and sinks. How did life get so complicated in such a short time?

It's been two years since Dad died, and a certain part of me believes he is still there in the world I left behind. I often have the urge to call him. I picture him in his armchair with a book, John Coltrane's Giant Steps, on the turntable. The book suddenly abandoned on his lap in anticipation of the difficult riff coming up, the piano straining to keep up with the Coltrane Changes. When it stops, Dad's eyes close as Coltrane's saxophone takes off at lightning speed. Those chords are so embedded in my brain that I can see Dad's fingers tapping on the armchair to their rhythm, his head moving slightly, as if in another world.

Alexander is gone more than a year, and there is a wounded part of me that never heals entirely. Whenever a scab starts to form, it gets ripped off by some reminiscence, by the lament of what will never be, or just by a leaf falling to the ground. The family that had existed without my knowledge are all gone, except for my grandmother Alice and Alexander's grandmother Sondra.

And there's William, a force of nature that has me caught up in its energy, spiraling with its currents, and leaving me breathless. What should I do about William?

My mental meanderings don't keep my hands from working. I mindlessly sketch the faces of the people in my life, sometimes combining features so that Alexander becomes Dad and William becomes Alexander. The profiles of Mrs. O and Sage, joined like Janus, fitting perfectly with each other. I flip the pages and am surprised to discover that the figure drawings I was doing last fall are actually self-portraits. One shows a haunted figure, eyes with black irises and eery white pupils, glaring over her shoulder as if she were being pursued by some demon. The figure's awkward, slightly bent posture is rendered in aggressive, jagged lines. It's the mass of Medusa-like hair drawn in meandering curlicues that identifies it as me. The wild, frantic tentacles suggest movement and vulnerability. It shows my desperation to escape from my own body.

Comparing myself in the mirror to this wretched creature, I can see I have matured. My body has more angles as I've shed pounds, making my breasts appear larger. Cheekbones have emerged, making my eyes appear larger too, no longer haunted but deeper. My demons have not defeated me.

An article appeared in the Times yesterday about a tragic incident that occurred in Florida. A youngster was accidentally killed by a security guard after he broke into an art supply store. It aroused a sense of urgency in me to do something. Kids shouldn't be getting killed for wanting stuff. This kid, especially, who was stealing cans of spray paint for graffiti. He only wanted to express himself through his art. I understand that need. I call Julian right away.

"Julian, I have an idea."

"That's great, Manon. What do you have in mind?"

"I want to help kids who don't have the means to fulfill their dreams to make art. I want to open a storefront studio space for kids. They would have all the materials they need as well as support from mentors. Can I do that?"

"Yes, absolutely; it's a wonderful idea."

"How do I start?"

"Let's have a meeting to discuss. When can you come to WWP?"

"How about tomorrow?"

"Okay, come at 11:00. In the meantime, start formulating your mission statement."

All afternoon, I'm channeling my younger self. What would I have wanted? Most of all, support. Nurturing budding talent is as important as enabling it with ample resources. This nourishment is vital to an artist's soul. I envision a friendly drop-in space, a mini Motherwell's Place for kids. A place to go to do art in an atmosphere where everyone supports each other.

Jacob Lawrence may never have become a celebrated African-American artist had his mother not enrolled him in after-school art classes at community workshops in Harlem. There are a lot of kids whose parents can't provide that kind of support, so many who could benefit from having drop-in places like that.

It doesn't take long for my vision to take shape. Sketchbook at hand, I start to draw a street scene, inserting a cheerful storefront poignantly juxtaposed among the row of dilapidated industrial low-rise buildings. I paint potted plants, venetian blinds, and tied back curtains on the windows, like decals. I add children of varying sizes in the kind of Cubist style that Lawrence painted. I imagine walking through the front door into a studio bright with color and light and smelling like the Blick store.

I'm doing this!

CHAPTER THIRTY-TWO

I spend the rest of the month in a small office at WWP working out the details of the foundation, and most evenings at Elderberry staring at the miracle of Alexa. As I coddle this beautiful infant, my breasts ache with a surprising and powerful longing to nurse. When I'm with William, his not so subtle prodding for us to have babies adds to this physical desire. I have no control over this strange new impulse, and I'm worried that I will allow myself to become pregnant. Should I now interrupt my new life or give it up for good to be something I have no idea how to be?

I try to put some space between us to give me a chance to breathe and settle down outside of the sexual temptation. William has no trouble filling the time that he would otherwise be with me. I chase the thoughts of Adrianna, or worse, Sarah, and others from my mind.

Spring has released the familiar, comforting scents of earth, hay, and lilacs. I'm up early, excited for my day, and immersed in the foundation project. Ideas are teeming in my brain. The work of organizing them and working out the details suits me. But I haven't abandoned my art; if anything, I am more prolific than ever, working evenings in my studio on the large canvas on the floor. It's thick with paint now, and the 'roads' are nearly obliterated by black figure-like drippings 'drawn' with a turkey baster. Each night I get re-acquainted with the painting, which seems to have a life of its own.

Whenever I need confirmation that one of my ideas is possible, I go to Julian. He educates me in the basics of running a foundation but spares me the bulk of administrative preparation by handing off some of that work to Nicole. Sometimes he sends me to Gerry Abrams' office to discuss liability issues. My idea of having a climbing rope hung from the rafter, for instance, as a material manifestation of the logo I've been working on is a hard no. I am forced to think more practically. Gerry drafts permission slips for parents, and we compile a code of conduct for the kids. I don't want to impose too many rules and intimidate them from coming, but Gerry insists that we need to make the place safe for everybody.

When I'm with Julian, he always asks about my art and wants to know what I'm working on. He reminds me that his friend David Zweig is eager to see my work. David's gallery of contemporary art is right in the heart of Chelsea, under the Highline on 10th Ave., a great location. It has a constant stream of tourists with disposable incomes looking to own a piece of art. But I'm reluctant to entertain the idea of a show, of exposing myself, only to turn my work into souvenirs or, worse, have them rejected and realize my greatest fear, that I've become a 'wannabe,' just as Dad feared.

My days are busy with running around on various missions for the foundation. Catching a glimpse of myself dashing by a store window, I realize that I have become one of those wealthy Manhattanites who I used to observe, wondering where they were all rushing to.

I've found a good location: a storefront in the South Bronx, just south of I95, at the end of a block of auto repair shops. There is a vacant storefront on the corner of Webster and E 176th St., with soaring ceilings and large plate glass windows facing both north and west. Across the street, construction cranes, like a herd of diplodocuses, hover above grimy brick buildings clad in scaffolding.

I invent the name Lofty Ambitions and design a logo that depicts a thick knotted rope ascending skyward. The end of it is out of sight beyond the lofty clouds, symbolizing the potential to climb to unlimited heights with a little support.

Each concept is infused with Alexander's altruistic spirit so as to create the same kind of environment that the Riding School enjoys: focusing on the kids, building their self-esteem, and unleashing their talents. I enlist William's help in planning the physical space. But the structures he wants to build inside the studio are over-the-top. I recall his grade school project, the wobbly structure of disparate objects balanced precariously on top of each other, which came crashing down, breaking Tommy Winter's nose. When we disagree, I have to strengthen my resolve to maintain my own vision of what I want to do. I'm learning about hard nos.

Instead, I asked him to design programs for the kids. He is especially good with these ideas. He promises to come and lead workshops. There will be other guest artists to work with the kids. I add a note to my to-do list to find Napoleon, a street artist I met in Brooklyn, to ask if he would consider doing a graffiti project with the kids. I'll need to find out whether permits are required.

I interview interns, hire staff, and explain my vision to them. I make sure they understand the fragility of budding talent and explain how to nurture young artists. Kids will come in to do art and have their confidence boosted. There will be scholarships and stipends for supplies or whatever is needed. I know Alexander would be thrilled with this venture, and he would have gotten a kick from the logo, which incorporates his hobby of knot tying.

At the end of a day of work, I head home, tired but satisfied with what I have accomplished. I settle in the cozy den with a container of double chocolate ice cream as my reward and listen to the exquisitely expressive guitar music of Andre Segovia, picturing Alexander's long fingers strumming and plucking out a melody. The sound of Mrs. O's puttering in the kitchen is comforting. A satisfying melancholy settles over me.

CHAPTER THIRTY-THREE

By the end of May, we will be ready to open our doors. Flyers have been distributed to local schools, and posters are displayed in stores and the lobbies of apartment buildings for blocks around. Children passing by have been pressing their noses against the window to see what's coming.

On the opening day, there are balloons flanking the entrance. There are a few kids already waiting outside when I open the doors at 3:30. There's milk, juice, and cookies for a small group of 7 - 12 year-olds. Most are bashful and unsure of what to do, except for one boy. His name is Jean-Michel. As we are introducing ourselves, he walks around and inspects the supply shelves, helps himself to a large drawing pad, chooses a box of pastels, and sits down at one of the tables.

"Welcome to Lofty Ambitions; my name is Manon, and this is Emily and Darren. They will be working on group projects with you." I let Emily take over.

"Today we're going to draw a traffic jam together," she says.

I help Darren spread some big rolls of paper on the floor, and then I move back to where Jean-Michel is working quickly, as if he wants to finish before he's told he has to stop.

"Now," Emily says, "look around and find some 'obstacles' to put down on the paper. Jars, cookies, cups, whatever is not too big or too small." Kids enthusiastically find objects that their brushes will avoid. One boy takes off his shoe and places it on the paper. Everybody laughs. Darren is preparing individual cups of primary colors for each kid and hands them out with brushes. Emily continues,

"Find a starting point and imagine your paintbrush is a car. Take it for a ride, don't lift it until you've arrived at your destination; and watch out for obstacles; don't get any paint on them." Journeys overlap as lines appear everywhere. Kids are scrambling over each other like in a game of Twister. The paper is filling up with crisscrossing 'roads' of color. "Now, let's remove the obstacles." The negative spaces left behind beckon to be filled. "Okay, now fill the spaces with whatever you think you might see on your journey. You can use pencils or crayons or paint, whatever you want." Soon, flowers begin to bloom, and houses and people appear. A busy two-dimensional world takes shape as cars, fire hydrants, stick figures, and swings in parks are created.

Jean-Michel is working on his own, intent on a complex drawing. When I approach him, he abruptly asks,

"What kind of name is Man-on?"

"It's French."

"Are you French?"

"No."

"Then why do you have a French name?"

"Apparently my mother loved the sound of it."

"Do you speak French?"

"Oui, un peu."

"My name is French too."

"And do you speak French?"

"Non," he says, pronouncing it with a nasal sound.

He grins at his own joke, exposing brilliant white teeth that shine in his caramel brown face. I am immediately smitten. He continues to work, making deliberate, easy strokes with pastels. Emily and I look at each other and smile in amazement at this young boy's obvious drive and talent.

Through the afternoon, the kids work at the traffic jam, creating their little masterpieces. The older ones start to get boisterous, and Darren calls them to attention.

"Listen up, y'all. You are free to use any of the materials here to make art. But there are rules." He points out the large poster outlining the code of behavior that must be adhered to while at Lofty Ambitions. Two troublemakers sneer at the rules and are asked to leave.

By closing time at six thirty, most of the kids have left, and there is only Jean-Michel working intently on another intricate drawing using black pastel, drawing Keith Haring-style stick figures over the colorful base of doodle-like sketches. They create a sense of movement like a hive of busy insects, a little creepy but executed with a precision unexpected in an eleven-year-old. When I tell him we are closing, he looks up at me with his dewy brown eyes.

"Can I just finish my drawing?"

I send everyone home and stay with him for a while longer, tidying the studio, surrounded by the quiet left by the kids' departure. In the half-light of dusk, I see the Bronx landscape through the window. The moody skies create an Edward Hopper-like atmosphere, which inspires me to create a palette of grey, umber, ochre, and forest green. A blank canvas from the supplies shelf becomes my new painting.

I outline the cityscape in chalk. Looking from inside out, I include the window frame to encase the scene before me: partially silhouetted buildings across the boulevard, their red brick muted by grime and shadow; cranes like futuristic creatures mimicking dinosaurs emerge in silhouette. Looming in the sky behind them, the I-95 overpass curves right and disappears off the canvas.

Before I know it, it's after seven, and a loud thumping on the door interrupts my flow. Jean-Michel is still busily working on his masterpiece. A young black man is rattling the door knob insisting on being let in.

"What do you want?" I yell through the locked door.

He looks past me, pointing to Jean-Michel, and yelling loud enough to be heard inside the studio.

"Yo, JM! Get yo ass over here!

"It's okay, Manon; that's just my brother."

I open the door, and he pushes past me toward Jean-Michel.

"You 'post to be home by five. I got no time to babysit your whiny sisters." Then, turning his attention to me, he screams, "What kinda place is this where you keep little kids so late? C'mon, JM, we're out of here, and you ain't coming back neither." He grabs JM by the collar and starts pulling him roughly toward the door.

"Please wait!" I touch his arm to stop him. "You're right. I never should have let him stay so late. I promise I won't allow that to happen again. Please let him come back. Your brother has real talent; you mustn't keep him from exploring it." He looks at my hand on his arm, boring into my flesh with his eyes, and I quickly pull my hand back.

"Who the hell are you to tell me what I must do?"

"M-my name is Manon," I offer him my hand and muster the temerity to ask, "and you are...?"

He ignores my extended hand.

"You own this place?"

"I run the foundation."

"Well, Man-on, lots of people have talent; it doesn't give them a pass to do what they want. If I let him, JM would be scribbling all day on whatever surface he could find. He needs to step up. I can't do everything."

All night, I agonize about this little boy. I wonder if he will show up tomorrow.

CHAPTER THIRTY-FOUR

The city is getting hot and grimy. Nevertheless, Sage is taking her vacation in New York. When I pick her up at the airport, we hug each other, and the warmth of her body transfers to me, coating me in caramel. I don't want to let go. On the drive to Elderberry, I fill her in on Lofty Ambitions, going on enthusiastically about the whole process of setting up the foundation and about the kids.

"The kids are amazing. They love coming to the studio and being able to express themselves freely, forgetting about their difficulties while they're making art. There are a couple who are really talented. An eleven-year-old boy, Jean-Michel, has done some remarkable conceptual work expressing ideas that elude verbalization, confronting themes of race and mortality. Stunning insights from a little black boy living in a harsh white world. He has grown attached to me, and although he's very confident about his work, he always seeks my approval. He looks at me with big chocolate brown eyes, and my heart melts.

"Then there is Isabella, an anemic twelve-year-old who rejects any help or encouragement. In a way, she reminds me of myself at that age."

"Yes, you were quite aloof. Your dad had a difficult time getting you to accept his way of doing things." Old feelings of rebelliousness make me shift a bit in my seat, and I quickly revert to telling her about my current passion project.

"If I had had a place like Lofty Ambitions to go to, I might have been more compliant with Dad's rules. Like Jean-Michel and Isabella, I had the will to create but was denied the means with which to succeed. Given the opportunity to do what drives them, these kids can overcome even the most heart-hollowing of childhoods. JM's inventiveness grows with each piece he creates, and Isabella has developed a technique all her own for drawing horses. She does what I used to do with Audubon's birds – copy and perfect. I've given her photos of Banjo and Arty to draw, and I'm astonished by how good their likenesses are. I can actually recognize Banjo's expression as he looks out from the page.

Other kids just like messing with paint and doing the projects that Emily, one of the interns, makes up for them. William has designed some group projects that require construction, which Darren, the other intern, works on with them."

"Your dad would be proud of you. He had a philanthropic streak, which he exercised by donating his time. Giving was one of the cornerstones of his character. I guess you get that from him."

Bitter resentment of him leaving me for more important things to do floods back, and I struggle to keep from drowning in this sea of need. I let it go. Dad was not who I thought he was. I wish he was just my father again, as he's always been, not a separate person who had a secret life of his own. Am I really anything like him?

"So, what do you want to do while you're here?"

She rhymes off her itinerary and, I have to smile at her ambition.

"I'm going to drag Peg out of the house and take her sightseeing. We're going to The Cloisters, The Brooklyn Botanical Gardens and have lunch at the Tavern on the Green in Central Park. Oh, and I really want to do a Circle Line Cruise around Manhattan Island. Then there's The Morgan Library, which has *The Hours of Katherine of Cleves.*"

"What's that?"

"It's an ornately illuminated manuscript from the 15th century that I've wanted to see ever since your dad told me about it. I imagine the colors and the glimmers of gold leaf will be spectacular to see in person. I also want to go to a play on Broadway. I hear *Rent* is the current big hit. We might be able to snag rush seats for a matinee."

"All that in how long?" I laugh.

"I'm here for two weeks if you all don't get tired of me."

"Great. Save time for me to show you William's *Kids in The Park,* down in Chelsea."

She asks about William

"He wants us to get married."

"You say that like he's proposed a death sentence."

"In a way, it *would* be the end of the relationship we have. Furthermore, he wants to have children. I'm not ready for that."

"Well, it sounds to me like you're fulfilled by the work you're doing. If William loves you, he'll wait."

"Do you really think so? Patience is not one of his virtues. Once he has an idea, he jumps on it; it has to be immediate and I know he's ready to have kids. You should see him around his nephews; he becomes a child with them, a sweet little boy."

"William is a great guy, and I hope you work out a way to be with him without veering off the path you're on. You positively shine when you talk about the foundation and the kids. It's changed you."

With this positive reinforcement, I resolve to tell William that I don't want to be married. I want to continue my work with the kids, even if it means he might let me go.

When we turn onto the gravel path at Elderberry, we see that Mrs. O is sitting on the stoop waiting for us. Sage rushes out of the car and they hug and nuzzle each other like bunnies, holding each other so close as to become one. In profile their curves fit neatly like puzzle pieces. The palpable passion between them makes me long for William. How long has it been since I've lain on his pallet quivering like a leaf after a carnal workout? Was it last Tuesday or Wednesday? What's he doing now, I wonder.

I've gotten so absorbed by the pastel drawings inspired by JM that I sometimes forget to eat and now the smell of simmering tomato sauce and pungent garlic emanating from the kitchen makes me salivate. Dishes of antipasto sit in the center of the trestle table, which is set for six. I grab an olive and debate whether I should serve myself some artichokes and my favorite spicy feta-filled peppers.

Leading Sage downstairs to their quarters, Mrs. O turns back and says,

"Julian needs some signatures, so he's coming by. I told him to stay for dinner."

Just then the doorbell rings. Julian stands on the threshold with his usual placid expression, his mat of dark kinky hair cropped close to his scalp revealing an appealingly round cranium. He's forgone his customary dress shirt and jacket in the July heat. I've never seen Julian dressed casually. His jeans and white polo shirt fit snug enough for me to see that he works out. Of course, he would.

Steph and Hedley come in through the French doors with three-month-old Alexa strapped to Hedley's front in a baby carrier. I beg to hold her even though she's sleeping. He scoops her out and hands her to me; the warm weight of her in my arms is soothing. Her face is cherubic. Her violet eyelids, feathered with long lashes, are so delicate I want to put my lips on them. She smells of that divine 'baby' smell that affects my hormones directly, creating a deep, inexplicable ache in me.

When Sage and Mrs. O come in, Alexa opens her eyes and looks in wonder at where she is now and, making eye contact, she tries to place who's face this is. I think she recognizes me because she doesn't cry. She doesn't complain as she is passed from hand to hand. Even Julian coos and pats her bum as he bounces on his toes.

After dinner, Julian and I are left by ourselves, and as he helps with the cleanup, he once again broaches the subject of 'showing' my work. He is my constant champion and insists that hiding my art is a travesty.

"Whatever you may think of art for sale, you now have a body of work that merits exposure to the world. Those abstract expressionist pieces you've been painting would be appreciated by lovers of art."

"They're not abstract expressionists. That's part of the problem. I don't want to be labeled."

"Labeled or not, you can't deny that there are people who would love your work, who would want to own it for their own pleasure. That's a gift you must give."

"I don't paint to sell. I've been privy now to the pretensions and intentions of the art world. I don't wish to engage with the power structures of it."

"Stop resisting this. Didn't Andy Warhol already settle the relationship between commerce and art? You are beyond commercialization. Your work is worthy of being seen. All the great artists had to have shows to be able to grow."

"It would require me to have an agent. I don't want anything to do with agents. I haven't met one that I'd want to work with. You're the only one I would trust to curate a showing of my work. Would you handle the process of mounting a show?"

"Well, I'm not an agent, but I do know people, and I would be honored to take on the job of introducing you to the art world."

Thus settled, I no longer have to think about it and can rest comfortably in Julian's capable hands.

CHAPTER THIRTY-FIVE

During the summer, I keep the studio open to kids all day. I've hired more staff, and the place is a hub of activity. The kids are busy on a joint project they are designing with Napoleon, intended for the side of the building across the street. JM participates by drawing black skull-like faces with spikes sprouting from their tops. He draws a series of identical simple figures with arms raised and feet pointing left. The little silhouettes resemble hieroglyphics marching at the top of the maquette. The kids are cooperative and encouraging each other, offering constructive criticism.

The younger ones are working jointly on a hands and bodies mural. Some draw around their own hands and feet. Some lie down and are traced by others; their giggles are as refreshing as a gurgling brook. They draw faces inside the traced heads, fill negative spaces with brilliant colors, and scribble all over, making charcoal 'signatures' until the work begins to look abstract.

JM is here every day, his brother having disappeared somewhere and his sisters in foster care. JM stays with his dad who suffers from mental illness and often forgets to supply basic necessities, so JM becomes the parent. Lofty is his refuge. He and I have begun experimenting with pastels.

One day, I take him to see Joan Mitchell's work at the Whitney. In many of her pastel works, eye-popping shades of yellow, royal blue, orange, and mauve are densely bundled against light backgrounds. The swirling masses seem to vibrate with life, drawing us in physically, leading our eyes around the canvas into the vortex, and they also draw us in emotionally, as we are awash with color. JM's body moves to a silent rhythm; I notice his eyes glaze over held-back tears. He is very sensitive. We relate in much the same way to art. I wonder if I was as emotional about it when I was his age. I take his hand, and he holds tightly onto mine.

Life has become routinely hectic. Both William's and my schedules require a conscious effort to plan getting together. As I'm leaving Lofty one windy October evening, I text him, asking him to come for dinner at the Colosseum, promising that I won't cook. He offers to bring Chinese, but by the time he arrives, it's almost ten and my anticipation has turned to frustration. Having been put into a grumpy mood, I decided this is the best time for me to reject his offer of marriage. I'll be less inclined to succumb to his persuasive charm and his intoxicating touch. He arrives with my favorite Chinese dishes from 'Birds of a Feather.'

It's been a week since I've seen him and laying eyes on him now weakens my knees, if not my resolve. I open cardboard containers of Thousand-Year-Egg and Tofu Rolls, Fried Eggplant Accordions, and Purple Rice. The pleasure of eating this food relaxes me, and my steely determination softens. I am awash in sensual pleasure, savoring spicy sautéed string beans, sucking the meat from crab legs, and brushing my legs with William under the table.

"You've been busy. I hear a buzz about Lofty Ambitions. Don't be surprised if the Art World descends on you to probe your secret to success."

"I have no secrets. The truth is that the kids are phenomenal; they make the place work. Being in their milieu is exciting." I make my awkward segue, "In fact, all I want to do is exactly what I'm doing. I don't want to get married." There it is, out of my mouth.

He takes my hand and gently rubs his thumb on the inside of my wrist, a sure-fire persuasion technique.

"But don't you want to make babies with me?"

"I'm not ready, William. I've got some kids in my life now who need me. And I've got Alexa to shower with maternal love."

His teal blue eyes turn crystalline, and he has that look that he gets when he is overwhelmed by emotion, why I love him. We are so drawn to each other that we abandon our chopsticks and begin touching, gently at first. I move to hug him for the hurt I've caused, to show him that I love him and he holds me achingly close. Then we are wrestling out of our clothes in the living room. Then we are wrestling each other in the bedroom. We are oblivious to the world, unaware of the huge storm brewing outside, and drained by our exertions. We sleep like babies through the night.

I awake in a panic that I'll be late in opening the doors at Lofty. I turn on PIX11 and get the news of the storm, which has dumped two inches of water on the city in just a couple of hours. There is no train service because the water is gushing into subway tunnels like in a disaster movie. The deluge has overwhelmed storm sewers, and the streets are flooded. Finding a cab will be impossible.

"Nobody will be going to the studio today," William says, "and it will be impossible to get around out there. I think we should stay in bed all day." He takes his time in making love to me again, making the case of why we should be together forever.

Just as William predicted, the success of the foundation comes to the attention of a journalist at *The New York Times*. Leticia Drake contacts me. She wants to write a feature article about Lofty Ambitions. I agree to an interview.

On the day Leticia visits, it is particularly hot and humid. The air conditioner in the transom above the front door only adds to the din created by ten kids, three interns, and a guest artist without cooling the air. The ceiling fan stirs the hot air, turning the room into a cauldron of creativity. Napoleon and his crew of five are painting the large mural they've designed on the wall across the street. The heat doesn't dampen their enthusiasm. I watch nervously as JM climbs a ladder to paint his silhouettes in the upper right corner.

"I'm surprised at how this many kids can work side by side without war breaking out," Leticia observes.

"It's a behavior we actively nurture. Everyone wants recognition. Support from peers is critical."

There are paintings, rudimentary clay sculptures, collages, and group work displayed on the walls and tables. I show her some of the completed joint projects. She listens attentively and takes some photos. I point out the supply shelves stocked with fresh canvases, sketch pads, rolls of paper, pots, paints, boxes of charcoal, and pastels.

"We try to provide a variety of materials, so they aren't limited by lack of supplies. The kids are so enthusiastic. They move gleefully from drawing to painting to sculpting, exploring their imaginations." She stops to pull out one of my own paintings stacked in a corner.

"This can't have been made by a child," she says. "This is very sophisticated work. Whose is it?"

I try to see my Bronx landscape through her eyes. Flat, opaque shapes in the blue light of dusk, the cranes sticking up behind them look somewhat like JM's motifs. I wonder if he got the idea from watching me paint this. I'm still not happy with it. The overpass sliding off the edge of the canvas seems awkward to me.

"Oh, that's mine," I say, taking it from her and turning it back to the wall. She pulls out another one, an abstract pastel in progress.

"And this?"

"Mine also, but it's not finished." I take it from her.

"Where can I see more of your work? Do you have a gallery representing you?"

"No, I don't. I haven't shown my work."

"But surely these pieces," she flips through the paintings in my office, "are not one-offs. Where do you keep your treasure trove?"

"I work mostly at my studio in Connecticut." I don't want this to be about me, so I show her some of JM's work. "He's got real talent and a passion for his art. I hope we can help nurture his gift so he can realize his potential – that is the mission of Lofty Ambitions."

CHAPTER THIRTY-SIX

Fall makes me nostalgic for my home on the Massawippi River. There is something about the moving river that is especially thrilling at this time of year as it carries the detritus of fallen branches and miscellany from upstream. The backyard will be carpeted in fallen leaves of red, yellow, orange, and brown. Trudging through them, they make that rustling sound that always elevates my mood.

Lofty can do without me for a while, and it seems William can do without me as well. With our disparate schedules, we've hardly seen each other over the last few weeks. I'm going home for a bit. There are things I need to do.

Sondra Whitehead Cameron has invited me to meet her, so I book a flight to Montreal. Arriving there, in my new persona, I rent a car and take a room at the Ritz for the night, remembering Jack Webb, wondering if I'll bump into him again.

The next morning, I cross the street to the Musée des Beaux Arts, where they are showing a Dianne Arbus collection. Over a hundred of her striking black and white photographs are on exhibit. Studying the eerie portraits, I begin to understand how she revolutionized portraiture. The oddity of her subjects juxtaposed in conventional settings is so jolting that you just can't look away. New York City is rich fodder for people-watching, and Arbus availed herself of the assorted faces she saw in public parks, seedy hotels, and even the morgue. They reveal the exotic buried in the familiar and enlarge our understanding of ourselves. Although I could look at these striking images forever, I tear myself away so as not to be late for my appointment with Alexander's grandmother.

I drive up The Boulevard to find Fordham Circle, a little pocket of imposing estates in Westmount. The Cameron residence is hidden behind a dense grove of conifers. A little early for our two o'clock meeting, I sit parked in the circular driveway in my rented BMW, trying to prepare myself for meeting Sondra. For Alexander's sake, I want to hear more about Gabrielle's origins, and I really want to know if Sondra had any personal connection with my father.

The house is impeccably furnished and immaculate, but the air in it is stale, a Miss Haversham-like atmosphere. Sondra herself looks fresh in a pale pink silk blouse with a sash tied in a bow, a soft grey cardigan, and a tweed A-line skirt. Her faded blonde hair, highlighted with silver strands, is parted on one side and coiffed in a vintage pageboy style. She greets me warmly with what seems to be an underused smile.

"Please, sit," she says, indicating the chintz sofa opposite the wingback chair that she takes. She strikes the same pose as she had for Pete's photo, her still-shapely legs crossed at the ankle. The practiced lady-like posture is reminiscent of a Dianne Arbus subject. Framed by the drapery of the bay window behind her, she is the perfect portrait of a lady. Looking deeper into her eyes, I can see the melancholy there.

"So, you are Gregory's daughter. I can hardly believe that he grew up to have a family of his own." I wonder why this seems incredible to her, and I can't wait to hear more.

As if in audience with a royal, I imagine how different this meeting is from one I might have with my own demented grandmother. The class disparities are stark. Where do I fit in?

Our conversation meanders from her brief happy time with Stuart to her subsequent loveless marriage. She relates the heart-rending sorrow of being forced to relinquish her beautiful baby girl. She never had any children after that. She wants to hear all about Gabrielle and Alexander.

"I didn't get to meet Gabrielle, but I understand she was a woman of great style and passion. Alexander adored her. Do you recall what became of her and my dad after their fathers dropped out of their lives?"

"I'm afraid not. When my parents discovered I was secretly meeting Stuie and Gabrielle, they sent me off to the Sorbonne to finish my education. I completely lost touch with them, but I don't imagine Stuie's girlfriend at the time was able to care for Gabrielle on her own. She was probably placed in foster care, and I imagine Gregory was too."

"Pete is still searching through Quebec's Child Welfare Agency; apparently, their document filing system is not the most organized. So that's all you know about them?"

"Years later, when I came back to Canada, I used to go wandering through the streets of Saint-Henri, and I did catch a glimpse of a young boy who looked like Gregory but never saw Gabrielle. I learned later, from your detective, that they had been living with their grandparents there. Had I persisted in my walks around that neighborhood, I might have caught a glimpse of her." Her placid face begins to crumple, her eyelids drooping, the rarely used smile reverts to deep lines around her mouth, and the melancholy filters through her eyes.

The woman who had opened the door for me comes to inquire if we would like anything, and Sondra asks,

"Would you prefer coffee or tea?"

"Tea, please," and almost immediately, as if both options were already prepared, the woman returns with a tray laden with gold-rimmed Evesham porcelain ware. I cringe at the memory of my paltry offering on Alexander's first visit.

"Please tell me about Gabrielle, about her marriage and her son."

"Sadly, I only got to know Alexander a few years ago when we discovered that we are related. By then both his parents had passed away." Carrying on the tradition of secrecy in our family, I don't mention suicide or the incestuous relationship that created Alexander. She doesn't need to know that her daughter deliberately ended her own life, and she is oblivious of the relationship between Dad and Gabrielle. "You would have been very proud of your grandson; he was a remarkable man, taken from us too soon."

After relating what I know about the Montgomery's and telling her about Alexander's accomplishments, I venture to ask if she had actually known my dad.

"I used to see him with Eddie all the time when he was just a little boy. When I first met him, his mother had already vanished. Eddie didn't know what to do with him, so he just dragged him along everywhere he went. He even took him to the taverns where he and Stuie used to go drinking. I remember telling him, *"Eddie, this child needs a bath,"* or pointing out that *"Greggy is hungry."* Poor little boy, he looked like he had the weight of the world on him, never smiled, never played, just clung to his father. I can't imagine what it did to him when Eddie was killed. He was only three or four years old."

My heart breaks again for the life my father had. My regrets for not being a better daughter mingle with retroactive respect and admiration for the man he became. I wonder if I'm anything like him.

With promises to stay in touch, I say goodbye, not knowing that this was to be the only time I see her.

֍֍֍֍

The house on Massawippi looks haunted. When I step into the vestibule, the air is as stale as it was in Sondra's imposing house. Even though it's quite chilly, I open the windows and check to see if the furnace is working. It's not.

When I knock on the Richardsons' door, they are happy to see me, gushing about how I've grown up and how successful I've become. I guess they've talked to Sage. Mr. Richardson is happy to come over and show me how to turn the furnace on. There is a washer and dryer beside the furnace, a workbench with tools that Dad puttered with, and one entire wall is covered in shelving cluttered with pictures, paintings, and other paraphernalia related to my art. I'll have to purge most of what's here.

Once the house is aired out and the heat is on, I begin to be more comfortable in the tiny bungalow. It feels like home again; all that's missing is Dad.

Surveying the place, I make a list of all that needs doing. By the time I sit in front of the fire in the living room with a hot cup of tea, the list is long enough that I realize nothing short of a full renovation will do. Ideas abound in my brain. I will turn this into my holiday cottage. The entire back of the house will be glass overlooking the river. There will be a multi-level deck along the full length of the building, bringing the river even closer. The kitchen and both bedrooms will have patio doors opening onto it. I'm excited to get started interviewing contractors.

It's almost three years since Dad died, and I haven't ventured to the cemetery once. Weeds abound, the invasive Creeping Jenny has established itself on my mother's gravestone, obliterating the inscription, and fallen leaves hide Dad's grave because I have yet to set a headstone for it. I don't want closure; I want him not to be dead, but my more responsible adult self resolves to get it done.

֍֍֍֍

While I'm away, Emily keeps me posted on what's going on at the studio.

"The kids ask about you. They want to know when you're coming back. William has come with a supply of clay and is conducting a workshop; he's waiting for you to come back too. JM hasn't been in since you left." This worries me, and I feel guilty for not being there for him. Calling his place is useless because nobody answers the phone.

Speaking to William from a distance makes me realize just how distant we are from each other. His exclusive world of influential people, art critics, and wannabes has also receded since I began my work at the foundation. I feel liberated. The only gift of William that I miss is his extraordinary talent for making love.

֍֍֍֍

On my first night back in New York, I go straight to William's studio. The place is lit up with candles everywhere, and the somber sounds of Beethoven's Moonlight Sonata build slowly to a crescendo and then taper to a slow discordant adagio. William has set a serious mood, and as he approaches me, I begin to tremble. He drops to his knees and buries his head in my crotch, his hot breath igniting me at my core.

"I've missed you, Manon. I want you close to me."

My knees weaken, and I sink to the ground with him. He takes something from his pocket – a wide stainless-steel ring embedded with three glistening baguette diamonds.

"I made this for you. Will you marry me?"

He puts it on my finger, and I instantly feel like a banded pigeon waiting to be dispatched. I emit some painful warbling sound, a disturbing combination of fear and desire. The allegro part of the sonata mimics my heartbeat and the urgent throbbing in my belly. As the piano builds to Beethoven's dramatic crescendo, William's capable hands bring me to climax just as the fingers tickling the piano keys create a tremolo. I want this, but I know William's vision of marriage and family is very far from what I picture. Finally, before I've even recovered from the orgasm, I answer,

"I can't."

CHAPTER THIRTY-SEVEN

December in New York brings the wet snow that dampens everything. It's different than the first snow I remember in Montreal that floats down in pretty flakes. Christmas business is in full swing with bright decorations and twinkly lights everywhere. Music filtering from all the stores entices people to come in and buy. The season's aggressive cheerfulness always makes me melancholy; the holiday emphasizes the loneliness of those without loved ones to celebrate with and takes me back to the many lackluster Christmases of my childhood, alone with Dad.

Now that JM's father is involuntarily confined at Bellevue Psychiatric Hospital, JM is spending most of his time with me. He avoids the hospital and his apartment for fear that Child Services will grab him and put him into foster care. He's living like a fugitive; his only refuge is the studio. His artwork is darker than usual; he uses black almost exclusively and makes his strokes sharp and angular. He breaks my heart. On one particularly frigid night, I take him home with me and put him up in my old room at the Colosseum. When I check on him later, he is curled up, head resting on his clasped hands, his face angelic in sleep.

After that, sleeping over becomes a habit. The change is good for him. He seems less wary than usual until his brother Blaze shows up at Lofty one day, looking for him. JM reluctantly goes home with him. I don't see him for a few days and grow sick with worry. When he comes back, he is so distraught about having to stay with his brother that I resolve to do something about protecting him. I call Gerry Abrams to find out how I could legally assume care for the boy.

"That's a huge commitment. Are you sure you want to take that on?"

"I'm already committed. He needs me, and I need to know he is safe. I can't work, worrying about him all the time. I need to be able to take care of him."

"We could apply for guardianship through the courts. Given what you've told me about his circumstances, I believe we can make a pretty good case."

We have become really close, JM and I. Our moods coincide, and we are there for each other when we get frustrated about our work. He has tremendous insight for a young boy. I make sure he is well nourished and has a somewhat regular schedule, which means no missing school. Parenting him comes naturally because I have come to love him. I draw on some of the methods Dad used to reign me in and have a new appreciation of just how difficult it must have been for him to raise me by himself.

One day, I take JM along to Motherwell's for a preview of paintings by Shoshana Popova, the new darling of William's crowd. Bored by her large pastel florals, JM begins to observe the people instead. At twelve, he's my height already, so we are face to face when he remarks, as guilelessly as only a child can, that William loves Shoshana.

Since I rejected William's proposal, I've been waiting for the guillotine to drop and sever our relationship at any moment. So far, he's carrying on as if I had not refused him. Still, my persistent insecurity about his fidelity is confirmed by JM's observation. Feeling suddenly queasy, I have to get out of the place.

"Are you ready to leave?" I ask.

JM takes my hand and gives it a comforting little squeeze.

The last few weeks of 2007 blur by in a bustle of activity. Lofty is busy with greeting card projects and street decorations around the studio. Gerry has managed to get a court date before the holidays, and JM is particularly anxious. He needs me more than ever. He understands that his future depends upon the whim of a judge. When I retreat to Elderberry, I take him with me, and his eyes are wide, taking in the Martha Stewart environment. Excitement is pitched, with Mrs. O planning a very special holiday for Alexa's first Christmas and Sage's arrival. A huge fir tree is already in the Great Room waiting to be decorated.

The holiday at Elderberry this year is both solemn and joyous. Alexander is missed, and Alexa is doted upon. At nine months old, she is irresistible. We try to make JM feel at ease, enlisting him in the business of tree decorating, which he takes very seriously. He paints pine cones in silver, gold, and of course, black, which has become his signature color. He picks the flutes, kazoos, and mittens from the box of decorations and hangs them, stepping back to see their effect, adjusting, adding, and taking away. Once the pine cones have dried, he hangs them carefully around the upper part of the tree, like a crown, returning them to their origins. He is patient with Alexa when she grabs them and tries to eat them. He pries them from her pudgy little fist and says patiently, "Not in the mouth." He seems more comfortable with her than with the rest of us and takes on a parenting role naturally. His eyes are always glazed with wetness as if tears are imminent. He never talks about his sisters, but I know he's thinking of them.

When I take him out to the barn, JM shivers; he is a little afraid of the horses.

"Do you want to go riding with me?"

"Nuh-uh. The only horses I know are the nags that pull the buggies with tourists around Central Park. They're a lot smaller, and nobody rides them."

"But Banjo is really gentle; we could both get on him and he'll take it nice and easy."

"No thanks."

Just then, Bobby and Macy run into the barn, chasing each other. They see JM and are curious. A new boy! They sniff and lick him in welcome. Now I see JM's expression soften, and a smile erupts on his usually serious face.

CHAPTER THIRTY-EIGHT

The first week of January brings unseasonably warm temperatures. I ride out in the fog of dawn, and I can see Banjo's breath like little clouds trapped by the moist air as he trots. My cheeks feel cold, but the rest of me is sweaty under my turtleneck and down vest. I am still incredulous that I am here atop this beast that has become my friend, here in this setting that now belongs to me. The life I had with Dad and even the life I had with Alexander is just a memory, and a new life has begun.

Now that I have so much to lose, I worry all the time about what new tragedy awaits me. Irrationally, I worry about Mrs. O's health, about Alexa having some tragic accident, and about JM's future. I don't want to lose any more people in my life. And then I think about the guillotine hovering above my relationship with William. I speed to a gallop, and endorphins course through me, clearing my head – I have a lot to be grateful for and a lot of work to do.

The patio doors are clouded with condensation, so when I enter, I'm surprised to see Julian at the trestle table drinking coffee and chatting with Mrs. O. and Sage.

"Where's JM?"

"He's at Hedley's cottage playing with Alexa," says Mrs. O.

Julian gets up when he sees me and seems as invigorated as I am from my ride.

"Manon, you know The New Museum, down in the Bowery?"

"I know of it, but I've never been."

"Their raison d'être is to be a catalyst for dialogue between the artist and the public. On December first, they opened their new building dedicated to mounting group shows organized around important social and political issues, but they also focus on presenting exhibitions of emerging artists."

It sounds like Julian is building to some climax, but with his abundantly detailed style of speaking, so much like Alexander's, it takes him a while to get to the point.

"Is there something I should see there?"

"Their inaugural show, *Unmonumental,* is an international group show. You should see some of the contemporary art by 'outsider artists' being shown. Beyond Surrealism, Art Brut, as created by these talented activists, gives us a glimpse into some serious European issues. It closes in February."

"Have you seen it?"

"I was there for the opening. One of my friends, Laura Hauptman, is a Senior Curator there. I talked to her about your work."

So this is what he's getting at. He's been so keen to get my work out to the public.

"Their fourth-floor gallery will be available in the spring. It's one of their smallest galleries but has ample room for showing up to forty paintings. The space is graced with a southern skylight that allows natural light to wash through it during the day."

"And...?"

"Laura has agreed to look at your work. They are very interested in presenting works by previously unknown artists. If she likes what she sees, which she will, she will offer you the space to exhibit it. It's a unique opportunity. I know we can put together a good selection of your work by that time." Julian's eyes shine with excitement. "Unlike most, it's a non-collecting museum and different from commercial galleries in that they are only interested in the aesthetic value of the art presented and the trajectory of previously unknown artists. I thought that might please you. I think it's the perfect venue for your inaugural showing. What do you think?"

What I think is that I must meet my destiny and put myself out in the world. I don't want to end up like Lee Krasner, waiting throughout her career to be celebrated, only to die just before her show at MoMa opened. After all, if this is my life's purpose, my identity as an artist should be tested by the public at large, and if validated, it would prove to Dad that I am not merely dabbling in paint. Julian is the only one I would trust to handle my debut.

"Okay."

Julian is so surprised and delighted that he spontaneously hugs me and then pulls back, actually blushing.

"That's great! We'll start by photographing the pieces you have here and at Lofty. Rebecca Reinhold, the photographer, is a friend of mine; I'll ask her to do a shoot. I also want to include some of your stupendous pieces that I saw in Montreal, and I'm sure there are other works I have yet to see, which we can include to create a true retrospective of your career. Let's go to Lennoxville to get them."

Since I need to check the progress of the renovations on the Massawippi house anyway, we decided to drive Sage back at the end of the week.

On the six-hour drive, I am in a cocoon of love and support in my Lexus. My confidence bolstered by my two champions; I feel very competent even driving the treacherous winter roads. I watch for black ice and try not to think of Dad's car crash. We review the delicious holiday dinners and the delightful ambiance of our Elderberry family. We reminisce about Alexander, and when Sage falls asleep in the back seat, Julian and I discuss plans for opening my work to the world.

None of my pieces are titled or dated, and Julian encourages me to think about each one so that we can properly label them. I try to describe my process, but it is with great difficulty that I can verbalize them at all. If it weren't Julian I was talking to, I wouldn't know where to begin. He enables me with his encouragement but is always reverent and sensitive to my emotions. When I tell him how I felt while painting Dad's portrait, he understands. He also lost his dad a few years ago and when he saw the finished portrait, he admits he was moved to tears. When I reveal my remorse for not having been a better daughter, he reaches over and squeezes my arm as I drive, a sweet gesture that touches my soul and somehow changes the dynamic between us.

When we arrive at my little bungalow, it's late and it is cold inside. I'm eager to see the new glass rear of the house. The change is dramatic. Even though it's dark and there is no deck yet, I feel the river close to me. Now that I know how to turn the furnace on, I get it going while Julian starts a fire and peruses the books and records, still as they were when Dad was alive. He sleeps in Dad's room, and I take to my juvenile bed, exhausted from the long drive.

In the morning, I note that even though the rear façade is on the west side, the glass lets in so much light that the house is no longer dingy. The fir trees near the house and the poplars along the river bank are encrusted in glittery ice; a silvery brush of frozen snow delineates bare branches. I find my old Sorels, don my down parka, and go out to inspect my old haunts. When I get back in, I find Julian has made tea and is sifting through piles of my watercolors and charcoal sketches. He wants to curate a coherent progression of my work.

"You haven't dated any of these. Do you think you can remember roughly when they were done?"

"I only remember going through phases, when I would work on one thing exclusively, interminably, until I got it right or left it frustrated." My childish diagrams of leaf structures delight him. "I did these when I was quite young, maybe eight or nine."

"What about these sketchbooks filled with drawings of Audubon's birds?"

"The birds were an ongoing exercise from the time I was about twelve."

"And these watercolor paintings of the seasonal flora? They're quite sophisticated."

"When I was in grade ten, I had an art teacher who painted watercolors, and she encouraged me to try the medium. That spring, I went out to draw every day, fascinated by the changes happening in my own backyard. I must have been around fifteen."

Julian is jotting notes on his Blackberry and taking photos with his digital camera.

He flips through canvases, admiring an unfinished painting of a ballerina painted in the impressionist style of Renoir, which I had abandoned because I thought it pretentious.

"I went through a phase of figure drawing when Dad brought home some full-length ballet videos. I wasn't very good at it."

"On the contrary, they demonstrate a real progression in your technique."

He even appreciates the childish Norman Rockwell-style paintings of happy families that I fantasized about when I was a kid.

"Oh, those are awful; I was just a kid wishing I had a family like these. I copied them from some old 'Dick and Jane' books from the library." He remarks on how expertly I created the pallets for the rosy-cheeked children and the healthy glow of the adults. We clash about what can and cannot be included. I put my foot down when it comes to these sentimental depictions of other people's lives that reveal my pathetic longing.

We have to be back by the seventh, so we load up the car with a dozen or so canvases, a couple of collages on Masonite boards, a portfolio full of drawings, and a stack of sketchbooks. We pack up some of the larger Rothco-esque paintings and have them shipped. I still want to cull this collection, especially the experiments in self-portraiture, the ugly renditions of my miserable teenage self.

We head back to Connecticut and continue battling about what is presentable and what is absolutely not.

"Manon, we've agreed that if we're doing this, I must have the final word. You'll make yourself crazy with the details of what, where, and how to mount your own work."

"Okay, but don't include my horrible 'blue' period."

"Just let me handle it."

I have left JM with Mrs. O, and when he sees us turn into the driveway, he runs out to greet me without the coat that Mrs. O is trying to thrust at him.

CHAPTER THIRTY-NINE

One of the first things I do when we get back is go to William's loft. I find him hard at work on the floor of the living room tapping numbers into a calculator. There are blueprint-size sheets of paper strewn around the large living room, a yardstick, and a huge protractor. He has won a city competition to create a sculpture to be installed in Central Park. The ambitious piece is a life-size bronze swing set with three swings frozen in motion: two kids swinging, one seat unoccupied, which some real child will sit on, no doubt just for fun, and one boy standing, pushing a toddler from behind.

"These 'kids' look less cherubic than your previous ones. Are they maturing?"

"They're growing old and I'm growing tired of them. I've created twenty-two since I first had the inspiration when my nephew was born, and I'm sick of making them. This is my final 'kids' sculpture. I want to make flesh and blood children. I want to make them with you, Manon."

He yanks my arm and pulls me down right on top of him on the floor. His mouth immediately finds mine, preventing me from objecting and turning our emotional battle physical. It's a winning tactic for him because inevitably, I lose myself to sensation and cannot muster a rebuttal. William manipulates me like a rubber doll; my arms and legs do his bidding, and I'm rewarded with multiple orgasms. Then, when I am lying in a limp heap on the carpet, he persists, "I know you want it too; let's not wait too long."

I try to envision the babies we would make; how beautiful they would be if they looked like him. But I just can't see myself in the role that Stephanie is playing. Alexa is a treasure, but she is a full-time commitment, and Stephanie is ten years my senior. Maybe in ten years, I'll be ready.

To change the subject, I tell him my news about The New Museum. Instead of being happy for me for this opportunity, he gets in a snit.

"You know you'll never sell anything from there. You should let Marty handle you if you want to exhibit."

"My goal isn't to sell anything; I don't want to be a pawn in the game of art sales. I only want some feedback from the general public."

"Well then, why didn't you let me hang your work at Motherwell's?"

"Because the people at Motherwell's are not the general public. I still regret letting you install the statue of me there and cringe whenever I see anyone scrutinize it. That crowd would look at my work and see it as naked as your clay version of me."

"Suit yourself, but what does Julian, the accountant, know about mounting an art show?" I feel like I have been slapped, but more than anything, I feel angry at his derision of Julian. Strangely, I want to defend him and feel even more committed to him putting my work out there.

"Julian is a sophisticated and discerning art collector. He has many contacts in the art world; he understands my inhibitions and is sensitive to my concerns. He will curate the exhibit with care."

I feel guilty for the pleasure I've taken from his lovemaking, and when he tries to touch me again, I turn away and leave the loft.

Preparations for my show are in full swing, but Julian has kept me at arm's length, only sharing scraps of the many details he's been tending to curating, photographing, framing, printing posters and postcards, compiling an invitation list for opening night. He's even writing a bio to include in the catalog, for which, I learned, he has consulted with Sage. I am grateful not to have to go through the anxiety of making all these decisions.

One rainy April day, he calls and asks if I could meet him at his place after work.

Julian lives in a brownstone in Brooklyn Heights. When I enter the front hall, I am immediately blown away by a huge David Hockney that overpowers the space with vibrant colors. He introduces his collection as if I were meeting his children. He has two of Cy Twombly's green paintings hung on one wall of the living room. Looking at them, I feel the coolness of a walk in the woods, and when I turn to the adjacent wall, I am surprised by one of Jasper Johns' iconic flag paintings. Seeing the texture of the hand-drawn stars and stripes in thick, waxy encaustic gives me a greater appreciation than merely looking at the flat reproductions I've seen. The sunroom at the back has a small wood wall sculpture.

"That's a rare work of Ellsworth Kelly's. It's called 'Concorde Relief I.' I have more of his work upstairs; come, I'll show you."

He takes me to the third floor, which is his bedroom. The large white wall opposite his bed has three minimalist, irregularly-shaped canvases: Red Panel, Dark Green Panel, and Dark Blue

Panel. They have a powerful effect on me, as if they are pushing against me, and I have to tauten my body to stay upright. When I turn around to look at the similarly minimalist space, the shapes remain burned on my retina. There is an enormous bed covered in a plain bedspread the same color as a Red Panel. There's not much else, no dressers or chairs, just a sleek teak night table and a floating teak shelf above his bed with neatly stacked ART news magazines, their spines creating a colorful op-art effect. The clean lines make for a surprisingly soothing environment, allowing the art to dominate. I imagine what it might be like to awake here and see the canvases lit by a rectangular shaft of light from the skylight.

When we go back down to his study, I notice beside shelves laden with legal textbooks are stacks of art catalogs. There's a series of black and white photographs of rugged landscapes and luminous skies, hung gallery style on one wall. Given his sophisticated collection, it's possible they might be Ansel Adams originals.

There is a card table set up with a mock-up of the fourth-floor gallery, complete with miniature photographs of my work hung on the perimeter walls and my large canvas isolated on one of the temporary walls erected in the middle of the space. There is a tiny glass display case with a reproduction of one of my sketchbooks opened to my studies of ballet dancers. There are even tiny people standing in front of the pictures. Confronted by the body of my work in miniature, I feel like I've stepped into an Alice-in-Wonderland version of my life neatly encapsulated in this tiny world. The exhibit is set up chronologically, and as I 'walk' through the space, the emotions I dealt with when making these works flood over me in waves: naiveté, insecurity, frustration, anger, pride, rebellion, remorse, sorrow. I begin to shake and feel a little lightheaded. Julian puts his arm around me.

"Are you okay? You look a little pale. Have you eaten today?"

"How did you do this?"

"One of Nicole's friends is an architecture student at Columbia; she did the scale models. If it looks good to you, then we really have to get down to naming the pieces so we can print up the labels."

"I can't believe you did all this work!"

Julian takes my arm and leads me from the room. In the hallway, there are more framed photographs. I barely recognize Nicole in a glamour shot, and there are other portraits, presumably of his family. There is one of a striking woman with prematurely white hair and piercing eyes that is signed and inscribed 'To Julian with love, Rebecca.' It occurs to me then that Julian has a lot of female friends.

"Come, I have some dinner for us, and we can discuss your large canvas, which will be the feature piece in the show. You have to call it something."

The large canvas that has been my daily practice forever, with intersecting 'roads' and 'highways' of color that freed me of boundaries and led me to the realization that marriage was not for me, is now rigid with layers of paint, each layer a new revelation hidden beneath the next.

"Let's call it Crossroads."

CHAPTER FORTY

While Julian is curating my existing work, I'm busy working with a new style and subject. When I saw William's recent sketches of the kids he's making for 'The Swing Set,' I noticed how their features have changed. An idea is unfurling in my imagination, at first murky and elusive, then crystallized, it bulldozes everything else out of the way – I want to make children too.

My afternoons at Lofty give me a unique opportunity to observe the faces and postures of the kids. I've begun studying and sketching them and am ready to start painting a few who are willing to sit still for me.

Of necessity, I must work quickly on my slippery subjects and thus have hit upon a new combination of representation and abstraction. Rapid brushstrokes, outlining limbs and torsos, black for detailing their features, and cubist blocks of color for their clothes. Because I have come to know these kids, my representations of them are emotionally intense. Frowns and worry lines are incongruous on young faces, self-defensive gestures, and sad eyes, even on smiling faces. I can relate to these themes of loss, anxiety, vulnerability, and fear, and I am surprised at how effortlessly I can render them.

One day, Isabella's mother comes to fetch her, with two of Isabella's tiny siblings in tow and a babe in arms. I am surprised at how young Carmen is to have a thirteen-year-old and struck by how old she looks. I'm captivated by the different shades of her children's skin, olive, caramel, and bisque. When I invite her in to pose with them, she hesitates by the door, searching the room. It's only when she sees Isabella's look, silently commanding her, that she agrees to sit. They settle into a pose, and when one of the toddlers starts fidgeting, Isabella smacks her little sister and tells her to sit still. The painting that results from this sitting is a variation on the Madonna and child pictures that have settled in my subconscious since I was just a child myself. I used to pore over the religious paintings of the Renaissance, both fascinated and horrified.

When Julian sees these latest works on a visit to Lofty, he gets very agitated, and I fear he thinks they are awful. They are certainly a departure from what I've done thus far.

"I had a call from Laura Hauptman," he says as he picks up a stray piece of paper and replaces it on a shelf. "She has to push your show to the Fall because they have a unique opportunity to mount an exhibit by an emerging artist from Romania before her work goes on tour this summer. But Laura has committed to reserving the fourth-floor gallery for you in September. I hope you're not disappointed."

This news is actually a relief. Now, I don't have to think about how my work will be received. I'll have the whole summer free of the fear that I'll be exposed as a fraud.

"I'm actually glad of this extension to refine our show, and you are so prolific, I can't keep up with you. We are going to have to erect more temporary walls to display these. I'll have to re-organize the layout. We'll need more time. How many have you done?"

"I have four that are finished and several in the works."

Julian's signature contemplative stance has his left hand on his waist, fingers at the back, and his right hand cupping his chin as he considers these new paintings.

"These are…they're extraordinary. You've moved to another level." And then, as if thinking out loud, he decides that the portrait of me and JM will be the centerpiece for this phase of my work. It's an emotional piece in which I've used a pallet of burnt umber, yellow ochre, and rich mahogany. Our shoulders are level as we sit on the bench, and I have my arm around him protectively, his head angled in towards me with the spongy mass of his curly hair pressed against my cheek, my eyes looking sideways focused on him, hinting at the concept of motherhood.

❁❁❁❁

Lofty has become a lifeline for some of the regulars who come to create. With the summer holidays approaching, I have to plan for keeping the place open all day so the kids will have a place to go to stay out of trouble. My worry for JM extends to some of the other kids on the edge. I need to step up the support they get by hiring more staff and maybe even opening a second location.

My work days stretch into the evenings, even though I'm trying to keep some semblance of a normal schedule for JM. At the end of the day, we go home to Elderberry for the respite that the country provides. I work in my studio all night while JM happily plays with Alexa and the dogs. He is thriving while I am depleting my energies. Mrs. O brings me tea and biscuits and expresses her concern.

"Manon, you look positively haggard. You need to slow down. Get Julian to handle some of the day-to-day operations, or have him hire people to hand it off to."

What I need is some of William's attention, but he is preoccupied with his 'playground' and likely with Shoshana as well. I have also been occupied with my responsibilities to JM and Lofty, and I'm still engrossed in my current obsession with painting children. I'm working on a portrait of Alexa sitting at the end of a path of flattened dandelions that have turned the meadow yellow. Her chubby face is serious as she examines one of them that has turned to fluff. I wonder if the lawn on Massawippi is similarly covered. The third anniversary of Dad's death is approaching, and I feel him pulling me back to Lennoxville.

Since we have hired Lillian Hernandez, one of the teachers at PS 136 for the summer, and with JM happily ensconced at Elderberry, I take off to Lennoxville for a change of pace and space.

CHAPTER FORTY-ONE

The three-level deck is ready but for the staining. It extends far beyond the original porch, accommodating the maple tree in front of the kitchen window by building around it. The trunk and crown serve as an umbrella, providing shade at the west end of the deck. The river has swollen and slowed from its early rapid spring flow, and the slip of sand has disappeared. I can sit on the bottom tier of the deck and almost reach the water with my outstretched legs. The cattails that I used to draw when I was a kid, making them look like hot dogs on spikes, have grown as high as ten feet, and I can smell the scent of woodland phlox from the opposite bank. I am home, and I imagine Dad is just at the library.

I return to Elmwood Cemetery and see that the headstones I've commissioned for both graves stand erect, their black marble glistening ostentatiously among the old moss-covered stone monuments. I place flowers at the base of each of them, feeling Dad's hefty presence hunching at my back. On the other hand, my mother's grave just leaves me empty and a little disoriented at the lopsidedness of our family.

I make my pilgrimage to the Musée de Sherbrooke, where the main floor is devoted to an exhibit of Tony Urquhart's work.

My first impression when I entered the gallery was that this couldn't possibly be the work of just one artist. The eclectic style of paintings and objects, ranging from abstract expressionist to representational, elusive renderings of landscapes, cages, and graves. The one constant in all of them is the use of color. Works on canvas and board, rondos, vertical oblongs, and various-sized rectangular shapes make up a stunning spectacle.

Further into the gallery, there are small boxes poised on pedestals with landscapes painted on all sides. In order to get the whole picture of these three-dimensional paintings, you have to move around and see them from every perspective. One of them is an abstract sea theme with four doors cut into it. When I look inside, the interior has rocks and painted waves, transporting me to my own little seaside.

These boxes fire my imagination, and when I get home, I immediately begin to make something. With Dad's tools and scraps of material left over from the deck construction, I try my hand at sawing, screwing, gluing, and painting the odd shapes I am able to build. They are grotesque and humorous at the same time. Being a thing-maker is satisfying.

❁❁❁❁

It's quiet at the library for a Saturday. Sage is sitting in her usual armchair reading.

"Look at you," she says, surveying me head to foot. I'm wearing my Katherine Hepburn pants, just for her, and a black silk camisole. "You have grown into a beautiful woman." She hugs me and then immediately asks, "How's Peg?"

"Mrs. O is good. She's her usual steady self except now, being in charge of JM, she has become more of a mother hen than ever."

I run my fingers over the spot on the library table that I had carved into when I was a young rebel. The wear and polishing over the years have improved my attempt at an etched flower. Sage prattles on about whatever news there is in Lennoxville. "Remember when your dad was advocating for a new wing for the library? Well, it finally got approved. There will be a two-story addition at the back with rooms for children's programs and book club meetings and a large archives area on the second floor. This is all Gregory's doing; I wish he could know that his vision is being actualized." I remember how I resented all the time he devoted to that initiative, and now I feel guilty again. "Oh, and I thought you might be interested to know that Mary Allidon is in town."

I haven't thought about Mary since Dad died, and yet I feel a little twinge at the idea that I may run into her. How would she judge me now? Would she be impressed with my work? She was the one person who thought I would become something. Should I call her?

As it turns out I do bump into her on Queen Street. She doesn't look like the Mary who was always perfectly put together, with every hair in place and her posture rigid. This Mary looks comfortable in her skin. Her haircut is designed to look windswept, and the extra pounds she's put on make her look voluptuous. This time, we greet each other with shy hellos. After an awkward moment of silence, Mary says,

"Do you have time for a coffee?"

My heart thumps with a brief resurgence of the old love I felt for her.

"Sure."

What kind of mechanism has eradicated her from my life these intervening years? When she relates all the things she knows of my life – about Alexander, my move to live with him in New York, and about my art practice – I realize I know nothing of hers. All I know is that she married some guy and moved to Arizona. There is a lot of catching up to do.

We've talked for over an hour. Mary is late for an appointment, and so we part with sincere promises to keep in touch.

Coming to Lennoxville has proved to be grounding. There is 'love' here. How did I miss that when I was living here?

֍֍֍֍

As I'm settling down with a cup of tea in the big wicker chair, I get a call from Julian. I am surprised to realize that I've missed him these couple of weeks. We have put our heads together so often lately, sometimes literally, bent over documents or drawings while working on Lofty business or my imminent opening at The New Museum.

"Manon, I need to see you. Is it alright if I come to Lennoxville?"

Julian arrives by hired limo from Montreal the very next day. He's dressed casually, which for him means a white polo and pressed jeans. He's let his hair grow out from its usual close cropping, and it now looks like a lighter, shorter version of JM's hair. He looks softer, more relaxed, and when our eyes meet his smile is wide and open. I'm glad to see him.

After a spaghetti dinner that I made from scratch, we continue our unabating conversations in the living room. While I settle into my corner on the couch, Julian peruses Dad's record collection, picks an album, and, as a melodic stringy intro begins, he takes a seat beside me, close enough that we are touching. He takes my hand as Nat King Cole begins to drawl the seductive lyrics of *'When I fall in Love'*. This intimacy is new, and I feel myself responding to his touch with a familiar flutter in my belly.

"Manon, I have to confess that you've fascinated me since I first met you, but it's recently since we've become closer," he rubs his thumb on my palm, "that I realize I'm in love with you. I've never been in love before, not really, but now, especially since you've been gone, I recognize my feelings."

Before I have a chance to respond, I feel him cup the back of my head and pull me closer. He leans over and kisses me, his soft, generous lips enveloping mine, his velvety tongue probing my mouth. I let myself be loved, and the physical sensation of his caress is more powerful, somehow than even William's expert dexterity. I feel I am in good hands.

This changes everything.

CHAPTER FORTY-TWO

New York in August is stifling. At Lofty, lethargic kids scribble and squabble without the energy to do any group work. When I get back, I'm chagrined to see the *Creating Monsters* project abandoned under a cabinet, unfinished. They were having such a ball with that joint project, a dice game where you have to draw the number of body parts (eyes, ears, limbs, etc.) that come up from your throw and then switch with someone until all the panels of the piece are covered with monster-like creatures. Either I put in central air or move the kids to the park to work. Instead, I decide to have the storefront windows replaced so that they can be opened awning style to let the breeze blow through. This is a big hit with the kids, and they are energized to begin a new project Emily has devised, busily clipping images out of magazines for a collage.

JM is growing as an artist and in size. He is now taller than me, and his long arms have become precision tools that execute his poignant, socially relevant paintings. He paints primarily in black with spots of primary colors to lead us around the canvas; his hard-edge style, the result of a methodical process, is reminiscent of Joan Miró's paintings. In fact, I have seen him studying Miró's work in the library at Elderberry.

The one he's working on now is more ambitious than anything he's tried before, a large canvas that he can master with his long reach. He's painted a mottled sky the color of concrete and a lumpy ground the color of mud. There are black birds flying, and two little black girls are holding hands, floating in the air, their dresses flapping in the breeze. There are floating rectangles with bars like the rudimentary prehistoric ones discovered in caves in France. His work is mature beyond his years. I am proud of my protégé.

Since I became his guardian in December, JM has turned thirteen, and like a true teenager, he has become very conscious of his appearance. He badly wants to get his hair done in twists. I try but quickly realize that African American hair is not to be messed with by an amateur. JM designs his style, and I take him to *'Flava in Yah Hair,'* a Jamaican barber shop in the Bronx. The washing, detangling, conditioning, and twisting will take a few hours, so I leave him and head down to Chelsea. I need to speak to William.

I am reluctant to just go to his loft unannounced as I normally would, for fear of walking in on him and Shoshana or whoever. I know that William hasn't been waiting around for me while I've been busy and away. His appetites are all too familiar to me, and I feel a little twinge of jealousy for whoever is benefitting from his prowess. I call first.

"William, can I come and see you?" This used to be shorthand for 'I want you,' so I regret my choice of words.

"When did you get back?"

"A couple of days ago."

"Did you want to come now?" I sensed some hesitation, so I abandoned my plan to visit him today.

"No, whenever...whenever you're free. I know you're busy with *The Playground.*"

"No, come by this afternoon, it's fine."

"No, let's have dinner later." This is shorthand for 'not tonight, dear, I have a headache,' backtracking my original signal.

This awkward exchange is already the writing on the wall that we both can read.

To keep my mind off William's busyness, I head over to Marmalade Vintage to see if I can find something interesting to wear for my opening. I can't believe it's really happening in just a couple of weeks. Hannah is at her usual post behind the counter, crunching an apple.

"Hey you, where have you been?"

"Just busy working."

"I've got some new acquisitions in your size. I'm still sorting through them, but have a look on the rack at the back of the store."

My eye immediately catches on a sleeveless Mondrian shift dress. The block panels are divided by graphic black lines, all of which are made of individual pieces of fabric integrated by invisible seams, not printed on. The two upper panels are in ivory and lemon yellow. They are underscored by a horizontal black line above the breast, separating them from the two lower panels, both in ivory, which are divided by a vertical black line. The beautiful simplicity of it appeals to me, and I go to try it on.

"Wow that dress is made for you! It's a tad long, but I wouldn't alter it. Instead, wear some heels to elevate it. Wait..." She rummages behind the counter where she keeps boxes of shoes and brings out a pair of square-toed black pumps with three-inch block heels. "You're lucky to be a designer size."

In the mirror, I see a woman I don't recognize as me. There is a blatant sophistication that this garment confers on me. I'll have to tame my hair into a tight bun to match the effect. I stand tall; the weight of the wool jersey fabric ensures that the dress hangs straight without breaking to distort the simplicity of the lines, even at my hips. The price is staggering, but I no longer have to consider the decadence of making such a purchase. I simply have to have it. Nevertheless, I play the game as expected and offer her half of what she asks.

"Oh, I remember what a hard bargain you drive. But since you were true to your word and have become a repeat customer, I'll let you have it at my cost plus 10%." Relieved at having made a deal, I walk out in my 'new' shoes to make sure they are as comfortable as they look.

When I meet William at the Mermaid Inn on Amsterdam, he is his ebullient self. He kisses me passionately, pulling me close, pressing at the small of my back. He's familiar with all the pressure points to my libido, and he just can't help himself despite the inkling of what's coming.

"William, I have to tell you something." I ease into the conversation, remembering his history of erratic behavior after his breakup with Sarah.

"I feel like oysters tonight!" he deflects with more shorthand.

"William, I'm in love with Julian."

"The accountant?"

"Well, it's hardly his only persona."

William stops short of asking me whether I've slept with him. He knows that his outrage would be rich, given his own 'sleeping' habits.

"You know you're breaking my heart," he says. His turquoise eyes glisten, and I want to pull his head to my chest and comfort him, but we are on opposite sides of the stainless steel table, a plate of freshly shucked oysters between us.

My mixed emotions roil in my belly, and all of a sudden, the quivering porcelain white delicacies make me nauseous. William and I want different things, and though I love him passionately, I can't sustain the turmoil of our relationship. Even with this Adonis in front of me, I find myself craving the steady, unhurried love of Julian.

When I mention my latest 'kids' paintings, his eyes melt in sorrow as if he just now realizes the loss of something. Then, after he fills me in on the progress of his big project, I venture to the subject I've had in mind for some time.

The second anniversary of Alexander's death is looming, and I feel the need to commemorate him to keep his spirit close. I ask William if he would make a small stone memorial. As I talk, I'm sketching what I envision.

"There will be two granite slabs, one to serve as a bench and one to support the monument." I describe a two-dimensional egg shape made of polished onyx with the arc of a fingernail moon cut out at the top left portion, the hole in my heart. The whole thing will only be thirty inches high by two feet wide with a simple inscription: Alexander Montgomery 1977 - 2006. It will nestle among the reeds by the pond at Elderberry, a favorite spot where I can be in the landscape with him. "Would you do it for me?"

"It's a no-brainer; of course, I will."

And with that, William and I part company.

CHAPTER FORTY-THREE

With over a thousand art galleries and more than a hundred museums, art in New York is serious business. On any given day, walking around Chelsea, you will see artists, gallery owners, and hangers-on, all dressed in black, crawling from one exhibit to another, judging. And that's not to mention critics from the *New York Times*, the *New Yorker*, the *Village Voice*, and other publications, experts poised to make or break careers. There are no smiles, lest the pretensions be exposed.

September 18th approaches and my anxiety about the opening has me roaming the trendy art precincts, dropping in at galleries to see work by famous and obscure artists, good and bad – all better than mine. I go to the Whitney to revisit the established American artists of our time, the likes of Edward Hopper, Georgia O'Keeffe, Jacob Lawrence, and Jasper Johns, and despair about my own abilities.

Curiosity overpowering apprehension has me heading down to the Bowery to see The New Museum. It's a seven-story building that looks like a Jenga game with stacks of blocks on top of each other, looking like they are about to topple. How appropriate. The façade is simply a fifteen-foot pane of clear glass stretching the full width of the building. As I enter, the grey concrete sidewalk gives way to the polished grey concrete floors of the entrance hall. The fourth-floor gallery still has the previous exhibit up.

I immediately encounter a giant painting with a nice balance between sweet chaos and something more disturbing. What looks like raspberry juice, or perhaps blood, oozes down the right side of it. The next works deal with what seem to be themes of survival and rebirth. One of the sculptural pieces has shrubbery growing out of the base. There are other items of oddly juxtaposed objects which have an organic feel to them. The works exhibited convey deep concepts relevant to our lived experience. I am dismayed as I try to think of what my work has to say – nothing profound, I fear.

When I get home and search for my abysmal Rothco studies, I realize they must be out for framing, and I'm frantic. I call Julian.

"I can't do it, Julian. I just can't put myself out there naked in the road, waiting to be run over."

"Please trust me, Manon. The show is looking great. We've already secured your 'Crossroads' onto a large wall right in the center of the exhibit. It radiates energy. The other pieces are being hung. The fourth floor looks like someone has opened a treasure trove of previously unknown work. Your talent and your versatility will blow people away."

"Please don't hang the Rothco studies; I want to destroy them."

Julian is my champion, but I worry that he is biased. I shudder at the thought of people scrutinizing my childish early work and of exposing my amateurish meanderings through techniques and subjects. I fear the show is a sloppy mish-mash of styles.

The trepidation of what's to come has me searching for razor blades, something I haven't done in years. It's only JM that keeps me from harming myself. The thought of disappointing him is devastating; he looks up to me and is beyond excited about the opening. He is inspired and is working fast and furiously on his own art. I think he should be the one exhibited. I think he is a genius.

꩜꩜꩜꩜

On the day of the opening, Julian arrives at the Colosseum in a limo to take JM and me down to the Bowery. My scalp tingles from the pull of the ballerina-like bun at the nape of my neck. The tingling extends to my whole body, manifesting a confusing mix of fear, anxiety, and excitement.

When we arrive, there are groups of people on the sidewalk with glasses of wine, chatting exuberantly. As we step out of the limo, they take sidelong glances at the three of us, wondering, no doubt, who we are. Posters are plastered on the building, and banners on some of the lampposts announcing;

Manon Mouland - Evolution of an Artist, September 18 - October 18

I feel queasy. JM holds my hand, bolstering me, telling me I'm a rock star, making me feel even more like an imposter. When we get off the elevator, we are greeted by Laura Hauptman.

"Welcome to your world, Manon!" She takes my arm and starts ushering me toward a group of people scrutinizing my 'Crossroads.' "I want you to meet ..." The formal introductions bypass my ears and are obliterated by the hum of voices chattering about my work. I walk away from Laura and leave Julian and JM to wander silently among the crowd, eavesdropping. My heart soars at hearing comments like:

"Brilliant!"

"Look at that saturation of blues..."

"Her use of light and space is wonderful..."

"I love how this piece is open to so many interpretations..."

Then, I am devastated by others;

"I don't get it..."

"This is awful..." and, of course, the perennial evaluation;

"My three-year-old could have done this..."

I duck out to the washroom and sit trembling in a stall, my hands sweaty, wishing to disappear. Indeed, I feel as though I'm disappearing into the blackness of one of my inept Rothco studies, my confidence shattered.

I don't know how long I've been in here when I hear my name.

"Manon, are you in here?" It's Stephanie. "It's okay, you can come out; there's no one in here but me."

Her voice, like a misty searchlight, pulls me from the black hole. She envelops me in a cloud of momminess, and I'm finally able to cry. Sobs come automatically, as uncontrollable as vomiting.

"You are a phenomenon. I always knew you were talented, but this collection is overwhelming. You should be proud."

"I am a laughing stock. I've laid myself bare, and people are ridiculing my work. I can't bear it."

"No, no, no. On the contrary. People are insecure when they see art that can make them nervous. When people are confronted by it, they often react by discounting the effect it has on them. It's only when it leaves them unmoved that the artist has failed. What I've been hearing in the gallery is that people are stirred into expressing their feelings. You are a big success; come and revel in it." She tucks an escaped strand of my hair behind my ear. "And you look amazing."

In the mirror, I don't see what she sees. My face is spotted with irregular red blotches; the gold flecks in my eyes have disappeared into the sooty brown of my irises; there are dark circles under my eyes, and more strands of hair have sprung from their restraint, breaking the illusion of sophistication. But my dress still drapes impeccably, camouflaging the turmoil beneath it.

"Come on, there are so many people who want to congratulate you."

Julian and JM are waiting nervously outside the washroom, and when I emerge, they both move to hug me at once. They usher me back into the gallery, which has filled up while I was hiding. There must be a hundred people here.

I begin to focus on faces. I am surprised to see Sage; I didn't know she was coming. She and Mrs. O approach, and a sense of calm descends on me in their presence. Laura touches my arm and winks. Nicole is here, beaming at me. As I progress, with Julian's hand on my arm, I see the back of William concentrating on my painting of Carmen and her children, and then I notice the cascade of red hair flowing down the back of the woman beside him. My heart momentarily constricts when I realize it's Sarah. Just then, Julian puts his arm around me, boosting my equilibrium. When William turns and sees me, he drops Sarah's hand and comes to congratulate me, his arms held out in an invitation to hug. Julian releases me, and I am surprised that I feel none of the old desire for him when his body touches mine. I'm looking over his shoulder at Sarah, who eyes me with something like contempt. My confidence teeters but is quickly righted by Julian slipping his hand into mine.

Gerry Abrams brings his wife Suzanne over to introduce us.

"I'm so glad to finally meet you," she says. "I've heard so much about you." Really? Does Gerry talk about me? What could he possibly have to say? "Congratulations. Your work is amazing. I love the children's portraits; they make me want to cry; they are so beautiful."

Marty Sheridan walks toward us, and Julian immediately runs interference by guiding me away to introduce me to a friend of his. And when Leticia Drake of the *New York Times* wants to engage me, he tells her she can contact him for more in-depth information about my work.

I look around the room, trying to find JM, and see he is surrounded by the Elderberry group with Alexa in his arms, her chubby little fingers trying to pry open his smiling mouth.

I feel a tap on my shoulder and turn to come face to face with Mary Allidon and I can barely speak for the lump that has formed in my throat. She introduces her handsome husband, Bill and gushes about my brilliant success. "I always knew you would do great things; you're amazing. Your Dad would be so proud of you." I wonder if this is true and a tinge of melancholy is added to my erratic moods.

Even Rosalia Menendes is here. "My dear child," she squeals dramatically. "I could hardly believe it was you when I saw the announcement for this exhibit. I just had to come." She takes me by the shoulders and delivers air kisses to both sides of my head. "Congratulations!"

When the gallery empties out, and Julian and I are the only ones left, our footsteps echo from the twenty-five-foot-high ceilings. My vintage pumps have served me well, but now I'm dying to take them off. Julian takes charge, ushering me out and into a cab headed for his place in Brooklyn.

I think I am spent, but when I'm finally under the red bedspread, unknown stores of energy are awakened by Julian's capable hands. He makes my body hum with his methodical anointment of love. I fall asleep as the pulsating of powerful orgasms wane, and I awake in the morning to more orgasms delivered by his uncommonly large, sinewy cock. His moans please me, his timing impeccable as we climax together. When I open my eyes, there is a shaft of light illuminating the Kellys, and a soothing sense of calm envelops me.

CHAPTER FORTY-FOUR

September is my favorite time in Elderberry, and this weekend, I especially appreciate the bucolic environment after the nerve-wracking week leading up to the show and then the actual opening, which did me in. JM and I couldn't wait to get out of the city. Outside my window, the landscape is muted, the greens are no longer vibrant, and the tops of some of the trees have been touched with gold. Sore from yesterday's vigorous workout riding Banjo, I linger in bed, waiting for the Sunday Times to arrive.

Although the feedback Julian's received over the last couple of days (while I hid at Lofty) has been positive, I am still anxious to see the review by Leticia Drake. I finally head downstairs to grab the paper as soon as it arrives. I peek in on JM, still sleeping like a baby, and my heart melts. No matter what happens, I have this lovely boy to cherish.

When I retrieve the paper from the front stoop, I carry the weighty bundle gingerly to the trestle table as if it contains a bomb. It sits there while I make my tea, a menacing presence waiting to be reckoned with. Finally, I sit and sip, take a deep breath, and resign myself to reading the critique. I bypass Current Events with the grim headline: *Suicide Bomber Attacks Pakistani Army Convoy,* and flip through the Feature articles, Editorial pages, and The Book Review. I fling aside the special weekend inserts to finally retrieve the Art & Design section. There it is **Manon Mouland - Evolution of an Artist.**

I imagine Dad at the kitchen table with his Sunday *NYT*, opening the arts section first and seeing my name in bold as the feature article. What would he think? Would I make him proud? It remains to be seen whether Leticia endorses me as a legitimate artist.

Right away, I am appalled to see reproductions of my early childish drawings that Julian insisted we include to give context to the body of my work. The other pictures they have reproduced are: 'Crossroads,' which looks like a dog's breakfast on the printed page, and 'Mother,' Carmen's wary expression looking directly out at us. The children's beautiful coloring is lost in the grainy grey reproduction. Before I settle down to read my fate, I skim the piece apprehensively to see what negative adjectives jump out at me. Finally bolstered by my strong tea, I begin to read.

Manon Mouland - Evolution of an Artist

Exhibits in The New Museum at 235 Bowery contain all things contemporary and modern in all media, but their main focus is to champion lesser-known artists. Manon Mouland is one of those hidden talents. A twenty-eight-year-old artist from Quebec, she has a body of work that could be attributed to a much older, more established person.

In this show of about forty examples of her work, we see the arc of an entire career. Without the benefit of art school instruction, her work is a collection of exercises in which she devised her own experimental techniques, which are interestingly unique. Although some of the work could be more refined, her drafting skill, even in her earliest work, is impressive and gives Mouland legitimacy as a fine artist.

The traditional definition of a curator is someone who is the custodian of a collection. In this show, Julian Fisher is more like the passionate conductor of an orchestra of artworks arranged chronologically, building to a crescendo with Mouland's most current works. At first, the chronological arrangement felt a little too regimented to me, but after a second visit, I could see how it showed Mouland's development vis-à-vis each theme. I saw the logic in it.

There are good things to be found in almost every piece. From exquisitely precise renderings of flora from an early age to pleasant pastoral watercolors showing an appreciation of beauty, she moves through the years, creating emotional pieces of yearning and frustration. The portrait of her father, simply titled 'Dad,' is fraught with pain and love. The painstaking magic realism of his checkered shirt is at odds with the more gestural rendering of his face. We can almost see the movement of his brow knitting into a scowl of disapproval. We get a visceral feeling of dread from the red flush of anger on his smooth-shaved cheeks.

As she moved from faux-naïve realism toward abstraction, she appears to have been set upon by forces she couldn't control. These abstract paintings reveal her lack of confidence through everything from color choices to brushwork. But by the time she paints the show's centerpiece 'Crossroads,' Mouland is able to lay her emotions on the canvas with more certainty. 'Crossroads' leaves us dizzy with emotion and wondering where the roads lead.

Another intriguing piece is Mouland's 'Urban Landscape,' seen through a dirty pane of glass. It exposes the rapid urban renewal of the Bronx, the replacement of old blue-collar tenements with unseen monstrosities to come, hinted at by the forest of looming cranes. With I-95 sliding off the canvas to the right, we are led to an uncertain, ugly future.

There are some abstract expressionist paintings where Mouland explores the limitless possibilities of layering rectangles onto fields of color. One of these large-scale color field paintings is called 'Blue Black.' Although it is characterized by rigorous attention to formal elements such as color, shape, balance, depth, and composition, it fails to draw the viewer into a 'zone.' Other works that teeter between representation and abstraction look less Rothko-esque, which is a good thing.

By far, the most captivating is the recent portraiture, including children, introducing themes of motherhood and desperation. In these startlingly vivid portraits, you can see Mouland's deep feeling for her subjects. The surface tension of these canvasses feels like her subject's souls may crack through them to meet ours. Revealing and confounding at the same time is the untitled self-portrait with a young boy. They are close both literally and figuratively, as is evidenced by their intimate pose: him leaning into her, his Afro pushed against her cheek, and her eyes looking sideways at him. The tenderness of her gaze rendered from somewhere beneath the surface pulled up possibly from the subconscious or perhaps the heart. These powerful renderings of human sentiment reveal such intensity that you may feel compelled to rush out of the gallery for a breath of air. Her keen eye and ability to bring out deeply felt emotions leave you wondering who Manon Mouland is and to what heights she will soar.

The first words that jump out at me are, "gives Mouland legitimacy as a fine artist." I want to stop reading right there and save myself from whatever harsher evaluations are coming. And just as I thought, Leticia recognized my pathetic attempt to elicit the kind of engagement in Blue Black that I strived for. I'm devastated that I have been outed as a failure in this, and I'm angry with Julian for having included it. The labeling and interpretations of my work are puzzling. Was I painting faux-naïve realism? How did she figure that my Bronx painting projected an ugly future? How embarrassing that she recognized the pain in the portrait of Dad. Can everyone see that? Even though they excited me at the time, all those abstracts I painted in Montreal didn't fool her; they were uninspiring, and my use of cheap acrylics never achieved the richness of color I was striving for.

Even though it's early, I hear Julian's Mercedes coming up the driveway. As soon as I open the door and see his wide grin, I start pounding his chest with my fists.

"I told you not to show my Blue Black! I told you it wasn't ready to be seen! I can't believe the world will look at it and those abstracts and see me as a 'dabbler.'" I finally break into sobs, the tension of the week spilling out of me onto Julian's chest. He receives it with the care that he has always shown; his arms surround me, and he buries his face in my wild 'morning' hair.

"Manon, you are a huge success. My phone hasn't stopped ringing since the opening. Alexander would be so happy with what you have accomplished; he really believed in you, as do I."

CHAPTER FORTY-FIVE

When Julian suggests we take a trip, it occurs to me that I've never been 'away on vacation.' The only memory I have of a vacation isn't even an actual memory but one conjured from the photographs of us on Parliament Hill for Canada Day when I was about three.

"We could both use a break after the exhibit closes. Nothing short of a complete change of scenery will quell the nervous energy that has built up over the last few months."

"But who would look after Lofty?"

"We wouldn't be gone long. Lofty will manage fine without you for a week. Where would you like to go?"

The first thing that comes to my mind is the stunning desert landscapes that inspired Georgia O'Keeffe. I've always wondered what it would be like there.

"Can we go to New Mexico?"

"Absolutely. It's the perfect time of year to go there."

From the plane, I can see the snow-capped peaks of the Rocky Mountains and feel a thrill as we descend into the Land of Enchantment at Albuquerque. We're doing a road trip and will head north to Santa Fe, Taos, and Abiquiu, but first, we head south to Casey Tank because I want to see the salt flats.

The detour is worth it. We drive until we are the only outcropping on the pristine flatness, which stretches to the horizon. When we get out to take a walk, our feet crunch crunch on the hard crystalline surface. I feel like a speck, a flaw in the perfection of this reflective landscape. The whiteness is blinding. We might just as easily have arrived at the North Pole. As the day wanes, the white plain turns a soft yellow and then pink. The pinkness permeates me, and I feel like I'm glowing.

The glow dissipates somewhat when we get back to Albuquerque and see the poverty in the neighborhoods we drive through. Julian suggests we leave early in the morning on the next leg of our trip.

Driving with Julian is comfortable; the atmosphere in the car is serene. We take turns in the driver's seat, and he often holds my hand while he drives. Although we talk a lot about many things, he seems to know when *not* to talk and just appreciate the never-ending vistas. We are in sync.

In Santa Fe, we visit the Georgia O'Keeffe Museum, a beige adobe building that turns red in the setting sun. Large and small canvasses are hung in such a way as to make you feel that you're walking from outside to inside. Mountains and sand dunes that look like folds of supple flesh, sunsets, and sagebrush lead us to giant white irises, red poppies, and purple morning glories, exquisitely simplified flowers with labia-like curled petals. "I'm surprised how moving it is seeing these in person," Julian says, and I can see his face is alive with emotion. I love this about him.

"I'm in awe of the saturation of colors. Her brush strokes are almost invisible. How did she accomplish that?"

"Practice, I think. Lots of patient practice. I'm sure you could master the technique if you wanted to."

We spend a couple of nights in Santa Fe at a five-star inn hidden like turquoise within the hillside. Our room has an antique rug, textiles on the walls, and a kiva, an in-ground fireplace stocked with fragrant piñon wood. We are bonded in our love of the beauty that surrounds us, and we make love like newlyweds, unable to keep our hands off each other.

We would stay here longer, but I'm so excited to go to Ghost Ranch, Georgia O'Keeffe's home in Abiquiu. We set off, after breakfast in bed, for the hour-long drive on a bumpy dirt road.

Her home is as minimalist as I expected, a tranquil whitewashed space with hardwood floors and an adobe fireplace, above which hangs a bleached animal skull. Wood-beamed ceilings cap the serenity. There is a careful assemblage of found objects and functional furniture. Seashells and rocks, gnarled branches, and animal bones are displayed on the mantel and windowsills, things that she scavenged from the desert. I can see the attraction of these shapes as subjects. White cotton curtains flutter in the gentle breeze. The environment is inspirational. I am determined to try my hand at simplifying my subjects and painting out the brushstrokes. It will be a Zen-like exercise.

Back in Albuquerque, we see a lot of little children begging on the streets. Their circumstances move me, and I speculate,

"I wonder if they had a place like Lofty to go to, would they stay off the streets?"

"I'm sure it would help some of them. There must be many budding artists in this 'land of enchantment.'"

"Could the foundation support such a place out here?"

"I love it that you're thinking big! I suppose it's doable."

Back in New York, at Lofty, I am swarmed by the kids in a warm welcome. They are excited to see the objects I have brought for them to draw: imitation animal skulls, antlers, horns, and shells purchased in the gift shop at the gallery. They are so keen to get started. I'm gratified to see the difference we've made in their lives. My mind is busy with the idea of doing this in Albuquerque. I love the idea of going back to New Mexico with JM and doing some good. How I have changed!

For years after I walked out of Champlain College until Dad died, I lived in a kind of purgatory. In the monotony of my days, I was a zombie. I got up, had my tea, went to work, came home, and mostly brooded on the riverbank, watching the water flow downstream, wishing I could float away with it.

Dad and I barely spoke after I quit school. He thought I was a failure, and I believed him. His disappointment in me was a malignancy that grew daily. The weight of it oppressed me. I ached all the time. The only thing that felt satisfying was cutting myself, something I thought I'd left behind in my teenage years.

I worked at my dead-end job at Michael's and saw people bringing in the 'masterpieces' they thought worthy of framing. All I could manage were incomplete studies of disparate objects, uninspired still lifes reflecting my own stagnancy. Luckily, I had the wherewithal to destroy almost everything I did in those years.

Now, I look back at that version of me, and it doesn't seem possible. I'm a completely different person. How did this happen?

Alexander happened. His generosity, his altruism, and his unconditional love helped re-shape me. I carry the great sorrow of losing him too soon, along with the regret that Dad is not here to see my philanthropic practice and my body of work, proof that I am not simply a flâneur.

Growing up, I always saw myself as a waif, unworthy of the love bestowed by a mother and a family. I operated under the conviction that I deserved the neglect and that the unsatisfied yearning to belong was my burden to carry forever. From the moment I broke my mother's beloved Meissen figurine, which I loved when I was little, my persona was sealed. I was bad. I fulfilled the expectation that I would misbehave and became selfish, indulging in hedonistic pleasures, looking for love, and rejecting it when it was offered. I can't even remember how many guys I dumped once they fell in love with me. Even William could not have me the way he wanted. But Julian has me. We fit together as naturally as Sage and Mrs. O. His love for me is as unconditional as Alexander's was, and my love for him is deep and steadfast.

My life is complete, and I can even say I'm happy, although there is that little stone that's settled in my chest, which aches from time to time.

AUTHOR BIO

Susan Hoffman is retired from careers in sales, design, and art consultation. A creative person with a keen sense of beauty and harmony, she reads, writes, and occasionally paints. Among her favorite pastimes are gardening, sewing, and cooking. She lives in Toronto with her husband. They have a daughter who currently lives in San Francisco, having moved there from New York, where she graduated from Columbia University with a Masters in Architecture.

Made in United States
Cleveland, OH
22 August 2026

43019516R00174